**Kari roared with laughter.**

Rob swung her wide, lifting her off the floor and twirling her. "Got another cake that needs decorating?"

"That's the sugar high talking—I think you may have licked one too many bowls of buttercream," Kari said. But her eyes were sparkling, and Rob knew it wasn't the buttercream that made his heart do a triple beat.

"There's sugar, and then...well...there's sugar," he whispered. He bent down to kiss her.

She tasted of sugar...vanilla buttercream, to be exact. She smelled of the stuff, which suited him just fine, because for that moment all he wanted to do was take in the scent of her, the taste and the feel of her. If he'd had to decorate a thousand more cakes, give him a kiss like this, and he was game.

Because it was plain and simple. He was addicted to the sugar high that was Kari Hendrix...regardless of whatever secret she might be keeping.

Dear Reader,

Until I had the privilege of working for the US House of Representatives, I had always thought a juvenile offense was no big deal. Wasn't it sealed away, never to haunt the grown-up, much wiser version of that foolish teenage self?

The answer, I found, was no. Even a misdemeanor arrest as a juvenile can come back to haunt a person in her adult years. Men and women in their twenties and thirties, in search of college loans, job opportunities, security clearances and other things that might improve their career prospects all told me the same thing: an arrest is still an arrest, a conviction still a conviction, no matter how old you were when it happened. Even an expunged record, I found, wasn't truly a clean slate. On a job application, you still had to check yes on that box that asked, "Have you ever been arrested or convicted of a crime?"

That's what my character Kari faces in *Out of the Ashes*: one bad decision so many years before comes back to haunt her. She's older, wiser and a good deal sadder for her bad decision, but it still impacts her present in ways she had no idea it would when she made it. And it has the power to destroy any chance of her future with Rob.

I hope you enjoy Kari and Rob's story as much as I enjoyed writing it!

*Cynthia*

# HEARTWARMING

## *Out of the Ashes*

——

*Cynthia Reese*

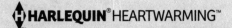
HARLEQUIN® HEARTWARMING™

Recycling programs
for this product may
not exist in your area.

ISBN-13: 978-0-373-36739-9

Out of the Ashes

Copyright © 2015 by Cynthia R. Reese

**HARLEQUIN**®
www.Harlequin.com

**Printed in U.S.A.**

**Cynthia Reese** lives with her husband and their daughter in south Georgia, along with their two dogs, three cats and however many strays show up for morning muster. She has been scribbling since she was knee-high to a grasshopper and reading even before that. A former journalist, teacher and college English instructor, she also enjoys cooking, traveling and photography when she gets the chance.

## Books by Cynthia Reese

### Harlequin Heartwarming

*Seeds of Trust*
*A Place to Call Home*
*What the Heart Wants*
*Man of His Word*

### Harlequin Superromance

*The Baby Wait*
*For The Sake Of The Children*

To my husband, my biggest fan.

This book, like the ones before it, owes a tremendous debt to the efforts of the best editors on the planet, Kathryn Lye and Victoria Curran. I am so thankful for their belief in my writing. Karen Rock has a huge part of this as well, as she helped me brainstorm the original story idea and the story arc for the Georgia Monroes.

Thanks, too, goes to Sgt. Tommy Windham and all the firefighters at the City of Dublin, Georgia's, Fire Department, to John Lentini of Scientific Fire Analysis, to Judge Sherri McDonald, and to Blake Tillery for their patient answers to my dumb questions. All mistakes are mine.

No man is an island, and no woman can truly write a book on her own: thanks to my critique partner Tawna Fenske, my beta reader Jessica Brown, my cheering squad and inspiration for big happy families, Leslie and the gang, and, last but not least, to those who have had to talk me down from the ledges—my sister, my daughter and my husband. Thank you for all the times you didn't strangle me when I replied to any request, "Not now, I'm writing."

# CHAPTER ONE

Smoke.

Ashes.

Kari Hendrix wanted to see neither ever again.

All around her in the predawn light were the loud industrial sounds of ventilator fans, the slap of boots against concrete, the beep-beep-beep of a fire truck as it backed up, the calls from one firefighter to another, the thwack and clank of fire hoses being rolled up, the pulse of red and blue lights streaking across puddles of water on the street.

And the wet smell of a building burned to a crisp.

*Make that buildings.* She shivered and wrapped her arms around herself to ward off a chill despite the late summer temperatures still not dropping below seventy-five at night. Almost the whole section of the downtown on one side of the street was gutted and blackened. Her little bakery stood smack in the middle, an even darker smudge against the rest.

Gone. Up in smoke.

She'd checked everything twice the night before when she'd closed up: the oven, the stove, the lights. She always did.

If there was one thing Kari knew, it was the destructive power of fire.

The scrape of boots on the sidewalk came nearer—next to her. She pulled her attention away from her ruined bakery and switched it to the man who'd walked up to join her by the fluttering yellow tape that blocked off the scene from civilians.

The first thing that struck her about him was how tall he was—a good foot taller than her 5'4"—okay, 5'3½"—frame. Beside him, Kari felt even more like a munchkin than usual.

Unlike the rest of the men on the far side of the tape, the tall man wasn't dressed in turnout gear. He wore no fire helmet or rubber boots, but he was in a uniform of sorts: khakis and a knit golf shirt with a shield of some sort embroidered on it.

She couldn't make out the logo because of the third thing she noticed about him: in his hands he carried two paper cups of coffee and had a blanket slung over one arm.

"You're Kari Hendrix." It wasn't a question, just a confident restating of a known fact. "Here. I figured you could use a cup of coffee."

Kari's hand reflexively took the coffee before she could get out, "What?"

But he wasn't done. With his free hand, he awkwardly propped the blanket, marked PROPERTY OF LEVI COUNTY FIRE DEPT, around her. Kari grabbed at it before it slipped onto the sodden sidewalk and pulled it gratefully around her shoulders.

The man made a quick save of her fumbling coffee cup. "Whoops. So much for my being a gentleman. You nearly lost the coffee and the blanket," he told her.

"Thank you," she replied. She peered at the stitching on the shirt, which stretched over a well-constructed chest that looked more like a triathlete's than a firefighter's. This guy was built like a tree. In the dim light, though, she couldn't really decipher the dark threads that made up the design.

"Oh, I'm Rob Monroe." He offered a hand, realized she had both hands occupied—one with the cup and the other anchoring the blanket. He grinned.

It was a good grin—the smile of a guy who didn't take himself too seriously and realized when he was being a goofball, Kari decided. It tugged at dimples and a cleft in his chin, and it showed off white teeth and the barest hint of stubble to devastatingly good advantage.

"Kari—well, you, hmm, you already know my name, don't you?" she asked. She felt her face heat up. Suddenly she could picture how she looked to this guy: she could feel her blond hair slipping out of its hastily-rigged ponytail, imagine her face bare of makeup and still streaked with the tears she'd shed earlier as she'd stood watching the fire in all its gut-wrenching destruction. "You have me at a disadvantage."

"The coffee and the blanket don't make up for that?" His eyes were dark—not brown or black, but she couldn't quite make out the color in the dawn light. But they were kind eyes. Intelligent ones.

Now they shifted beyond her, not apparently expecting an answer to his question, and they locked on the smoldering remains of the downtown section that had burned.

She followed his gaze. It was hard to watch it now that she'd looked away. She'd almost hoped that it had been a nightmare that she could wake up from and it would be gone.

But of course it wasn't. No, the fire was out now and the firefighters were gathering up their equipment, tromping around the half-burned walls of the buildings, over rubble.

"Want to take a closer look?" Rob Monroe offered suddenly.

Kari opened her mouth, but nothing came out. Did she? Yes…and no. Even from here, she could tell nothing would be salvaged from her shop.

Still, she wanted to know what she'd done—or hadn't done—that had turned her dreams into ashes.

"Okay," she got out. "But can we? The chief told me to wait back here."

Rob lifted the tape and jerked his head for her to go on. "I happen to have a little pull with the chief," he said. "He's my brother."

"Oh. Are you—you're a firefighter, too?" She glanced back over her shoulder.

Rob reached over and righted her coffee cup again—as she had again been on the verge of dumping it.

"Sorry. I seem to be a bit of a klutz today. I'm not usually," Kari told him.

"It's like that at four in the morning." Now he walked beside her, matching her step for step, even though he could have easily crossed the distance in a fraction of the time it was taking her.

Especially when Kari's feet felt nailed to the ground the closer she drew to the burned-out storefront.

"Do you know?" she blurted out. "How it started? What did I do? What did I leave on?"

Rob cast an appraising look her way, one eyebrow hiked in question. "You think you left something on?"

"I checked. Everything. I always check. But I must have, right?"

It was the only thing that made sense to her. More than one firefighter had said enough in passing to let her know that the fire had started in her bakery. So she must have done something wrong. She'd left something on in the oven, or maybe her old coffeepot had shorted out, or…something.

The acrid smell of drenched ashes and soot assailed her even more strongly now that they were just outside the front door of her shop. Rob drew up short, staying put. Kari was grateful for his consideration, because without a moment to collect herself, she would have surely burst into tears or succumbed to the roiling nausea in her stomach.

The plate glass window with the stenciled name of Lovin' Oven was no more—splintered into pieces. Inside, the shop was inky-black, lit only by a few klieg lights and the sweeping beams of a firefighter's flashlight.

Even so, Kari could see only the barest scraps of the gingham tablecloths she'd had covering the window's deeply bayed display shelf. The window display with the four-tiered mock cake—nothing but a form made of hatboxes and decorated with frosting to showcase her skills—was no more.

A man almost as tall as Rob appeared out of the shadows. Even in his turnout gear and soot-covered face, Kari recognized him as the man who'd warned her to stay back what felt like hours earlier…the chief. Rob's brother.

"I told him you'd said I should wait—" Kari rushed.

But the chief—Daniel Monroe, she remembered now, waved her words away. "Rob said he was going to take you through it."

Kari gulped. Usually she was stronger than this, braver. She'd had to be braver for years now, so there was no point going all weepy over a fire. Nobody had gotten killed in it, thank goodness. And at least she'd been able to pay the insurance.

Rob cocked his head. "See? I told you I had pull." He clicked on a huge and battered flashlight that rivaled a small baseball bat in size. "But we do need to be careful. Here—why don't you leave your blanket and the coffee with Daniel?" He winked at his brother. "You won't mind holding it for us while we're in there, will you, bro?"

"Why not? You've left me holding far worse bags over the years, now, haven't you?" But Daniel's retort was devoid of malice… Kari found herself wishing she and her own brother could joke around like that. She handed him her coffee and slid off the blanket, shivering at the cool air.

Kari stepped through the door to an interior she would have never recognized as her very own shop. Black water was everywhere, walls were gone, tables reduced to ash and rubble.

The precious glass display cases she'd found online and got her brother to help her haul them home—gone. The kitschy fruit prints she'd framed on the walls—gone.

And the farther she went into the bowels of the beast, the worse it got.

The kitchen area in the back, smelling of burned sugar and flour and plastic, had taken on an apocalyptic appearance, all scorched earth and none of the cheerful, neat work space she'd left just a few hours earlier. Kari stood beside her Hobart floor mixer and slid a hand over its fire-blistered paint.

Gone. All gone.

She hadn't even realized she was crying until Rob squeezed her shoulder. "Hey. If you want to do this later…"

He was so kind. As if he didn't mind in the slightest standing by a squawling baker as she wept over her floor mixer. Kari swiped at her eyes and choked back her tears. "No, I'm—it's okay." She whirled around to escape his intense look of compassion, only to stumble and nearly fall on something in her path.

"Whoa, there!" Rob saved her from a nasty spill in the soot. He shined his light onto what had caused her to stumble: her bookshelf of cookbooks, now charred almost beyond recognition.

"Oh, no…" Kari hadn't even thought of them—all these cookbooks, collected over the years from the first time she'd ever baked a cake, destroyed in seconds. "My recipes… all my recipes! Gone!"

"Wait—see? Not all gone." Rob bent over and scooped up a thick book and flipped it open. Sure enough, though the edges of the pages were scalloped with an ugly carbon-black from the heat and flames, many pages were readable. "You'll need to let them dry out, of course, because they got an extra good soaking."

She couldn't help it. She grabbed that cookbook and pressed it to her, giving up on holding back her tears.

"Your favorite cookbook?" he asked.

Kari managed a laugh, then sniffled. "Cookbooks are like children or dogs. You can't have a favorite. They're all my favorites."

"Hmm. I had no idea." His smile was sweet and patient. Kari realized that daylight was filtering through the front windows. "Come on." He waved her toward the delivery door. "I want to show you something out back."

Carefully she made her way there. Outside, a hulk of scorched metal lay in a heap near the remains of what had been a wooden door that Kari had daily battled with.

"What?" she asked as she joined Rob, who was staring at it intently.

"You don't recognize it?"

She frowned. It had been white, maybe, or the lightest of blue, a tank of some sort…

A chill went down her spine.

A propane tank.

"Is that what I think it is?" she asked.

"What do you think it is?" Rob evaded answering her question.

She knelt down for a closer look.

Yes. A small propane tank, like the ones you'd see at a convenience store, ready to be taken home and hooked up to a grill.

But she had no grill. Her bakery ran on natural gas and electricity, not propane. She'd not had any need for a propane tank.

Jammed into the tank's collar, next to the valve, was a scrap of metal and a heap of ashes.

She straightened up, her heart sinking to her toes. "It looks like a propane tank. For a grill."

"Yep," Rob agreed.

"It's not mine."

"That a fact?" he asked.

Now she met his eyes, and she could tell in the gray light of dawn that they were blue, a very dark blue that she hadn't seen ever before—but she'd seen the speculation that filled them in others' eyes—plenty of times.

"Is that what started the fire?" she asked. "This tank?"

"I couldn't tell you yet. I've only just started to investigate."

"Investigate? You?" Now it was Kari's turn to look speculatively at her companion.

"Didn't I tell you? I'm the fire marshal and arson investigator for Levi County."

A renewed wave of nausea flooded through her. "Arson?" she asked and sagged against the scorched cement of the exterior wall. But she hadn't needed to ask him to repeat it. She'd heard it the first time.

"It looks that way. That tank's valve is open, and it appears to be the remains of a road flare stuck in there."

Kari's knees wouldn't hold her up any longer. She found herself sliding to the wet ground, the masonry wall digging into her back as she descended. "Not again," she whispered. "Oh, please, not again."

"Again?" Rob knelt down beside her.

"You might as well know…" She stared down at the cookbook in her arms, the one thing she'd been able to salvage from the ashes of her fresh new start.

"Know what?" Rob prompted.

"You'll find out soon enough. I was convicted of arson when I was fourteen years old."

## CHAPTER TWO

ROB SAT BACK on his heels, stunned. Had she really said what he thought she'd said?

Yes.

But she'd said it in a curious, distancing way. Not "I started a fire," or "I burned down a building."

No. "I was convicted." That was how Kari Hendrix had put it.

He took in her eyes. They were gray and flat and dull, devoid of the hope he'd seen sputter in them when she'd found the cookbook.

So the question wasn't if this was arson. Rob switched his gaze away from Kari and back to the propane tank.

Revenge. That was the first thought that popped in his mind when he'd made his initial sweep after the firefighters had put the blaze out. He'd seen the way-too-obvious point of origin—an open valve on a propane tank, the remains of a safety flare jabbed into the tank's collar—and it was impossible to miss the "take that!" message the arsonist had sent loud and clear.

Rob had taken Kari through the building in hopes she could fill him in on who it was she'd so badly ticked off. A boyfriend? A customer?

But now…

Now he had to consider whether Kari was the culprit. The propane tank was easy enough to acquire, as well as the safety flare. She owned a bakery—and any food-based small shop hemorrhaged money like nobody's business at first. And she certainly knew the lay of the land and when no one would be around.

Means, motive and opportunity…and a past criminal history, albeit self-confessed.

Her head was bent, and Kari appeared to peer deeply at her knees as though the secret to the universe were there. He could see the fabric of the denim stretched over those knees was thin and threadbare—not some high-dollar distressing of the jeans, but literally worn through.

Kari hadn't done this.

Rob knew it. It was a bone-deep knowledge he couldn't explain, but he was just as certain that Kari Hendrix had not set this fire as he was that his big brother Daniel would throw back his head and roar with laughter at his conclusion. Daniel was always telling Rob that *Rob* was the cynical, suspicious one.

Still…

"Ahem. I should read you your rights," Rob said. Funny how his voice seemed to strain and crack. "You have the right to remain silent—"

Kari lifted her head. Her mouth twisted in a grimace. "Yeah. I know. And whatever I say, you'll use against me in court, and I can have an attorney—you'll even give me a really, really bad one since I can't afford one. I know the drill."

"So? Did you? Do this?"

"No." There was no equivocation, no hesitation, no fancy I-swear-on-a-stack-of-Bibles, no how-dare-you outrage. Just a plain and simple, no-frills, direct, "No."

"Do you know who might have?"

But now Kari lied.

Not at first. Her initial headshake was vigorous and heartfelt. But somewhere in mid-shake, a lightbulb must have gone off. She froze—just for a split second. He could see more pain flare up in her eyes, the deep anguish of betrayal. And for a moment he was sure she was going to spill out a name.

Instead, she pressed her lips together in a tight, thin line and clutched the cookbook to her chest. "How could I know who burned this place? Why would they want to?"

"That's what I'm asking you. Do you have trouble with your landlord?"

She laughed. It was a dry, bitter sound that would have been more fitting for a jaded seventy-year-old than someone Kari's age. Kari pushed herself up to a standing position, wobbly on her knees, but still pointedly ignoring Rob's outstretched hand.

"I take that as a yes?" Rob pressed.

"My landlord, as you probably already know, is Charlie Kirkman, and everybody has trouble with Charlie Kirkman. And when you ask around, you'll probably find the customers who heard me screaming at him the other day when he refused—again—to send somebody to look at the roof. Or the air conditioner. Or the vent fan. Or the water heater. But if everybody who got into a screaming match with Charlie Kirkman burned his buildings down, Charlie Kirkman would have no buildings left to burn."

She was right about that, Rob knew. Charlie was as skinflinty a landlord as he'd ever come across. Rob had had dealings with Charlie—and not in a good way—when he'd followed up with Charlie's residential tenants about fire safety complaints. And he knew that Charlie was famous for finally getting around to repairing the problem—and then upping the rent and gleefully evicting the poor tenants.

So it was par for the course that Charlie's commercial ventures would play out the same way.

"Why'd you keep renting from him, then? Why not move somewhere else?" Rob asked.

Kari shrugged slim shoulders. "Location, location, location. I haven't been in business long enough to have a reputation yet, or a real customer base that would follow me if I moved. The location was perfect. Plus, I'd signed a year's lease. It won't be up for... gosh, another six months."

Rob couldn't believe that the Lovin' Oven had been in business for six months already and he hadn't availed himself of its goodies. But he hadn't. Maybe it was because he could get all the free dessert he wanted at Ma's...or maybe he'd somehow looked down on a boutique bakery that sold things like four-buck cupcakes that couldn't be any better than the boxed brownies he made for himself whenever he had a snack attack.

*If I'd known the cupcakes were baked by someone like you...*

Rob gave himself a mental slap upside the head. What was he thinking? Four-buck cupcakes were four-buck cupcakes, and a suspect was a suspect.

Even if he knew she wasn't.

"So what next?" Kari asked wearily.

"Next? I investigate. You say you didn't do it, so that leaves me with no choice but to find out who actually did it."

Rob could have sworn that Kari flinched at his words.

"I'd like to go home now," she said quietly. "Is that okay? Can I?"

"You're not under arrest."

"You read me my rights," she pointed out.

"Because I'm very careful about procedure. It would be like you—I dunno—reading a recipe before you start baking a cake."

An even bleaker look filled her eyes. She made her way to the shop's back door and leaned against the blackened doorjamb. "I won't be baking anything for a long time yet.

Maybe ever. The insurance—the insurance won't pay if arson was involved."

"Not if, Kari. It was arson. There are no ifs, ands or buts. It was definitely arson. If you tell me—"

She whirled around. Anger tightened the grim lines of her face. "I can't. I can't tell you what I don't know. I can't tell you why anybody would want to hurt me like this. I hate fire. I hate it. It destroys everything."

And with that, she pushed past him and made her way down the back alley behind the burned-out hulls of the buildings. In the shadows formed by the dawn's gray light pushing through the gaping holes of the buildings, Kari Hendrix appeared small and frail and bowed over with pain. And she was running—running away from something? What?

Rob was determined to find out.

"SO LET ME get this straight," Daniel said, his words laced with amusement. Rob's brother leaned back in his squeaky desk chair and stretched out his feet on an open desk drawer.

"What's there to get straight? And are you asking as my brother or the chief of the fire department?" Rob stretched his own feet out on the concrete floor of his brother's office at the fire station.

Daniel shrugged. "Brother, chief, what does it matter? I'm curious. You know it's arson, I know it's arson, and the owner of the business where the fire originated tells you she was convicted of arson, but you believe she didn't do it? Wait. Who are you and what have you done with my got-to-believe-the-worst-in-everybody little brother?"

"I know. It's not like me. If there's one rule, it's usually that the business owner or the landlord did it. But Charlie Kirkman is too stingy to properly insure his buildings, and… Daniel, you just had to be there. I mean, it doesn't make any sense for her to spill it all. It was a sealed juvie record, and I would have had to move heaven and earth to get it unsealed. I might not have even thought to look at it first if she hadn't said something."

"So maybe it's all an elaborate ploy to make you think she's innocent."

"Now you sound like me, and you're always accusing me of being cynical." Rob chuckled. He took a sip of bad firehouse coffee and grimaced, but swallowed another gulp down. He was on his third cup just for the caffeine's sake. The downtown fire had started way too early. "Here's what really doesn't make sense. If she'd wanted to burn that place down, she could have left a cake in the oven or something on the stove and walked away. Nobody could have proven it was anything but an accident. This?" Rob shook his head. "A propane tank and a safety flare? It's too obvious. Too stupid. Too brazen. And she—she would have known she would wind up a prime suspect."

"But you just said you would have never thought to check her out—"

"Maybe not, but it would have come up, eventually. I do my job, Daniel, you know that."

Daniel considered him. "Yeah. You do. And you're good at it."

For a moment, Rob let his thoughts wander back to Kari, weighing everything she'd said, every expression on her face. She'd been such an open, honest book. Everything—the pain, the misery, the fear—had been right there, as easy to read as one of those first-grade Dick and Jane primers.

The fear.

Kari had been afraid. Of what? Of who? It hadn't been a mortal fear, but more of a fear of having been betrayed. What had she said when he'd first mentioned arson?

*Not again. Please not again.*

"So what's next, Rob Roy?" his brother asked him.

A momentary flicker of annoyance at his family nickname distracted him from his thoughts about Kari. Rob pulled his focus together and considered Daniel's very valid question.

"Hmm. First I have to figure out exactly what sort of hole Kari Hendrix was in. Oh, and Charlie Kirkman. You never know. Even Charlie might have decided that a little insurance was better than fixing something—and maybe if that block was leveled, he could sell it. Maybe Kari—or some of his other tenants—didn't want to leave. Or maybe somebody had it in for Kari."

"I never knew cupcakes could be so deadly," Daniel quipped.

Rob lifted his shoulders. "You got me. I'm not much for cupcakes. Give me a brownie any old day. But you know what I mean."

"How long do you think it will take? To close the case?"

Rob rubbed at his eyes and considered whether another cup of coffee would help keep him awake. Fatigue and lack of sleep were catching up with him, and he still had the rest of the day to get through. "Probably not as long as it will take to write it up whenever I do figure it out. And definitely not as long as the grand jury and the trial will take."

"I know. You're always right, so why do those pesky lawmakers insist that you give the guilty party their day in court, huh?" Daniel grinned and winked at his brother. Then his smile faded. "I'm just kidding you, you know that, right? I meant what I said a while ago. You *are* good at what you do, Rob."

For a long moment, Rob didn't say anything. He looked past Daniel to the credenza behind him, loaded down with family pictures. There were Daniel and his new fiancée and her daughter, beaming at each other. There was a picture of the Monroe brothers, all around Ma—her birthday, Rob recalled. And at the far end, off to itself, almost as a shrine, stood a 5x7, a formal shot of their dad in his dress blues, back when he was chief.

Back when he was alive.

Before another arsonist had taken it upon himself to set fire to a building that had come crashing down on Rob's dad—on all of the Monroes, come to think of it.

Rob stilled. An awareness, a memory, flickered.

He'd pulled the case file of that unsolved arson some months back and had been going through it again during his rare down times. And now he remembered.

That arson. It had been started with a propane tank, too.

## CHAPTER THREE

"Did he do it? Mom! You have to tell me!"

Kari's mom didn't answer, just protectively pulled the opening of her terrycloth robe together with a shaking hand. "I—Kari—I—it burned? Your shop *burned*?"

Now Chelle Hendrix tottered past Kari, a hand raking through her bottle-dye blond hair. Kari wheeled around to hear the clatter of the coffee carafe rattling as Chelle managed to pour coffee into a mug, her hand shaking.

Kari started to speak again, but Chelle held up a finger, then went back to her coffee. She poured a boatload of sugar into it, then a flood of cream. After giving it a brisk, businesslike stir, she held the mug up and took a quaff from it like a man stumbling into an oasis after being stranded in the desert for days.

Fortified, Chelle tottered back to the kitchen table and sank with a sigh into a chair. "Now tell me. Seriously? Your shop? It burned?"

"Mom… I am so sorry. The first thing that I thought about was your retirement money."

Chelle would have wrinkled her forehead in shock and horror, but her Botoxed facial muscles wouldn't cooperate. Her throat moved in a visible gulp. "Oh, honey. Don't you worry about me. Sure, I borrowed against my 401(k), but it's you who's been putting all that hard work into making a go of it. How horrible! Now grab a cup of coffee and sit down and tell me all about it."

Thinking about coffee made Kari think about Rob, and thinking about Rob made her think about the case he was probably busily building against her as she stood in her mother's kitchen. "I don't want coffee. I don't want to sit down—"

"Well, you're giving me a crick in the neck, honey. Sit. If you don't want coffee, fine, but at least sit."

Kari sat. Her mother quickly grasped Kari's fingers in her own perfectly manicured hands. "Kari, what happened? Did you leave something turned on? No, I know you didn't—you're so careful. I'll bet it was that wiring. I knew that old dump of a building was a firetrap."

"No." Kari swallowed, tried to get the lump in her throat to dislodge. "It was arson. Somebody—" her voice trembled over the word *somebody*. "Somebody took a propane tank, leaned it against the back door and stuck a lit safety flare in the top of it."

Chelle recoiled. For a second, she just stared at Kari with rounded eyes, her hands clenched into fists against her robe. "Kari… Kari…you don't honestly think…"

"Where's Jake, Mom? I need to ask him—"

"No." The word was harsh and sharp and brooked no argument. Sometimes her mother dispensed with her dithery ways and allowed an iron maiden to peek out. "No. You will not."

"Mom—"

"He's back, Kari. He's back, and he's doing fine. We're all—we're all doing just *fine*." Kari's mom's eyes grew shiny and wet with tears. "What you're saying…it just isn't possible. He was young, Kari. It was a *mistake*. A stupid, stupid prank that went all wrong and his friends—oh—his *friends*!" A shuddering sound of disgust escaped her mother's lips.

Kari put a palm over her eyes, which felt

as raw as if they'd been sandblasted. Now was not the time to argue about Jake. It had been a mistake all right, taking the fall for his crime.

Kari still remembered standing in front of the judge that day, reciting the words she'd rehearsed for her confession. It was supposed to be simple: she was a juvenile first offender, sure to get off easy for a property crime. It was Jake who would get sent off if he were found guilty—and he was guilty.

But, her mom had explained, Jake would get sent to real prison—doing real time, since he'd turned eighteen. And her mother assured her that Kari wouldn't—probation, that's all, just like Jake had his first and second time before a judge.

Only the judge hadn't given Kari probation.

He'd given her four years in juvie.

Four years of hell.

It had taken Kari a long time to even be able to speak to her mother…much less Jake. In fact, it was only in the past six months that Kari had reconciled any small bit with her brother.

Her mother spoke now in a firm voice. "Kari, Jake wouldn't have done this. He

loves you. And you know he feels awful…
just awful about what happened. Why, he
was telling me about how that Charlie Kirkman was treating you, how he wanted to ram
that man's words down his throat." Kari's
mom's eyes rounded again. "You don't think
*Charlie Kirkman* did it, do you?"

"No, I don't think that." Kari couldn't look
at her mother for another second. More for
something to do than anything else, Kari
stood and poured herself a cup of coffee.
She'd give anything to have one of her bear
claws or Danish rolls to go with this—

No point in thinking about that.

"I'm sure Jake will be just as horrified as
I am," Kari's mother said. "Oh, Kari, grab
that box of croissants there. We'll have some
breakfast."

Kari followed her mother's pointing finger to the top of the fridge, where a clear
plastic grocery store bakery container held
a few croissants. With a sigh, she yanked the
things down and plopped them on the For-
mica tabletop. "You couldn't have bought
some from me, Mom?"

"Well, actually, these were leftover from
the office brunch—I *told* them we should
have had you cater it, but the girls at the of-

fice said that there wasn't enough in petty cash. Besides, they're not that bad."

Kari bit into one. The pastry was tough and greasy, not at all flaky like the croissants she strove to make. She scanned the printed ingredients list: hydrogenated soybean oil, high fructose corn syrup, refined flour, soy flour.

She dropped the half-eaten pastry on her napkin. It was disappointing to the taste buds, a little stale, nothing like a fresh croissant. A good one was light and flaky and loaded with real butter. So what if they took hours to make? Better to have one really good croissant than a whole bin of these.

"See?" her mother said. "Not bad at all."

What could she expect from her mom? Kari asked herself. Her mom always tried her best, but the results never turned out well.

True, such meals had been made lovingly and had been more than enough to keep Kari fed for the fourteen years she'd lived with her mom...and when she'd been in juvie, even her mom's cooking had seemed way better than the glop they served.

Her mother reached up and caressed Kari's cheek. "Oh, sweetie. This is horrible for you. But—I know! You can cook here! Why, this kitchen would do, wouldn't it? It would be much better than trying to cook in that oversized kitchenette in your apartment. And that way you could bake all your cakes and keep your orders up—you've got the Gottman wedding to do, right? You can bake it right here."

Kari couldn't help but smile. "I might have to take you up on that. It will probably be a while before I'm back on my feet again."

Her mom brightened and waved a hand around to encompass the kitchen. "Why, you've got everything you need, right here—and barely used at that. Isn't it a good thing I was such a bad cook?"

Kari squeezed her mother's fingers. "You're not a bad cook."

"Nope, next to you…you make those lovely little cupcakes that everybody always raves about. Oh, honey, where did you get your cooking mojo?"

Not for the first time did Kari utter some words of thanksgiving to Alice Heaton, the cook at the youth detention center where Kari had been incarcerated. If it hadn't been for KP duty and a birthday cake, Kari might never have found a way to survive her years behind bars…or a way to make a living.

Well, strike that. She'd *had* a way to make a living, but now? Not so much.

Kari flicked the croissant with a fingernail. This was not breakfast. This wasn't even really food.

"I think I'll take you up on that offer to cook. I can make something better than this," Kari said. She sprang from her chair and busied herself with rummaging through her mother's cabinets.

"Oh, sweetie, you don't have to cook—" her mother protested. "You've been through so much."

Kari shrugged. "It helps me, Mom, the cooking. Cheap therapy, you know?" she tried to joke.

"Except for my hips," her mother said. "If you really want to, I have some blueberries in the freezer. They've been there since the first of the summer, though."

"Perfect. I'll make us some blueberry muffins."

What Kari really wanted was to tackle a brioche or a croissant or even a Danish, something that would require thought and energy and concentration. She'd welcome anything that would distract her from her worries.

But her stomach was rumbling in protest from the Franken-croissant, and muffins would be quick at least. Kari began dumping the ingredients into a bowl.

"Where's Jake, Mom?" she asked again.

Her mother set her coffee mug down with a thud. "Out. Out with friends."

Kari tried to suppress the predictable irritation that flared up within her. Jake acted as though he were still seventeen, not almost thirty. He was three years older than her... but she felt eons older than twenty-six.

"I tried his cell phone, but he didn't answer," Kari said.

"Oh, well, you know Jake...maybe he ran out of minutes."

Kari stirred the batter a little more energetically than she normally would have. It sloshed onto the counter, and Kari made sure to wipe up the spill. "He'll never grow up, Mom, if you don't let him."

"Let him! Kari, my goodness, of course he's grown up. He's older than you—what, twenty-seven?"

Kari leveled a gaze at her mom. "Try

twenty-nine, Mom. And he still hasn't figured out what he's going to do with his life."

"Oh, now, that's not true. He's registered for classes at the college."

Despite Kari's best attempts to level it, hope rose within her. Maybe she was wrong. Maybe Jake had nothing to do with this fire. Between that and the magic of baking, some of her pent-up tension began to melt away.

"Of course… I don't like that boy he's hanging out with these days," her mother added in a murmur, completely destroying the peace that had begun to settle over Kari.

"Mom—" Kari bit her tongue and forestalled any additional reminders that Jake was way past requiring—or even wanting—assistance on the playdate front.

"Don't say it, Kari. You've made it perfectly clear that I need to be tougher on Jake. But I don't want to break his spirit…you know how sensitive he is."

"He's a guy, not a horse," Kari protested. She began to pour the batter into one of her mother's muffin tins.

As she slid the muffin tin into the oven, the back door swung open. She straightened to see Jake framed in the morning light of the open door.

He stood there, stock-still, all muscular legs and bare arms in his cargo shorts and rumpled T-shirt. He looked as though he'd just rolled off somebody's couch.

Even so, with his hair all ruffled and his clothes a wrinkled mess, he had that angelic-choirboy look that made girls his age flock to him and old ladies beam at him with trusting adoration.

Jake *was* beautiful, her beautiful, gorgeous brother. If he'd wanted and had lived in a larger city, he was so arrestingly attractive that he could have landed a male modeling gig.

Next to him, Kari had always felt a little…dull. Not so shiny. Not so pretty. And yet, just like everybody else, when she'd been fourteen, she'd wanted to be in his orbit, soaking up the glamour-by-association cachet having such a good-looking brother had afforded her.

"Hey, Kare, what are you doing here? I figured you'd be downtown." He did a double take, his eyes rounding. "Oh, wait, man, you don't know? It was a fire—wicked bad. One of my buddies told me—we went down there. Sick, man."

Relief flooded through Kari. Jake hadn't

set the fire. How could she have so instantly blamed him?

*Because he set one years ago.*

"I know. I came to tell Mom."

"Somebody said it was arson." Jake's words came easily. Unlike their mother, he didn't stumble over the word *arson*. "What? Old Charlie decide the insurance money was better than the rent money?"

Kari set the timer on the oven and waited to compose herself before she turned back to face him. "I don't think it was Charlie. Why would he burn a perfectly good building?"

Jake snorted and flopped down into a chair beside their mom. "You cooking? Righteous. I'm about to starve. And I can't believe you're calling that dump a perfectly good building. Just yesterday you and he were in a screaming match about everything that was wrong with it."

Kari felt her stomach churn. That very public argument was one more nail in her coffin. It was her motive. She could hear the DA's opening argument already— revenge because her landlord wouldn't repair the building.

She met Jake's eyes. They were coolly speculative. "Jake…"

"You didn't light it up yourself, did you, sis?" her brother asked.

"No!" She began dumping the dirty dishes in the sink, rinsing them out and loading them in the dishwasher. "Of course I didn't."

"So, was it? Arson?" Jake pressed.

"Yes, Jake, it was, but don't badger your sister. She's got a lot on her shoulders."

"So do you, Mom. I mean, she burned up your retirement money, didn't she?"

Kari slammed the dishwasher door shut a little too hard. "I did *not* burn—"

"Relax, sis. It's too easy to get your goat." Jake gave her that crooked little grin that worked on so many people—for at least a while until they realized that he had no interest in actually following through on any of his promises. "I was just joking."

"Jakey!" her mom scolded. "Don't even think about joking about this. Kari could get in real trouble—and think what she did for you. You should be grateful. If the police knew…"

Jake fixed Kari with a level stare. "But they don't know. And they wouldn't believe her now anyway. And, Mom," he added, not moving his gaze from Kari, "I swear, scout's honor, it wasn't me. You can't keep blaming me for every fire in a fifty-mile radius."

Kari wanted to believe Jake. And she understood well enough how badly it felt to be the usual suspect in whatever trouble that surfaced.

His mom rushed to smooth things over. "Of course it wasn't you, nobody said it was you—"

"Sure sounded like that to me," Jake grumbled.

"I tried to call you—" Kari began.

"See? You're still trying to pin it on me!" he snapped.

"No, that's not what I—"

The doorbell rang—the front door bell. Jake was apparently ready to snatch at any excuse to end the conversation, because he leapt out of the chair and said, "I'll get it."

As he went down the hall to answer the living room door, Kari's mom hissed, "Now, see? You've hurt his feelings."

"Mom, I didn't—"

But Jake's voice rose and fell in counterpoint to whoever was at the door. Something about the timber of that other voice—male, deep, the barest hint of amusement in it, caused Kari to stiffen.

She heard Jake say, "Sure, she's in the kitchen. You're just in time for whatever she's cooking. C'mon."

Footsteps sounded closer and closer as Jake approached the kitchen with his companion.

She froze and watched.

"Hey, Kare...somebody here to see you. Didn't know you had a boyfriend."

Jake strolled back into the kitchen. Kari looked past his shoulder to see none other than Rob Monroe in his wake.

"Pardon me for tracking you down," the arson investigator told her. "But I have just a few more questions for you."

# CHAPTER FOUR

ROB TOOK ADVANTAGE of Kari's flustered silence to let his gaze slide around the kitchen. It was straight-up middle class suburbia, updated sometime in the past few years with granite counters and stainless steel appliances, but Rob knew a working kitchen when he saw one. And this kitchen? It wasn't a working kitchen.

This one wasn't like Ma's—it showed none of the telltale wear that a kitchen offers when it's used every day. No, Chelle Hendrix's kitchen looked fresh out of a home improvement store brochure. And there was something about it that made him think that the whole thing was a wannabe setup. The appliances didn't look substantial enough for the industrial look they aspired to. The floor and the cabinets and the hardware were all too…shiny, perfect, basically unused. There were no scuffmarks, no scratches, no worn finish around the doorknobs. Ma's kitchen was scrupulously clean and cared for, but worn around the edges. This kitchen? It was too pretty to be a working kitchen.

But it sure smelled like a working kitchen. Something golden brown and delicious assailed Rob's nostrils—blueberry muffins, if he knew his baked goods, and thanks to Ma and a family of good cooks, he did.

The guy who'd let Rob in—there was enough resemblance in the face to peg him as Kari's brother—lounged against the too-pretty stainless steel fridge. "So, cool, you're with the police, huh? I thought you were Kari's main squeeze."

Kari coughed in embarrassment. "Jake, Mom, this is Rob Monroe. He's—what did you tell me? Fire marshal and arson investigator? He's determining the cause of the fire at the bakery."

"You mean the whole downtown, huh, sis?" her brother corrected.

There was something of a smirk in that correction. Rob couldn't explain the instant and visceral dislike that flared up within him at Jake's response. Maybe it was because, despite all the teasing that the Monroe brothers inflicted on their sisters, they knew the value of basic human kindness. He'd never kick Maegan, Cara or DeeDee when they were already down.

But not everybody was like him or his brothers. He pushed the thought away and concentrated on Kari's reaction. Her head bowed, and she managed a tiny nod.

"Yes. You're right, Jake. It wasn't just my shop that burned. Thanks for reminding me not to be so self-absorbed."

Rob did a double take. Kari's tone was completely devoid of sarcasm—in fact, a mix of humility and gratitude bubbled up out of her words.

If he'd been surprised that she hadn't clocked her brother, he didn't miss the flash of irritation in Jake's expression.

"Oh, yeah, Miss Goody Two Shoes. Guess you'll be wading in and saving the day, huh?" Jake retorted.

Kari's mouth compressed in real anger. Before she could say anything, Chelle piped up, "Jakey! Don't poke fun at your sister!"

Chelle could have been talking to a nine-year-old, not someone about Rob's age. But it must have given Kari the distraction she needed, because Rob heard her draw in an audible breath. He looked around to see her place both hands on the counter and press down hard. Control was obviously very important to Kari Hendrix.

"You're right, Jake. You know me way too well. I really should do something for those folks. They'll be going through and trying to salvage things now—right, Rob? The buildings have been released? People can go through them?"

Rob considered this. "Yes and no. If the building in question is structurally sound, then they can go in during daylight hours. But some of the structures will need to be reinforced. And…well, yours is a crime scene."

Kari bit her lip. "Right." She turned to her mother. "Mom, do you mind if I use up the rest of the blueberries and the flour? I'll buy you some more. But I want to make a big batch of muffins for my downtown neighbors… Jake's right. It's not just about me. They're going through the same thing I am."

Chelle waved her hand expansively. "*Mi* kitchen *es su* kitchen, I told you that. Jakey, go get some money out of my purse and run to the grocery and get her whatever she needs, okay? She'll make a list."

Jake barely concealed a roll of his eyes. "Sure, sure. I'll grab her a superhero cape while I'm at it. I think they've got 'em on aisle three. Hey, sis, just text me the list, okay? I'm outta here."

He sauntered out of the kitchen, presumably toward wherever Chelle kept her purse.

The timer beeped on the oven. It galvanized Kari. She called after Jake, "Wait! The muffins! You said you were hungry?"

His reply wafted back toward the kitchen. "I'll grab a honey-bun or something." The front door banged shut.

Rude. Just plain rude and inconsiderate. Ma would have skinned any of her children who turned down home-cooked food as it was coming out of the oven.

*Not everybody was raised by Ma. You can't judge people by Monroe standards. Isn't that what you're always telling Daniel and Andrew?*

Rob drew his thoughts back from his brothers and pinned his attention on Kari. It wasn't hard to do—not with her pulling a delicious-smelling pan of muffins out of the oven.

These were huge, puffy confections, studded with steaming volcanoes of blueberries. His fingers itched to snatch one up.

Kari must have read his mind. "You'll have one, won't you, Rob?"

"Uh, sure. If you have enough."

"Don't worry. I'm cooking more for the downtown folks." She smiled—a sweet curve of her lips that warmed her face in a way he hadn't seen on her before. "Can I get you some coffee?"

"I guess I'll take you up on that muffin. I don't know, though, about the wisdom of me having more coffee. I've had something like six cups already since four, and I'm wired as a coat hanger. Maybe I'd better just have some water."

"Milk," Kari said instead, firmly, confidently. "Milk would go better with the muffins, and you look like the sort of fellow who would enjoy a glass of milk."

"Yeah. That sounds perfect." He pulled out a chair beside Chelle and watched as Kari deftly turned the muffins out in a wide shallow bowl. They came out perfectly, like something that would be in the pages of a cookbook or a magazine. His mouth watered as Kari set the bowl down on the table between him and Chelle. With quick efficient movements, Kari grabbed a stack of small plates from the cupboard.

"Let me get that milk," she added as she set the plates down beside him with a clatter.

Kari was back in a flash, pouring two glasses of milk. As she handed him the milk, Rob saw that her face was still suffused with that warm expression. This was a different Kari from this morning, a confident, poised Kari who seemed to feel comfortable in her own skin, doing what came naturally to her.

Feeding others. Taking care of others. Rob had seen that same level of comfort and confidence in his mom and his sisters and even his brothers as they'd done the same thing.

The Monroes were like that, too—squirmy when the microscope was turned on them. He understood how a person could be uncomfortable with attention focused on herself, and then completely at ease when she could focus on the needs of others.

"Oh, Kari, you outdid yourself on these," Chelle told her after an enthusiastic bite from her muffin.

Kari smiled, ducked her head. "Thanks, Mom," she murmured as she tested one for herself.

Rob liked that. No "aw, shucks, it was nothing," no "These? These are horrible!"

Now he tried one of the muffins. It was like biting into a piece of paradise: warm and comforting and with a burst of summer as a blueberry exploded into his mouth. The balance of sweetness and earthiness mingled perfectly, along with just the right cross of crunch and chew.

"Wow." He managed to swallow the bite of muffin and not instantly stuff the rest of it in his mouth. Self-control. That was the ticket.

"You like it?" Kari glanced at him shyly.

"It's head and shoulders above my attempts. But then, I do use one of those boxed mixes," Rob admitted. He took a bigger bite of the muffin, trying to decide if it would be bad to eat two or three or the whole bowlful.

Kari shuddered. "Ugh. Really—I know I'm talking myself out of a job here—but muffins are just as easy to make from scratch as a box. And so much better."

"You'll have to teach me sometime."

Chelle scarfed the rest of the muffin and said with a wink to Rob, "Oh, you can't trust Kari. I follow her same recipe, and mine never turn out like this. She leaves something out when she writes it down."

"I don't," Kari protested with a laugh. "You saw me, Mom. You saw me cook them in front of you. Just follow the recipe and don't overmix. That's the only secret."

At the word *secret*, some of Kari's confidence seemed to wilt. It was as if she had been instantly reminded of the morning's events. She put down the half-eaten muffin and stared across the table at Rob.

"So you had some questions," she said.

Rob let the sweetness from the muffin linger in his mouth for a second longer before he washed it away with a swig of milk—and like the muffin, it was perfect: not too cold, not too warm, no ice to mess it up, an exactly appropriate amount of bubbly froth ringed around its surface.

He dragged his thoughts back from the task of filling his belly…and from his appreciation of the woman who'd provided the food to do that. "Yes. Oh, and you'll need to give a formal statement sometime today. You left this morning before I could finish."

"Ha. That's a polite way of putting it. I tucked my tail between my legs and ran," Kari said. She toyed with a muffin, shredding it between fingers that were long and slender but still managed to look as though they could manhandle a bowlful of bread dough.

"Well…yeah. Mind telling me why that was?"

"It was—just too much. That bakery is my

dream, the goal I've worked toward since I was fifteen. To see it all up in smoke and know that somebody intentionally did it..." Kari trailed off.

"But you did the same thing, didn't you?" Rob scrutinized her face for any reaction his provocative question gained him. "You burned down someone's dream, right?"

He'd not been able to pull up the case, so he was flying blind here. He had run Kari's name through the system, and it came up clean except for the sealed record she'd had as a juvie. Not anything else—not so much as a parking ticket in the years since she was fourteen.

That was odd. Usually juvie for a kid that age was a first stop on a long path to the revolving door of prison. Either Kari had been scared straight or she'd not belonged there to begin with...

*Now, that doesn't make any sense. She's a self-confessed arsonist. Of course she belonged there.*

The reaction that Rob had hoped to provoke didn't disappoint. He could have slapped her and got the same expression for his trouble: first the slack-jawed expression that followed any low blow, then the in-drawn breath, the narrowed eyes and compressed lips.

"I never—" she snarled.

Her mother quickly wrapped her fingers around Kari's in a tight squeeze. It seemed to deflate Kari. Pain pushed away the anger around Kari's eyes. She closed them, then dropped her head.

"It's okay, Mom. I'm…" She freed her hand from her mother's, and Rob noticed the red imprints of Chelle Hendrix's fingers on Kari's.

Kari put a trembling hand up to her forehead and leaned against it. "That's fair enough, Rob. I guess you think it doesn't matter, that what happened was only what I deserved."

Kari's listless words shamed Rob. "No. I'm not saying that at all. You paid your debt for that fire. And I can see from your record—or the lack of one as an adult—that you've mended your ways. Plus, there are other victims besides you, Kari."

She raised her head. "But I'm the one you're investigating." It was a flat statement of fact, delivered with a direct and unflinching stare.

Rob shrugged. "You said you didn't do

it. And that you have no idea who would."
He couldn't keep a faint trace of incredulity at this last out of his tone. To cover it—surely, yeah, just to keep his hands busy—he reached for another muffin.

"I don't. I don't know anything about who set that fire."

The second muffin tasted just as delicious as the first one had, but the tension in the room took some of the joy out of it. Rob noticed how both Chelle and Kari seemed on tenterhooks, poised to run or flee or… something.

"Besides the ever-generous landlord, Charlie, have you had any run-ins with anyone else? Owe any money to…hmm, highly motivated lenders?" Rob drained the glass of milk and wanted more. Before he could even put the desire into a complete thought, Kari had risen from the table and pulled the milk out of the fridge.

Was it reflex? Or an attempt to distract him while she thought through her answer?

Whatever her motivation, Kari brought the milk to the table and refilled his glass. She returned the jug to the fridge and shut the door with a crisp thud. "I borrowed the money for the bakery from my mom—who borrowed it against her 401(k). So unless my mom has Mafia leanings—and that's what you're thinking, right? Some sort of loan shark? The answer is no."

Rob focused his gaze on Chelle. She'd completely destroyed the paper napkin she'd been holding since Kari had pulled her hand free. It showered on her table like a mini snowstorm. "That right?" he prompted her.

Chelle jumped. She looked guilty as sin, to the roots of her pseudo blond hair. "Oh, yes. I borrowed the money. Kari's been paying me back with interest—the same interest that I'm being charged. I can show you the paperwork, if you like?"

"I would like. Very much." Maybe Chelle burned the place so that she could replenish her 401(k)? "Had she kept up with the note?" Rob pressed.

"Yes. Every month without fail—Kari's actually the one who makes the payment. Let me… I'll just go get that paperwork." Chelle fluttered her hands, releasing the final blizzard of paper napkin. She pushed her chair away from the kitchen table and strode out of the room.

"Happy?" Kari snapped to Rob. "Satisfied that my mom didn't torch the place to get her money back?" She didn't bother to take her chair again, but instead paced back and forth, armed with a dishcloth and wiping up imaginary specks of dust from the counter.

"Hey, I'm just doing my job." He held up both palms to ward off her sarcasm.

Her face fell again, with that same deflation that had occurred a few moments before when he'd reminded her about the consequences of her own arson. She put down the dishcloth and sighed. "Yes. You are. I'm sorry. This is—it's hard."

"You have to know how I'm going to see this, where my thoughts are heading," Rob pointed out in the gentlest tone he could muster. "If you didn't do it, and your mom didn't do it, somebody still did. And whoever it is has it in for you. I can't believe Charlie is the only person you've had cross words with."

"I can't—" Kari leaned against the counter, put her fingers to her mouth and closed her eyes. "Sure, I've had angry customers, disappointed customers, people who are after me to pay bills, but I can't imagine that any of them would think burning my bakery— burning half a city block—would be the answer."

"So you do owe money?" Rob's scalp

prickled. Now they were getting somewhere. Maybe with Mom out of the room, he could get to the bottom of this, get a viable suspect.

"Sure." Kari shrugged her slim shoulders. "What bakery doesn't? I have to buy the raw materials before my customers pay me, and sometimes it takes weeks on a big order before I do get paid. My suppliers—flour and sugar and all of that's not cheap. And I have to keep the lights on and the gas paid. Plus… well, I've had to do repairs, since Charlie wouldn't."

The buzz of excitement within Rob fizzled. She was right; a regular creditor would take a merchant to small claims court and send a report to ding her credit rating. Creditors were more interested in getting their money, not in making a statement with arson.

In his mind, he turned over the few facts he knew for certain about the case. If not money, which was the number one reason for arson, then revenge.

Come to think of it, the whole setup *did* scream revenge.

"What about that other fire?" he asked.

Kari jerked with surprise, banging her elbow on the edge of the counter as she did.

"The—the other fire?" she repeated, rubbing the injured elbow.

"Yeah. The one you set. Could this be related to it?"

"I've already told you I didn't start this fire—"

Rob noted the neat evasion and stopped her with an interruption. "Tell me about it. That fire. The one you set. Who did it hurt?"

Her face completely closed down. "It hurt everybody."

"No, I mean, who was the victim? There were two fires serious enough to get a first-time offending juvie a felony conviction for arson that year. Both big arsons. One was a convenience store. The other was a big warehouse fire. I know you didn't set the warehouse fire—that was the fire that killed my dad—since you were already sent off by then. So it was the convenience store fire, right?"

"Wait…" Kari's head tilted and she frowned, as if she were trying to hear something said at a great distance. Her fingers, their knuckles white, dug into the countertop as if to keep her upright and prevent her from sliding to the floor. "Wait. There was *another* fire that year? Your dad? Your dad got *killed*? In an *arson*?"

## CHAPTER FIVE

A WEEK AFTER the fire, and Kari still felt as though she were in disaster mode.

A trickle of perspiration coursed its way between her shoulder blades as she manhandled a huge cardboard box from her apartment's kitchen to the front door. It wasn't that the box was heavy, or that the distance was great. No, the box was awkward in its oversized dimensions, and negotiating the tight turns between her kitchen and the front door—

*Not my kitchen. Not anymore.*

The realization hit her with an almost physical force. She was actually doing this, packing up her bits and pieces of the scraps of the life she had salvaged from the first fire, and moving back in with her mother— the ultimate cliché, the ultimate punch line of so many bad jokes.

The very thing she wanted least in the world to do.

Kari hated being like Jake, freeloading off her mother's generous spirit. Her mom had worked so hard as a single parent to raise them without any help. And look how the two of them had repaid her: both of them bouncing back every time they needed a roof over their heads.

Well, no, actually, this was the first time that Kari had ever taken up her mother's repeated offers. But she had accepted her mother's loan—and look how *that* had turned out.

The box slipped in her sweaty palms, and Kari tried to save it from falling by wedging it against a doorjamb. Just as she had righted it and was attempting a more secure hold, the doorbell rang.

She groaned. "Door's unlocked!" she called out.

Whoever it was apparently didn't hear her. The knocking resumed, louder this time. She called out again, "Come in!"

But the only sound she heard was a rattling of the doorknob—which meant that the door *was* locked after all—and more knocking. Kari took up her burden again and started making her way, slowly and ponderously, toward the front door. "I'm coming! I'm really coming—just give me—"

The box slipped from her grasp, its contents of pots and pans clattering down the hall and into the living room. Kari kicked aside the cardboard and stepped over three sheet pans, a roasting pan and a cupcake-shaped Bundt pan. She yanked open the door.

To see Rob Monroe on her stoop.

The last time she'd seen him, he'd revealed that his own father had died at the hands of an arsonist. No way he'd ever feel any sympathy for someone who'd pleaded guilty to arson. No way he'd ever give her the real benefit of the doubt, no matter what he said.

Just as she expected, he'd asked—though she knew it was not really voluntary—for her and Jake and her mother to come down to the station and sign formal statements. The machinery of the investigation had switched into gear, so she shouldn't have been surprised that the guy showed up again with more questions.

"Gosh, are you happy to see me, or do you always break out the brass band when you have visitors?" he quipped.

"Huh?" His words were at such a paradox

with what she'd been expecting that she was rendered speechless. A strand of hair fell into her face, and she swiped it out of the way.

"The noise? It sounded like a thousand cymbals just a minute ago."

Kari looked over her shoulder. "Oh, that— it was a box I was trying to get to the car." To punctuate her statement, the lid of a pan slid off something else and banged loudly onto her hardwood floor.

*Not mine. Not anymore.*

Kari shook her head to clear away the negativity. "You might as well come in. I've got about a thousand baking sheets to pick up."

She left him to see himself in and squatted over the scattered contents she'd dropped. It surprised her when Rob knelt down beside her and began handing things to her.

"Baking pans for the baker?"

It occurred to her that maybe he'd think she'd moved these out of the bakery before she'd torched it—or had it torched. "Well, yeah, but these are old ones, not the nice ones I had at the bakery. These were the ones I used at home—the ones I picked up along the way, you know?" She let her fingers slide over the battered quarter sheet pan she'd found at a yard sale. It was a far cry from the heavy-duty professional pans she'd lovingly used at the bakery. "I can't believe…"

"Hey, at least…" Rob's hand closed over hers. "At least you still have a pan or two, right? Or do you want to hit me for saying 'at least'?" He made a playful ducking move and shielded himself with his free hand.

She laughed. It sounded rough and broken even to her own ears, but it was definitely a chuckle. "No, I believe I can resist the temptation. Do you frequently provoke people to use violence?"

"Andrew, my little brother, says I have the art of pranks down to a science, so he might volunteer to clock me for you. My big brother tells me that I could annoy a saint, and I guess he's right. Ma sure has put up with a lot from me, and she'd definitely make the saint category."

"What, with your sunny personality?" Kari felt her knees ache in protest to the way she was kneeling, but she didn't want to move. Any shift might make him move his hand from hers, and for some reason, the sensation it telegraphed to her nerve endings—calm, confidence, competence—washed over her. She didn't want that feeling to stop.

"No, believe it or not, I'm the cynic of the family."

"You?" Now she did move, out of surprise. "But you—well, you're so—well, so *sunny.*"

She watched as he picked up the pan and dropped it with a clang into the box. Kari saw his frown—not of displeasure, but of thoughtfulness. She could practically see gears turning over in his mind.

"Thanks?" Rob said uncertainly.

Had she missed something? Insulted him in some way? "I didn't mean—it's just that you're always joking—well, not always—"

He lifted an eyebrow wryly. "Ma does say my smart mouth will get me into trouble."

The word *mouth* was a mistake. She found herself fixated on his lips. Usually they were as changeable as quicksilver—a crooked grin here, a broad smile there, a tiny knowing smile. But now… He wasn't smiling, not exactly. The corners were lifted up, showing the hint of a dimple, and revealing a sliver of strong white teeth.

And he was close enough to lean over and kiss her.

"Uh—" Kari scrambled for a lid at the far edge of the living room, underneath the window. Anything to get her mind off the inappropriate thoughts she was having about the guy who probably was employing his investigative skills to put her behind bars again.

"So I take it you're going somewhere?" Rob commented to her back.

"Another genius deduction on your part?" She returned with the lid and another pan— not to mention her composure.

"I am a detective, after all. Don't try this at home, kids." His quip was accompanied with a grin and a clang from yet another of her kitchen bowls. "Empty living room, box full of kitchenware, and bam, it just occurs to me that maybe you're moving. Where's the new nest?" A beat of silence, and then a tinge of suspicion crept into his next question. "You're not leaving town, are you?"

"My mom's." Just saying the words made the defeat sting all the more. "I'm moving to my mom's."

He seemed to digest the words, chewing on them, staring at her as though he understood how ashamed she felt at this latest mess she'd found herself in.

"So you really do have money troubles?" Rob closed up the battered lid of the box.

"No more than usual—it's not the rent here. I can afford the rent, just barely. No, it's…well, my kitchen here is so tiny. I don't even have a dishwasher."

He wrinkled his brow. "I don't follow."

"State laws say that I can use a home kitchen to cook in, you know, to bake, but I have to *live* there. It's the whole cottage industry law—as long as it's home-baked goods in a regular home kitchen, then I don't have to meet standards for a commercial kitchen."

"So…you're moving in with your mom to use her kitchen?"

"Yeah. Just, well, until I can—" Her face heated up. "Until I can save up to find me a new location that will pass a commercial kitchen inspection." It smacked of Jake's wheedled promises to their mom—just until I find another job, just until I save up for a deposit, just until I pay off these guys I owe.

"Or the insurance money comes in," Rob added speculatively.

Kari couldn't repress the snort of derision that bubbled up from her insides. "Yeah, right, like that's going to happen. I can tell you when insurance is going to write out that check—half past never."

"But you did have insurance, correct?"

"Sure. The whole bit, even paid extra for

coverage in case of work stoppage. But it's *arson*, Rob. And they'll take one look at my record…" Kari shook her head. "Never mind. It is what it is. They'll pay or they won't. I've submitted the claim, so the ball's in their court."

"They won't pay out until my investigation is finished," he reminded her.

"I know that. So how can I help?"

Did he look surprised at her offer?

"I just had a few more questions."

"Let me guess. You're going to be like that old TV detective that was constantly going, 'Just one more question, Miss,' aren't you?" she asked.

"Ma always said I was the curious type," he acknowledged.

"Ma—whoever Ma is—is right on the money."

"Ma is my mom, Colleen Monroe. She raised nearly all of us by herself after my dad was killed."

Kari's stomach turned at the thought of someone dying because of a stupid fire. She hated fire. Making a conscious effort to shift her attention to something else, she asked, "Who's all of us?"

"Well, there was me and my brother

Andrew, and you've met Daniel. And I have three sisters. Daniel had moved out—he was actually a professional baseball player in the minor leagues when it happened. But the rest of us were still at home."

"That's—that's quite a big family."

"What about you? Do you have just the one brother?"

"Jake? Yes. It's just me and him."

"How old is he, anyway?"

"Believe it or not, he's three years older than me. He just—Mom says he hasn't found his true calling in life."

"But you don't believe that." It was a statement, not a question. Kari narrowed her eyes at his too-keen observation.

"I guess I'm hoping for Mom's sake that he'll find that true calling sooner rather than later," she said. She made to pick up the box, but Rob closed his hands over hers.

"Allow me. Unless you want to give me another rendition of Clash of the Cymbals."

"No way. It sounded like I'd let a two-year-old loose in my cupboards. If you don't mind, I'd appreciate it—my car is just outside."

"Wait, not the vintage Mustang convertible? Man, now that's a car I could get excited about—"

She laughed. "No, that's my next-door neighbor's—he's going through a midlife crisis. No, mine's the brown minivan with the peeling paint. The back door should be unlocked."

He pivoted with the box. "Just put it anywhere?"

"Wherever you can find a spot. I'll be there in a jiff—I need to grab a few last things from the bedroom."

Alone, she made one last tour of the empty apartment. It was a good thing she hadn't had the money to buy a lot of furniture or bric-a-brac. She couldn't have afforded the storage costs, and her mother's house didn't have the space.

With a lump in her throat, she surveyed the sunny rooms she'd first seen just six months ago. So much hope. So much promise.

"I'll be back," she whispered. "Maybe not here, but some place like this. Some place better, even. It's not forever. It's for now."

And maybe she'd even believe that eventually. But at the moment, Kari would have to pretend that she did.

She tightened her hand on the handle of the big shopping bag with the toiletry items she'd waited to pack last, then turned for the door.

It was as she was locking the door for the last time that she spotted what Rob was doing.

The box was on the sidewalk. The doors to the van were open—all of them.

And Rob was very carefully, very thoroughly, searching her vehicle.

# CHAPTER SIX

"HEY!"

Kari Hendrix's outrage was near palpable as she closed the gap between the two of them in a quick jog. "What are you doing?"

Rob laid the blanket he had in his hand down on the floor of the mini-van. "Shifting some things around. You did say anywhere."

"No! You were searching my van! You were—you used me! You were looking for evidence—"

Rob squashed the guilty feeling that was worming its way onto his face. "I was doing what you asked. But should I, in my official capacity as an investigative officer, ask if there's anything in this vehicle you mind me seeing?"

Okay, so he *had* taken advantage of the opportunity to do a quick toss of the vehicle. He was law enforcement, and she knew it—or she ought to. He'd found nothing in the vehicle the least bit suspicious. The only evidence he'd found pointed toward a careful and frugal lifestyle—that and a predilection for toffee bars, if the little trashcan's cache of candy wrappers belonged to her.

"Well—no—it's just—" Her expression was still full of wounded betrayal. "You could have told me that was why you came. And then I would have been prepared for you pawing through my things. That's—that's one of the things I hated most about juvie. They were always hunting and searching and—nothing was ever mine."

The words rang true, even to his cynical self. Or maybe it was because he had searched the van and come up empty.

"I'm sorry. I was here. You had given me permission to go into your van—and my nosiness got the better of me."

"It's your job. I guess I just allowed myself to forget that." This last she said with a baleful resignation. "So was that the reason? That you came?"

"Er—no." Rob busied himself with putting the box in the van. "I really did have some more questions."

She pushed past him and dropped the bag in her hand into the seat. When she saw his eyes trail the path of the bag, she gave an exasperated sigh and upturned the bag, emptying its contents. Shampoo, toothpaste, deodorant and other toiletries fell out.

"See any matches?" she snapped.

For the first time ever, he regretted his devious cleverness when it came to his job. He had a reputation for being able to charm confessions out of arsonists—he'd even been called into neighboring counties to help out with the odd case. And this, today, had been something of the same. She'd offered, and he'd taken the opportunity to dig around.

"Look, I said I was sorry," Rob told her. "Maybe I wasn't completely on the up-and-up with you, but if you've got nothing to hide, then no harm, no foul."

"Just because I've got nothing to hide doesn't mean I don't value my privacy—or a little trust. You really are cynical, aren't you?"

"Hey, you should look at it from the bright side—at least now I *know* you're not hiding anything in your van," he countered.

Kari rolled her eyes. "Oh, wow. A cynic who's a closet Pollyanna. How many times do I have to tell you? I didn't burn my bakery."

"So who did? Give me one solid lead, one

good suspect." Rob heard the near pleading in his voice, and it scared him. He wanted her to be innocent. He wanted her to have nothing at all to do with the downtown fire. "Tell me who hates you enough to destroy your business and do a decent job framing you."

Her anger faded to misery. "I can't do this, Rob. I didn't do it when I was in juvie, and I won't do it now. I won't get myself out of hot water by pushing someone else in."

Rob shook his head in frustration. Looking at Kari Hendrix's earnest face was only serving to confuse him. He kicked at pebbles strewn across the pavement by Kari's beat-up van and pinched the bridge of his nose.

"And besides," he said in a sour tone that he hated, "you don't know anything to tell."

She jumped—just a little jump, but one that he saw out of the corner of his eyes. Oh, yeah, Kari Hendrix had at least one suspect in mind. So who was she protecting?

"That's right." She nodded her head a little too vigorously. "I don't know anything at all to tell."

"Well, then. I guess it's a good thing that I am a real, bona fide investigative officer, because…" He leaned forward, close enough to inhale the sweet flowery scent of her hair. "I will find this person, Kari. I will. With your help, or without it. It's only a matter of time."

ROB WENT BACK to the basics the next morning in his cramped windowless office. First he wiped the whiteboard clean of his previous scrawls and notes held up by magnets. And then he began again with what he knew.

The fire was arson.

The MO was a propane tank and a highway flare.

The motive—just looking at the MO— was probably revenge.

He swore as he looked at the vast amount of white space left on the board. In the past week, he'd found nothing—absolutely nothing— to point him in any direction except Kari.

And yet, conversely, he'd found nothing to tie Kari to the fire. In fact, he'd found direct evidence giving her a fairly solid alibi: a surveillance video from a business across the street from her house had shown her working in her yard the afternoon of the fire, going into the apartment and not coming out until after the fire engines had been paged.

And the apartment didn't have a back door. He'd verified that today, though he'd already spoken to Kari's landlord earlier in the week.

True, there were windows on the back, but they were high off the ground with no good access point for a woman as petite as Kari. She would have caused an almighty racket if she'd come down on the bank of metal trash-cans along the rear of her apartment. He'd canvassed her neighbors—nobody had heard anything or seen anything. And one of those neighbors was a nosy Ned with a telescope on his deck and a roaming sort of eye.

Plus, Rob kept coming back to what he'd told Daniel that very first day: if Kari Hendrix had wanted to burn down her bakery, she could have figured out a way to make it look like an accident. The setup that had been used to start the fire, that MO so clear-cut a case of arson, was a clear threat or warning if he'd ever seen one.

Somewhere, somehow, in this entire week of digging, he'd missed something. He knew it.

So it was time to get off his backside and apply some elbow grease and shoe leather to the problem. He would go back and re-canvass the business owners and employees downtown. Surely, someone had seen something.

Maybe it was the fresh air or not being cooped up in the office, but Rob instantly felt more cheerful as he strolled down the sidewalk in the direction of downtown Waverly.

The walk from his office was just long enough to lift his spirits—to Rob, Waverly was the right size, not too big, not too small, and the downtown part with its wealth of locally owned businesses had always been his favorite. He passed the carefully tended planters the Waverly-Levi County Garden Club kept overflowing with cheerful red geraniums and nodded to a rail-thin septuagenarian sporting a dapper fedora who was propped up against them.

As he waved away an inquisitive bee, he spotted a group of toddlers cooling off under the interactive fountain in the pocket park just at the edge of downtown proper. Their moms sat nearby, laughing as the kids opened their mouths and drank in the cool water. Something about the kids' exuberance, their innocence, made Rob chuckle, too.

The burned-out remains of the buildings loomed ahead, but not even they could dampen his suddenly ebullient mood.

What did poke the air out of his bubble was the big zero that he turned up with his recanvassing. Besides Charlie Kirkman, the landlord, no one had ever seen anybody give Kari Hendrix so much as a hard stare.

For his last stop, Rob ducked into a jewelry store across the street, one with a good vantage point of the Lovin' Oven's front door. It was owned and run by the Sullivans, the same couple who'd been there since the 1960s.

"Well, if it isn't young Mr. Monroe!" Hiram Sullivan greeted him from behind the counter. "Make my day, sir, and tell me that you have finally been caught, and you're here to pick out an engagement ring."

Rob laughed. The engagement ring deal was Mr. Hiram's running joke with him— he said the same thing every time Rob came in. "You know me—a rolling stone, and all that. Nope, today it's all official business, I'm afraid, but Ma's got a birthday coming up, so maybe I do need something after all."

"Ah, a good woman, Mrs. Colleen is, and a very wise one. I saw her earlier this week with Mrs. Kimberly. Your brother and she have their bridal registry picked out." Mr.

Hiram nodded toward the tables of china near the front of the store.

The idea of Daniel picking out china and other frou-frous boggled the mind. "Just let me know what they need toward the end and put me down for it—I know beans about wedding presents."

Mr. Hiram nodded approvingly. "An easy customer. Now what is it that I can help you with in your official capacity?"

"I came back to ask again about the fire."

Mr. Hiram tsked and began polishing his spectacles with a jewelry cloth he'd pulled from his apron. "A sad thing, isn't it? Is it wrong to be glad that it was on the other side of the street? At our age, we couldn't start over. Our whole life is in this shop."

"And you've seen nothing out of the ordinary? Not in the weeks leading up to the fire?"

"No, like I told you before, nothing that stands out. No sinister folks—how do you law enforcement people put it? Casing the joint?"

The words sounded ludicrous coming out of the old man's mouth, but Rob managed to suppress all but the smallest of grins. "What about Kari Hendrix? And the bakery?"

Mr. Hiram pursed his lips, considering. "A nice young woman, if you ask me. Hardworking. Reminded me of Mrs. Sullivan at that age."

"How so?" Rob leaned forward on the jewelry counter.

"Well, she did so much of the work. The curtains—did you know that she sewed them herself? And every week she'd put in a new display in the window. She was there every morning when I opened up, and she stayed late a lot of nights. And have you sampled her wares?" Old Hiram kissed his fingertips and closed his eyes in satisfied memory. "That woman knows her way around a kitchen!"

"Did other folks appreciate her good points?"

Mr. Hiram frowned. "You mean did she have a good business?" He cocked an eyebrow. "Not at first. It was slow going, and you could see how dispirited she was. She'd come out and give free samples on the sidewalk—we looked forward to those, but my wife always said we shouldn't be greedy. I liked the little mini blueberry muffins the best."

"Her muffins *are* good," Rob conceded. "So business was bad?"

"Lately, no. She'd gotten on a roll…it was steady, and improving. A few days before the fire she came over with a basket of goodies for me and the missus, and she was excited about the orders she was getting—the mayor's daughter had ordered her wedding cake. Kari was sure it was a good sign."

"Obviously she didn't know the mayor's daughter. Now, that one is a diva if I ever saw one," Rob commented.

"Oh, yes. Changed her mind three times about her engagement ring, and I thought she'd drive my wife mad going back and forth about the china. But I could see why Kari thought it a good omen—if she pleases Mattie Gottman, she has a shot at the wedding cakes for all eight of the girl's bridesmaids."

"Eight?" Rob choked. "Who needs eight bridesmaids? I pity the poor guys they rope in for groomsmen."

"She'd wanted ten, but two girls had the temerity to say no." Mr. Hiram dusted his fingernails against the twill of his apron. "Can you imagine?"

"Saying no to Mattie Gottman? It takes

a strong man—believe you me, I've had to do it. Not for the faint of heart." Rob considered the import of what Hiram had told him. Kari had been given the golden ticket to high-society weddings, at least here locally. It would have translated into more work for her, he knew that.

So that was another nail in the coffin for the theory of Kari burning down her own business. Who would want to let down the mayor's picky daughter? Or ruin her growing business, for that matter?

"Did anyone *not* like Kari?" Rob asked. "Anyone who saw her as a threat or her business an obstacle?"

Mr. Hiram screwed up his face in concentration. For a long moment, he just shook his head. A thought must have occurred to him, though, because his bushy white eyebrows sprang up in a classic "aha!" move. "There was a young man who seemed to agitate her—a repeat customer, I suppose. He's been around more the past month or so. Tall, shaggy blond hair, wears T-shirts and those awful cargo shorts that hang from the waist and show off your underwear—oh, and flip-flops with socks."

That sounded like a spot-on description

for Jake, Kari's brother. "Could you pick him out of a six-pack if I brought you one?"

"A six-pack?" Mr. Hiram frowned. "Of… beer?"

"No, I mean, six photos of similar looking men. Sorry. My police lingo got the best of me."

Mr. Hiram had the audacity to smirk. "A six-pack, hmm? I shall have to remember that term. It will impress my wife—she's always reading those police procedurals." He began dusting off the spotless display case. "Why, yes, I believe I could. You bring your, eh, six-pack over to me and I shall give it a try."

"And what made you think this fellow agitated Kari?"

"Well, they seemed to disagree, for one. They were talking excitedly the day of the fire. Oh, wait! I suppose you've checked out Mr. Charlie Kirkman? Because he certainly had a contentious relationship with all of his downtown tenants. And he was arguing with Kari that same afternoon."

Rob sighed to himself. The brother and the landlord—nothing new at all in the way of leads.

"Yes, Charlie Kirkman's been cleared of

any direct involvement…and we can find no financial trail to indicate that he hired someone to do the job. But, er…" now Rob put his fingers to his lips and glanced ostentatiously to either side and said, "keep that under your hat, will you?"

Mr. Hiram nodded. "You have my word. Let's see…let me think." Now in an absent-minded way, he pulled out a tray of watches from the case and began polishing them with his jewelry cloth.

He'd made it to watch three before he said, "No, I can't think of anyone who seemed to have a cross word to say about Miss Kari Hendrix. She does so many nice things for so many people. When Jack Stewart—they own the little bookshop down the street from her—wound up in the ICU, Kari made up a basket of treats for Mrs. Stewart and took it to her in the hospital. The only way I found out about that was when Mrs. Stewart came in here to buy a little thank-you gift for Kari. And Kari's always donating things to the Downtown Association for raffles and fundraisers. Look—there she is now—see Kari?" Mr. Hiram gestured with the cloth in his hand over Rob's shoulder.

"She's handing out treats for the business owners who are still trying to salvage things."

Rob turned to see where Hiram was pointing. Sure enough, there was Kari, with a big basket lined with a gingham cloth, doling out…not muffins. A glazed pastry of some sort, from the looks of it.

"Well, how could I have forgotten!" Mr. Hiram murmured to himself. "Alan Simpson—he owns the pawn and gun shop next door to Kari. He'd been after Charlie to move Kari down to another spot, so that Alan could expand the shop. I didn't think about that until I saw them together just now. See? Kari's handing him—oh, my, do you think she'll bring one of those bear claws of hers over here?" The jeweler's eyes sparkled with anticipation. "I could do with a little midmorning pick-me up!"

It was as if Kari had read the old man's mind. Rob saw her smile and nod at Simpson, then cross the street and head straight for the jewelry shop. A moment later, the bell jangled and she came breezing in.

"Mr. Hiram! I brought you a—" The bright smile on her face froze as she spotted Rob.

"A bear claw!" Mr. Hiram either didn't notice her sudden stumble in speech or chose to ignore it. He put the watches back, deftly opened the walk-through gate between the counters and met Kari on the customer side. "I was just telling young Mr. Monroe here that I hoped you'd remember me."

"Would…would you care for one?" she asked Rob. She held up the basket with a great deal less enthusiasm than she had for Mr. Hiram.

"Oh, you must try one!" Mr. Hiram urged. "They are addictively good! Why, my wife buys a half dozen once a week, just as a treat for me."

Rob picked up the pastry and bit into it. A rush of butter and sugar flooded through him. The bear claw melted in his mouth.

"And I thought Ma was good in the kitchen. Is there anything you can't cook?" he mumbled around the mouthful of heaven he was devouring.

Kari's cheeks were rosy pink, and she ducked her head. "Sure. I'm not really a cook. I'm more of a baker. So, you know… if it doesn't involve flour and butter, sometimes I—well—I'm glad you enjoyed it."

She made a show of handing another pastry to Hiram and wringing out a promise that he would save it for his wife. With that done, Kari practically sprinted for the door. "See you around, Mr. Hiram!"

"Wait, Kari, I'll walk with you." Rob brushed off the glaze from his fingertips and hurried after her.

Out on the sidewalk, he saw how she bit her lip—an anxious habit he'd already noticed the previous times he'd been around her. "I assume this has something to do with the investigation?" she asked.

"Yeah. Tell me about your relationship with Alan Simpson."

Kari seemed genuinely startled by the question. "Mr. Simpson? Who owns the gun shop? He's my neighbor—shop neighbor, I mean. I don't know him well, but he seems nice enough."

"He wasn't pressuring you to move to another location?"

Kari shifted the basket to her other hand and let out a breath of what sounded like exasperation to Rob. "Not pressuring, exactly. He wanted to expand his shop, but Charlie let me have the space because I agreed to pay a higher rent for it."

"Do you think Simpson would have resorted to scare tactics?"

"Huh? You mean, did Mr. Simpson start the fire to burn me out? Why would he do that? His own shop suffered almost as much damage as mine—plus, he had all those bullets in there! He talked about how scared he was for the firefighters because he was concerned that the bullets would explode from the heat."

"Maybe he didn't bargain on it being such a big bang?" Rob countered.

Kari shook her head, a firm, decisive no. "Not in a million years. All he had to do to get me out of there, whether I agreed or not, was to offer Charlie more money. You know how Charlie Kirkman is."

"But you had a lease, right?"

Kari snickered. "And since when does any lease from Charlie not contain a few handy loopholes for him, hmm? No, Rob. I don't know who burned these buildings, but it wasn't me, and it wasn't Alan Simpson, and it probably wasn't even Charlie. Like I told you yesterday, I just don't know who could have started that fire."

Rob had to admire the way she refused

to throw anybody under the bus. Most people—and he had to admit that the majority of the people he interviewed in the course of a day's work were of the criminal variety—wouldn't have been so considerate. No, they would have jumped on the prospect of a pushy neighbor with the enthusiasm of a duck on a june bug.

Still, it didn't help further the investigation.

"Kari...everybody I talk to keeps saying how nice you are, how you don't have a single, solitary enemy. So why would someone go to the risk and the trouble of burning down your business?"

"Maybe it was a prank gone wrong," she said. "Do I ever know a thing or two about that." Kari closed her eyes, apparently visualizing her own crime of arson so many years before. She opened them and fixed Rob with a glare. "But if it is, if it's a kid out there who didn't realize the destructive power of fire, well, maybe he learned his lesson. Because I for one realize exactly how destructive time behind bars can be. It wouldn't fix anything, Rob. It wouldn't rebuild these buildings. It wouldn't pay one dollar to replace what was destroyed. If it was a prank, let it go. Just… please. Don't make some other kid endure what I went through."

And with that, she did a crisp about-face and hurried up the sidewalk away from him.

ler from one of the vendors. "I'm
out...it will come. I've been driv-
f crazy worrying about it because
t to do this investigation. But right
ding here with you, you make me
at it will all work out."

eamed. "Why, sure, it will. You've
ugh harder times than this, don't
at? Now you tell me all about it
poke around and explore this place

th that, Alice led her off to the tall their sparkling jars of preserves
te-season produce spilling out of
baskets and bins.

only much later, when the sun
rise in the sky in earnest and the
emed even thicker, that Kari actu-
nbered her original intention. She
colorful booth filled with jars of
wire baskets with smooth brown
bed of ice. A handwritten placard
nt of the red checked tablecloth
d Locally Grown—Pastured Eggs.
ft Alice at the booth with home-
ps and her assurance that she'd
in a moment. She hurried up the
een the stalls, working her way

## CHAPTER SEVEN

KARI SHADED HER eyes as she searched the
early-morning crowd at the weekly farmers
market and adjacent flea market just off the
Waverly downtown area. Alice Heaton had
said she would meet her here, but Kari couldn't
spot Alice's roly-poly frame—she was even
shorter than Kari—among the early morning
bargain hunters.

Alice had been the only good thing about
juvie—the one saving grace. The cook had
found her sobbing on her birthday, homesick
as all get-out and had hauled her up to her
feet. "You want a birthday cake? Well, all
it takes is flour and sugar and butter. Why
don't you come on and we'll bake one together?"

Her call yesterday had been just what Kari
needed. In the three weeks since the downtown fire, Kari had been going all out, trying
to deal with fulfilling orders and wrangling

with the insurance company—and its elusive insurance adjustor.

But Kari still wasn't sure she'd been wise to agree to meet Alice. After all, she had cakes to bake and piecrusts to roll out.

A tap on her shoulder made Kari wheel around. There Alice was, all 4'10" of her, her cheeks round and flushed, her eyes full of their usual gentle smile.

"Well, aren't you a sight for sore eyes! No, let me look at you—girl! You've grown. Seems like yesterday you were nothing but a snip of a thing."

She let Alice wrap her in a hug and she tried not to cry. This woman had believed in her, had given her a chance, had given her a life, when no one else had.

Alice patted her on the back. "Now, now. You cry if you need to. You don't mind these folks. We'll find a quiet corner and just talk if that's what you'd rather do. It is hard, I know. That bakery was your dream, and you worked hard to make it a success."

But even if Alice had given her permission to fall apart, Kari couldn't do it. Not here. Kari gazed at the bustle all around them. Little kids were dashing here and there, sporting handmade toys and finds from the jumble

sale, while their paren
fruit and vegetable st
vilion the city had bu
Few towns as small a
such a vibrant local

Still…she had a k
"I'm okay, Alice. I'
come, but I may n
spend. I've only plan
with another supplier
have a lot of free tim
I've got three cakes
ble batch of cinnam
cupcakes—"

Alice tucked her
always were a hard
sun is out, it's a gor
get all that baking
Edison invented t
we could work aft
Didn't I tell you th

Kari smiled. "O
sorry, Alice. I'm s

Now Alice sob
cause I stopped by
you get a check
pany?"

Kari breathed

mulle
not su
ing my
they've
now, s
believe

Alic
come
I know
while
togethe

And
bles wi
and the
bountif

It wa
began t
crowds
ally rem
spotted
jams an
eggs on
on the f
proclaim

Kari l
made so
come bac
aisle betw

past the people inspecting late summer tomatoes and peppers and the very earliest of
the fall butternut squash.

"Excuse me, are these eggs organic?" she
asked the woman sitting behind the table.

The woman, her dark hair shot with silver
and pulled back in a bun, looked up from the
knitting she was clacking away at. "Organic?
Well, no, not technically—it would cost us
too much money to get the certification, but I
can assure you, they're from pastured chickens, and we use organic principles."

Kari smiled. Something about the woman
seemed familiar. Maybe she'd been a customer? "I've definitely heard that before—
the cost to get certified can be rather high. I
guess for my purposes, I'm more interested
in how the chickens were raised rather than
if you actually can call them organic."

The woman nodded. "We have a farm
right outside of town—try to grow as much
as we can of what we need. Say, don't you
own that bakery?"

"You mean the Lovin' Oven? Yes."

The vendor tsked. "Now, that was a shame,
that fire. Awful. I do hope you're going to
be able to stay in business. Our Taylor sure
does enjoy your cupcakes."

So she was a customer after all. "I have a terrible memory—I seem to know you, but I can't—" Kari shrugged, embarrassed.

"Oh—you probably don't know me. I've only been in your shop maybe twice. But now, my daughter DeeDee and my grand-daughter Taylor? Maybe you're thinking of her. The one who has the corn allergy?"

"Oh, yeah!" Now the pieces of the puzzle clicked into place. "Sure, I remember—so DeeDee is your daughter?"

"Yes, ma'am, and we are eternally grate-ful to you for the times you've been able to bake something safe for Taylor. I bake, mind you, but she does like fancy things."

"It's truly my pleasure," Kari said, sat-isfaction warming her. "And I hope your eggs will fit the bill. I'd like to buy local if I could."

"Well, now—the person you need to talk to about those eggs would be my son—he helps me out with them. Let me see—"

Now it was the woman who was shading her eyes and searching. "Wait, there he is."

She pointed to another vendor's stall two or three booths down, but all Kari could see was a sliver of broad shoulders in a plaid shirt through the crowd of bodies. "I don't—"

But the woman had a more efficient way of communicating with her son. From her apron pocket she produced a cell phone. "What did we ever do before these things came along?" she said with a wink. A quick call later, and the woman said, "He'll be here in a jiff. Whatever questions you have, he'll be happy to help. We'd love to have your business—you must use a lot of eggs every day."

"Yes, I do. But farm-fresh eggs are a luxury I can't always afford. The price here seems more than reasonable."

"It's a shame to charge more when all that those chickens do is live off our land—and we have plenty of eggs. Ah, here he is!"

Kari looked up to see none other than Rob Monroe bearing down on her.

KARI WAS STILL befuddled a few minutes later as they sat on a bench away from the various market-goers. She was trying to focus on what Rob was saying.

"So, no, not organic, but almost, if there's such a thing. We're organic in spirit."

"I can't picture you raising chickens," she blurted out.

It was true. She couldn't. Fighting fires, investigating arson, sure, but chickens?

"And why not? Don't I look like a chicken man?" Rob's eyes crinkled at the corners, his smile lighting them up. "I've been raising chickens since I was in fourth grade. It was my 4H Club project all through middle school and high school. I took blue ribbon prizes for three straight years—although, I have to admit, my dad helped me with my first project."

"Wow. That must have been nice, having a dad around."

For a split second, a shadow passed over Rob's face, and she recalled that his father had died in a fire. An arson.

A shiver ran through her.

"Your dad wasn't around?" Rob asked.

"Uh, no. Don't get me wrong…he's not a bad sort. It was just, you know how divorce is…"

"Not really. My parents stayed together, and I've never been married. Came close once, but…it didn't work out."

Kari nodded her head toward a little girl about four, happily digging in the soil of the community flower garden. "I was about that little girl's age when Dad left. My mom caught him with his secretary. Before then, things were…well, Jake says they were picture-perfect, but it can't have been like that if my dad decided to fool around with a woman nearly half his age. He was a manager at a plant here, and he arranged for a transfer to another facility owned by the company."

"So do you see him?" Rob's voice was gentle.

"Not much. Having kids wasn't anything he ever really wanted, I guess. He married the secretary, and moved up the company ranks, and then a few years later, she found him with his new secretary. He didn't marry that one, at least…but they're together. Out in California."

"Ouch. That had to hurt."

Kari shrugged. "Truth be told? I barely remember him being at home. Now, Jake… it really bothered Jake. Still does, I guess. And I think that's why my mom…"

She realized almost too late that she was about to confide in Rob about why her mom had asked her to take the blame for that first arson. That first arson—now Kari couldn't help but wonder if Jake might have had something to do with the downtown fire.

The thought ate into the scant hold she had on her self-control. Kari couldn't even entertain such an idea sitting so close to Rob Monroe. What if she let something slip? She didn't know what would be worse…that her nagging suspicion was true and Jake had resorted to his old ways again, or that she might hang a completely innocent Jake out to dry.

Kari glanced up at Rob to see if he had noticed she'd become distracted.

He hadn't seemed to. His eyes were fixed on the little girl who appeared oblivious to anything but digging a very deep hole. "I can't imagine any man turning his back on his children. My dad wasn't like that at all— we were the most important things in the world to him, us and Ma. And that's how I think it should be."

Something about the emphatic way he said that made Kari's heart beat a little faster. She liked how he brooked no argument about commitment and responsibility.

Kari traced the bench's rough wooden slats that lay in the space between her and Rob. "To be fair, he did pay child support.

And he sent us presents, you know, for birth-days and Christmas. He actually offered for me to come out to California to see him—"

She stopped again, remembering how those plans had come to nothing because she'd ended up in juvie.

"Sounds more like an uncle than a dad," Rob protested.

"I guess so. I never thought about it like that, but you're right. Like I said before, he's not a bad sort. Just somebody I don't know really well."

She felt Rob's gaze on her, made it a point to meet it so that he wouldn't feel the need to pity her.

But it wasn't pity she saw in his eyes. It was wonderment. "I'm lucky, so lucky—my brothers and sisters and I. I should tell myself that every day. I had Dad for sixteen years, and he made every moment of those years count," Rob said.

"He died when you were sixteen?"

"Yeah. That summer."

She sat back against the bench. That sum-mer, she'd been incarcerated, scared to death, not yet taken under Alice Heaton's wing. And yet…on this gorgeous fall day with a robin's-egg-blue sky arching up and over them, she was out of that torment. Prison was behind her. She'd been given a fresh start.

But Rob would never have another chance to help his dad raise chickens.

"Hey, what's all this about?" With his thumb, Rob carefully brushed away a tear she hadn't even realized she'd wept.

"I can't—well, you." She ducked her face away to hide the fact it felt all hot and sticky with unshed tears and embarrassment. "You saying you're lucky to have had your dad when you lost him at such a young age. Jake—Jake is not like you at all. He's so bitter about Dad...and Dad's not even...well, dead."

"I imagine that might be harder, if you have less, hmm, what do they call it? Closure," Rob speculated.

"Maybe. Or maybe you're a different sort of person. Alice says..."

"And Alice is?"

"Oh! Alice!" Kari leapt to her feet. "I left her at the homemade soap booth on the corner."

"Who's Alice?" Rob asked.

"My friend—oh, no, she'll think I left without saying goodbye—"

"No need to panic," Rob said equably. "She's probably still here. What's she look like?"

Kari rattled off a description, and as she did, a girl with long blond hair cruised by on a bicycle. Rob beckoned her over, and at once Kari recognized her as DeeDee's daughter Taylor.

"Hey, Taylor, have you seen a lady..." Here, Rob recited Kari's description of Alice to a tee. "Can you go check by Mr. James' soap booth?"

"Roger that!" Immediately, Taylor pedaled hard, as though she were on a life-or-death mission.

Kari watched her go. "I didn't mean—gosh. When faced with a task, you Monroes are hard-core."

Rob smiled at her teasing. "So who's Alice?"

"The best friend a person could ever have," Kari said staunchly. "She was the head cook when I was in juvie. She taught me how to cook and bake and...and then when I got out, I worked at a bakery that a friend of hers ran—she recommended me for the job. I was there for several years, until she retired and handed the business over to her son."

Kari felt her face flush anew at the memory of the son firing her the day he took over. "We don't need any ex-cons around our cash drawer," he'd said. "Maybe my mom took in Alice Heaton's sob-story cases, but I don't have to put up with you a minute longer."

She'd been devastated—and her former boss had been enraged at her son's decision. There'd been nothing for it but to hang up her apron and clear out.

The mention of juvie seemed to startle Rob. It was as though he'd genuinely forgotten that she had been incarcerated. He looked as though he were about to say something, stopped, then started again.

"You say you didn't start the fire. Okay. But you know, it would help if you'd cooperate with me."

"I have. Every time you come and talk to me, I tell you everything I know. What more can I do? It wouldn't help you if I made up stuff."

Rob stood up, stuffed his hands in the pockets of his jeans. He took another long look at the little girl still digging in the flower bed.

"Fair enough. But why do I have the feeling you're not actually doing that? Telling me everything you know, I mean?"

*Because I'm not.*

Before she had to answer him, Alice came toward her, her hands full of the bags and parcels she and Kari had found during their trip, her face aglow and intent on Taylor. Taylor was pedaling slowly beside her, talking nonstop. Alice had that effect on young people. Something about her made kids just spill their secrets.

*Like Rob Monroe. He's the same way.*

The thought brought Kari up short. Maybe she'd be better to limit the time around him because before she knew it, she might spill secrets that weren't entirely hers.

"Just let me know if I can get any eggs. And tell…Mrs. Colleen, right?"

"Everybody calls her Ma. She'd be offended if you didn't."

"Okay, Ma, then. Tell her I said thank you."

With that, she hurried toward Alice, and away from Rob Monroe, hoping to make her escape. In her haste, she tripped over her own two feet and fell to the ground.

As Rob and Alice rushed over to help her

up, mocking laughter floated over from the pavilion.

Jake's laughter.

She spotted him, leaning against one of the tent's support columns, his arms folded across his chest, his T-shirt looked as though he'd slept in it. Scrambling up, she said to Rob, "I am so—thank you—I'm okay."

"You just have to overlook my sister," Jake observed. "Kari can be a klutz. Witness having two buildings burn on her watch."

ROB FOUND HIMSELF gripping Kari's arm a bit too tightly as he waited for Jake to stop smirking. He willed himself to ease up, smiled at Kari, made sure she was steady on her feet and then released her arm.

He didn't like this guy. He hadn't liked him when he met him, and the feeling lingered right through the formal statement Rob had taken from him early in the investigation. It was a gut feeling that could have simply been in reaction to Jake's self-absorption and amusement at being intentionally cruel to his sister.

Rob had known guys like Jake—not a bully, exactly, but someone with a quick, cutting remark ever at the ready. True, Rob had spent his share of time on the bench outside the principal's office, but it wasn't because he'd been insulting his classmates—at least not the defenseless ones.

No, Rob had gotten into trouble for using his wit to take guys like Jake down—either with an equally smart remark or an elaborate, well-timed prank that showed them for the empty windbags they really were. His big brother Daniel, weary of having to rescue him from the fallout of all those pranks, had dubbed him Rob Roy, after the heroic outlaw.

Nickname or not, Rob couldn't stand back and let people get pushed around.

The same urge to protect the vulnerable was what prompted him to jab back at Jake.

"Jake, have you noticed anyone who might have a problem with Kari or the bakery? You hung around her shop a lot, right?"

Just for an instant, he'd seen Jake startled—and not in a good way. Rob felt the back of his neck prickle with awareness: he'd gotten a little too close to something for Jake's comfort.

He pressed his advantage. "So? Can you help your sister out, buddy?"

But he'd overplayed his hand. Jake now had regained his bored expression and shrugged one shoulder. "What could I know about that fire? I told you everything in my statement, man."

"I didn't ask about the fire. I asked if you'd seen anything or anyone suspicious."

"Didn't you know, bro? My sister's a big-time hero. Everybody loves Kari. Who'd want to hurt her?" Jake dug out a crumpled pack of cigarettes from the side pocket of his cargo shorts.

Rob heard Alice and Kari's twin sharp intakes of breath at Jake's remark.

Kari didn't deserve this. These were low blows, and yet she seemed to go out of her way to be kind to people—witness the treat baskets she'd taken to the downtown merchants, and how she'd not wanted to hurt Alice's feelings.

Not to mention the tears that had sprung to her eyes when he'd talked about his dad. Kari definitely had a tender heart.

"Kari, honey," Alice said, busily brushing off the dust and dirt on Kari's jeans. "Let's get you to your car and if you can't drive, I'll drive you."

Rob kicked himself for not offering that a half moment earlier. Kari's face was crimson with embarrassment at the fall or Jake or a combination of the two.

With an awkward goodbye, she and Alice took off, and left Rob eying Jake.

Jake…yes, Jake was a different kettle of fish altogether, and arson conviction or not, Rob thought, give him Kari any day.

# CHAPTER EIGHT

ROB'S CELL PHONE rang even before he could unlock his office door the next morning. He juggled the keys and the phone with his hands until he could maneuver both.

"Monroe," he said into the phone.

"Hey, Rob! Tried calling the office, but you weren't in yet," boomed the voice of Chase Chatmon, an ADA with the county prosecutor's office. "I thought you were usually the early bird."

"Yeah, well, I had a few stops to make first. And, hey, it's not even eight thirty yet. What's up?" Rob pushed open the door and groaned at the stack of paperwork on his desk. "Please don't tell me I have to be in court today."

"Not today. Nope, I have something for you—those warrants you asked for? On the Hendrix family? To check their financials? The banks and the credit card companies have released the info."

"Great. I appreciate you going to the judge and getting it together for me."

"You probably would have gotten the stuff even sooner if you'd asked the judge for the financials of those other business owners at the same time. You should also know he didn't like the request to open Kari Hendrix's sealed record—he hasn't said no, mind you, but he still hasn't said yes. So on the financial warrants, I consolidated both asks, and when he saw you weren't picking on one family because of a juvenile offense—"

"I have to check, Chase. It's a reasonable assumption, right? If someone burned down a building before, then—"

"Preaching to the choir, preaching to the choir. Anyway, all of this—the financials for all the Hendrix crew, the pawn shop owner next door and the landlord—all of that is wrapped up with a bow. Want me to swing by and drop off your Christmas present early?"

Rob glowered at the paperwork he'd rather avoid. "I'll be here. With all this stuff stacked up, who knows when I'll dig out."

"Well, I'm warning you, this is a positive blizzard of paperwork I'm bringing you. The banks and the credit card companies are burying you with all the statements and loan info. Oh, and you're cleared to run a credit check on all the people in the warrants. It's lucky that I have a shovel in the car if I need to rescue you from that avalanche of paper."

"Since it was your office who sent most of this paperwork already on my desk, it's only fitting. See you in a bit."

CHASE WAS AS good as his word—including the part about the blizzard of paperwork. He had a file box full of papers from various financial institutions that he dropped with a thud on Rob's desk. He gave it a pat. "Ask and ye shall receive. Hopefully they sent you everything that you requested."

"If not, I know where the complaint department is," Rob replied with a grin. He abandoned the half-finished form on his desk and ripped off the box top.

"Eager, aren't you?" Chase asked.

Rob realized he was eager—eager to rule out Kari as a suspect. But to Chase, he said, "I've just been at a standstill without this. You know how hard arson cases are to prove—I have to tie the motive to the individual. Something in here has got to pop."

"You look like the proverbial kid in a candy store, so I'll leave you to it, then. Let me know when I need to show up to work out a plea bargain deal. My boss says he needs it yesterday."

"No pressure, huh?" Rob muttered as he began to scan the credit card statement he'd yanked out. But Chase had already banged the door shut behind him, leaving Rob alone to peer into the murky waters of Kari Hendrix's financial habits.

And they *were* murky. She carried a sizable balance on her credit card, but the interest rate seemed reasonable enough. That was a quick indicator to Rob of two things: one, that she was smart enough to choose a good card to begin with, and two, that she probably hadn't missed a payment.

Another scan, this one on her current charges, revealed the beginnings of a pattern. Kari used the card to pay for basic things, such as gas for her vehicle, online orders for what looked to be baking supplies and the like, albeit along with a few exorbitant big-ticket service charges recently to a local plumber and electrician. Even with the repair service charges, it looked like her latest payment covered the rest of the month's expenses and something toward the interest and the balance.

A flip back through past statements validated Rob's theory. Six months earlier, when she'd first opened the account, she'd amassed the initial bloated balance. That statement was rife with orders from kitchenware suppliers and other industry wholesalers.

Rob turned to the computer and eBay to see if he could track down by the item numbers what she'd bought. A few minutes later, he'd uncovered a used Hobart mixer, a countertop convection oven, a pasta roller with an electric motor, and a few other similar items.

He realized tension was easing out of him. It caught him unaware. He remembered the genuine wounded expression on her face when he'd accidentally implied she'd set the fire. He *wanted* Kari to be innocent. He *wanted* her to be nothing more than a victim.

*Buddy, that's a recipe for disaster. You know too well how an investigator can find what he wants to find.* Forcing his mind open with the mental equivalent of a pry bar, he went back over the credit card statements and then her bank statements with a fine-tooth comb. For all Rob's scrutiny, he could turn up no purchases of a propane tank or anything that shouted "roadside flare."

He leaned back in his chair and considered this. Just because he hadn't found it didn't mean it wasn't there, especially the roadside flare. That, she could have had before she opened the bakery.

And, he conceded, Kari could have paid cash for the propane tank.

Still, Rob had to admit he was relieved by what he hadn't found: a real motive for burning the bakery. Based on the cash flow of deposits and credit card payments minus the debits, including a faithful payment in full to her mom each month on her mortgage note, a rough calculation showed that Kari was beginning to make a profit—at least before the latest repair bills.

He couldn't help but be impressed. A bakery showing up in the black after just six months? That took discipline and hard work—oh, and good cupcakes.

The memory of those cupcakes, with their buttery texture and their perfect balance of sweetness and the tang of vanilla, taunted him. He found himself wondering if maybe she had some left over. He could swing by Chelle's and ask Kari about the—

No. He had to be honest with himself. Any "swing by" to see Kari was just a made-up excuse, even for the cupcakes.

Rob wanted to get to know her better, to fall into the easy conversation that they were lulled into when the subject got away from the investigation that had brought them together in the first place.

That was an excellent reason for avoiding Kari altogether until he could sort out this mess.

His stomach rumbled in protest. "Cupcakes!" it seemed to demand.

Or was that his heart?

With a groan, he dove into the box of financials with the sincere and fervent hope that someone else was stupid enough to write a check for a propane tank and note it on the memo line.

And if not? Well, he'd check every surveillance tape still available at every convenience store in town until he could say for certain—under oath in a court of law—that Kari Hendrix did not buy a propane tank, at least not within the county limits.

KARI FELT THE warm September sun bear down on her shoulders as she focused on not dropping the three large white cardboard boxes in her arms. Jakayla, the owner of the ice cream stand and bait and tackle shop, had called her in a panic this morning needing cupcakes for her son's daycare the next day.

Jakayla finished ringing up the last purchase of the day—a half bucket of fresh worms and a waffle cone with a double scoop of vanilla for good measure—and sent the happy customer on his way. She blew out an exaggerated sigh and rolled her eyes. "Whew! You don't need a part-time job, do you, Kari?"

Kari's stomach flipped as she set her cupcake boxes down on the counter by the dusty jars of pickled pigs' feet Jakayla kept more as a conversation piece than an actual sales item. Kari hoped she wouldn't need to resort to a part-time job. She hoped the trickle of new orders she was getting would be enough to keep her afloat until more orders started coming in. Or until this investigation was over and maybe the insurance would allow her to reopen her shop.

"You're short of help?" Kari asked,

deflecting the question. "I thought what's-her-name, Tina Williams, worked for you at least part-time."

"Man, am I! Tina just went into labor this morning, three weeks early. Everything's all right with her and the baby—an eight-pound boy, by the way—but it's caught me off guard, I can tell you," Jakayla explained.

"And I should tell you thanks for remembering me when you needed cupcakes."

"Remember? How could I forget? Demetrius asks every time we drive by your place if we can't stop in for more goodies—oh, gosh, your bakery." Jakayla's face fell. "Could you save anything?"

"Some cookbooks, a few stainless steel bowls—honestly, that's about it. But whatever I can, I will. I'm just glad you called me."

Jakayla lifted up the box lid and filched a cupcake. "Oh, these are so *cute!* Look at that little race car!"

"You said a mix of things would be fine, so I hope it's okay that they don't all match," Kari said.

"They're great—the kids will have their choice."

"Now, these are all peanut-free—no tree

nuts, no peanuts, no cross contamination. But they do contain egg and dairy," Kari warned. She tapped the little stickers on the side that indicated the egg and dairy.

"You remembered. Thank you—Demetrius has a friend or two in his class who have nut allergies, and I never know what's safe."

"My pleasure," Kari replied.

"It'll be the best birthday Demetrius has ever had." Jakayla pointed at the invoice Kari had discreetly taped to the top of the box. "This is the amount, right?" When Kari nodded, Jakayla pulled out her checkbook and started writing. "My phone died on me—Demetrius is at that stage where he wants to see what things look like on the inside, and I made the mistake of using one of his favorite cartoons as my wallpaper. Wouldn't you know? Kid tried to get the cartoon character out." Jakayla shook her head. "So I'd lost your cell phone number, and your shop number is disconnected. I'd tried everywhere to find you—and nobody could tell me your new location or a phone number. I was beginning to think I'd have to disappoint Demetrius when Rob Monroe showed up yesterday."

Kari's scalp prickled. "Rob Monroe?" Her

throat went dry, and she found it hard to get the name out.

"Yeah, you know, I knew he worked with the fire department—it's practically a family tradition for the Monroes. But I didn't know he was a—a—oh, here's his card. Rob Monroe. Cause and Origin/Arson Investigator? What is he, some sort of fire cop?"

"He was here?"

"Uh-huh." Jakayla ripped out the check and handed it to Kari.

Kari took it with numb fingers. "And he told you where to find me? How did you... know to ask him?"

"Oh, girl, I didn't. He came in here asking about propane tank purchases—you remember the cage of tanks I keep? It's a great draw—guys come here for the tanks, and nine times out of ten, they leave with a bucket of bait or a sweet treat, usually both. Anyway, Rob had your picture with him, and I said, 'I know her! She's my baker! And by the way, do you know how I can get in touch with her?'"

"Wow. What a referral," Kari managed to joke.

"He said that your shop got torched on purpose. That's a bummer. And he had to rule you out, you know, so you could get your insurance settlement."

A flood of gratitude at Rob's kindness welled up within Kari—he'd couched the question in such a way that she didn't look like Felony Suspect Number One.

"So I let him look at all the surveillance tapes and gave him my propane-tank log, and he seemed happy as a clam—and he gave me your cell phone number. Two happy customers!" Jakayla's smile flashed brightly. "Make that three—Demetrius will be so thrilled. You tell me when you get back into your shop, now—and I'll be sure to come by and order something—although gracious, goodness, my hips sure don't need any more temptation." She slapped her palm against the offending curve.

"Hopefully they're finishing up the investigation, and I'll be back in my shop very soon," Kari assured her. "I'll let you know. But in the meantime, feel free to share my cell phone number with anybody who may need baked goods, okay?"

"Sure will!"

Kari gave her a wave and started for the walkway to her van, but Jakayla's next words, delivered in a teasing lilt, made her pause. "Rob Monroe sure did seem interested in you," Jakayla said. "He seemed awfully smitten for a cop. Anything going on there?"

Kari felt her face heat up. "No—no, he's just a nice guy, that's all."

"Hey, there aren't that many nice guys left—I know, I got one of the last good ones," Jakayla cautioned her. "All those Monroe boys were raised right. None of that drinking or carousing around."

"Uh…" Kari shook her head. How to dance around this one? "You know, I didn't go to high school here. I was…"

Instantly Jakayla's face registered bemusement. "You didn't? Did you move here later? I thought you had family here."

"Well…" Kari didn't want to lie, but she didn't want to remind Jakayla of her past. The woman may have heard and forgotten about it, or never connected it to Kari to begin with. "My mom is from here. But my parents were divorced."

Jakayla flapped her hand in a never-you-mind manner. "Well, here's the honest truth, all you need to know is those Monroe guys are all nice and all firefighters. If he's as sweet on you as he seemed to me, then maybe you'd better snap him up."

Kari pressed her lips together and ducked her head. She focused on the concrete pad out under Jakayla's shelter. There were so many reasons Rob Monroe and she would never make it as a couple—her past, for one.

"I've got my hands full as it is—adding dating to the mix would stretch my juggling skills a wee bit too far," Kari tried to joke.

Jakayla shook her finger at Kari. "Still, it's a real good thing that you hadn't bought a propane tank lately."

Kari frowned. "I haven't ever bought a propane tank."

"Yeah, I meant—well, you know, Jake came in that time, got a tank for you. Remember? Y'all were grilling steaks? For his birthday?"

Jake's birthday was in December, and she'd marked that with a stilted phone call of well wishes. She had most certainly not grilled steaks for him.

"Last year?" she asked.

"No, no...about a month ago, now. His *birthday*." Jakayla repeated the phrase insistently as though it was supposed to jog

Kari's stubborn memory. "Or…no, maybe it was a friend's? He was with some buddies."

Suspicion pooled in Kari's gut, as nauseating as sour milk. Had Jake bought a propane tank? Had he started the fire after all?

# *CHAPTER NINE*

ROB WAITED WITH his brother Daniel in the DA's dingy and cramped conference room. The DA had called an impromptu status meeting on the investigation, and now Rob cooled his heels as he sat, more fidgety and anxious than he cared to admit. He flipped through his notes, straightened the pertinent financial reports into an even neater stack on the scratched woodgrain surface.

"Isn't that stack straight enough?" Daniel observed from his seat across the conference table. "That's the third time you've done it."

"What's he want, anyway?" Rob burst out. "If he wants the case solved, why jam me up and waste my time, calling me in and then making me wait on him?"

Daniel shrugged. But then, as fire chief, Daniel was used to being called in front of whatever authority wanted to quiz him—county commissioners, city manager, county manager.

Rob, too, had a murky chain of command. Ostensibly he was head of the Origin and Cause Investigative Division—but the arson squad was really just him. He reported to both Daniel, as the fire chief, and the DA, who would bring Rob's cases to court eventually.

Still, it was odd for the DA himself to wade in. Usually Rob did most of his work with an assistant DA. Chase had been the one assigned to this case.

"It's a big deal, Rob Roy," Daniel reminded him. "Half the downtown was torched. And Franklin does answer to the voters."

The door opened, and in swept the chief District Attorney Sam Franklin, his white hair high and away from his lined forehead, his pinpoint shirt still crisp and unwrinkled even midmorning, the cuffs precisely rolled up. Chase followed behind like a duckling keeping up with its mama.

"Rob, Daniel. Thank you, boys, for coming in. Chase tells me that you haven't closed the downtown fire case. I want to know what the holdup is."

Rob managed to bite back a "can't arrest an unknown" retort. "Sir," he said. "I am following every lead. Diligently. But you do know how tough arson cases are—"

"So you know who the culprit is, and you're just nailing down the evidence?" Franklin cut in.

"Uh…that would be a no. Sir." Rob fiddled with the papers on the desk to avoid meeting the man's gaze. He realized what he'd done and lifted his chin up, giving him a direct look back. "I can bring you up to date, if you'd like."

Franklin sighed, glanced at his watch, and sat down in the chair at the head of the table. Chase took a seat next to Rob and flipped open a notebook.

"I'm listening," Franklin said.

Rob drew in a breath. "Indulge me if I tell you something you already know, because I don't want to leave anything out. The fire started at the service door of the bakery, approximately 3:00 a.m., by means of a propane tank and a safety flare."

Franklin waved his hand impatiently. "Yes, yes, I'm familiar with this. Chase has kept me in the loop, and I do read the newspapers. How'd you proceed?"

Rob stared down at the papers again to give him a moment to gather his thoughts. "I focused in on the bakery owner, Kari Hendrix, to see if she had any financial motive or opportunity to set it. Video from a security camera put her at her apartment the whole night of the fire, until she came out after the fire department had responded to the blaze—a neighboring shop owner called her and alerted her to the fire."

"So she couldn't have done it herself, then. Airtight alibi? No way to leave by a back entrance?" Franklin prodded.

"Airtight, sir," Rob agreed. "No back entrance, and no neighbors heard or saw anything—and believe me, I raised a ruckus going back through that alley—dogs, cats, even a parrot that squawked loud enough to raise the dead. Plus, there's a sort of voyeur type who knew a little too much about Kari's comings and goings. Bordering on stalkerish, if you ask me. Anyway, he verified that he'd been up late—watching the stars, he said—and he saw no movement in that back alley."

A flutter of thanksgiving pulsed through Rob that Kari was away from that weirdo. Maybe it had been a good thing she'd had to move in with her mom.

"Okay, so could she have paid to have it done?"

Rob pulled out a summary on his notes from the financials. "As you can see, sir, she had no large amounts of cash withdrawn from her bank, no checks written to individuals. The credit card charges to repairmen checked out, and they verified that it was for parts and labor for various repairs to the store."

"Hmm." Franklin scanned the sheet, the corners of his mouth pulling down in disappointment. He tossed it aside, and it slid a few inches toward Daniel. "But she's done this before."

It always came back to that, even for Rob. He felt ashamed, since there was so little evidence against Kari.

"Yes, sir. But say for instance she somehow managed to get out of the apartment and start the fire. She had to acquire the propane tank from somewhere."

"You track the tank? Is there a way to do that?" Franklin mused.

"There are serial numbers and the like, sir. But I couldn't tell what company had manufactured the tank or filled it. I theorized that perhaps I could find a clerk who remembered her—or some of the other people I was looking at—getting the tank, even if she didn't have a paper trail. I couldn't find a check or credit card purchase that reflected a propane tank purchase."

"What about checks for cash? Or cash advances?" Chase interjected.

"I thought of that. Kari doesn't do that—she either pays with a check or with a credit card, and she only has the one credit card."

"Dang, she's clever, then," Franklin bit out. "Maybe she had an accomplice."

Rob couldn't help saying, "Maybe she's innocent. Sir."

Now Franklin steepled his index fingers together and squinted at him. "Rob." The word was gentle and easy, all warning signs for anyone who knew Franklin even peripherally that the next words needed to be heeded. "You sweet on this girl?"

"No, sir!" Rob protested. "I just—can't seem to find any hard evidence linking her to the crime."

"Besides the fact that she was nearly bankrupt, and she's solved her problems with a set of matches before," Franklin muttered. "You called her Kari a couple of times. I notice things. I'm wondering if you haven't let your…bias…cloud your judgment."

"Sir, I will admit to being impressed with anybody who works as hard as Kari Hendrix does and has a reputation for making everything right with her customers. She's smart, and she's built up the beginnings of a solid business in the six months she's been in operation. I don't know very many who could break even on a bakery as quickly as she has—you said bankrupt, but that's not an accurate picture. If it hadn't been for Charlie Kirkman's refusal to pay for some major repairs, she would have been turning a profit."

"Maybe," Chase interjected, "Charlie was the one who started the fire—after all, he wouldn't want to sink any money into a building he was planning on burning down."

Franklin guffawed. "Charlie Kirkman doesn't want to sink money into any building ever. Stingiest man I ever saw. No, sir, he wouldn't part with the money to buy the tank. He'd use somebody else's kitchen matches, if I know that boy. Besides, we wouldn't be talking about you chasing your tail, would we, Rob, if you'd found anything linking Charlie to this thing?"

Rob had to concede the point. "I looked

hard at Charlie. He was out of town that night, and he has nothing in his financials that looks like arson-for-hire or the purchase of a propane tank. Plus, the buildings were actually under-insured—Charlie and his skin-flintiness, as you pointed out."

"Chase said something about the pawn-shop owner?" Franklin prompted. "What was that?"

"Er. Nothing, really. Another dead end," Rob admitted. "He'd wanted to expand into Kari's—Kari Hendrix's shop. But he's already got an offer on a larger location around the corner. I don't think it's him, either."

Franklin shook his head in disgust. "So... nothing. You got nothing. Except a girl who has burned down one building just like this one—"

"Sir, I can't say that for sure. I don't know the nature of that fire. The investigation's records are sealed—the whole thing, because she was a juvenile."

"But she confessed. She pleaded guilty."

Now Daniel spoke up for the first time. "And she served her time, sir."

Franklin huffed. "I can't believe it. You two boys—of anybody in the whole wide world—ought to hate an arsonist with passion. And there are the both of you defending her? A self-confessed arsonist? Same as the coward who killed your father?"

Rob felt himself come halfway out of his chair, but saw his big brother wave him down.

Daniel's reply to Franklin came in measured tones. "If I might, as fire chief, put in my perspective?"

"By all means." Franklin made a show of looking at his watch again. "What's another five more minutes of wasted time?"

"I agree with you, sir, that my brother seems…a little protective of Kari Hendrix. Still, I have to concede that he's looked high and low for a connection. Rob?"

"I thought I'd found something yesterday," Rob told the DA. "I went to every convenience store in town, every hardware store, every business that sold propane tanks that matched the one used in the fire. Kari's brother Jake bought a tank at that bait and tackle shop on the outskirts of town about three weeks before the fire. He paid cash for it."

Franklin gawked at him and threw out his hands in a wide palms-up move. "Well, there you have it, plain as day. She had help!"

"Uh, no, sir. The number on the tank used to start the fire did not match the number on the tank he bought—plus, it wasn't the same make. This tank—the one used in the fire? It was older, like it had been around for a while."

"Maybe she stole it."

"Maybe the *arsonist* stole it, yes," Rob ground out. In a more controlled tone, he added, "But, sir, even if I were willing to swear that Kari Hendrix started that fire, which I'm not, you've got no case. She has no motive—no financial gain, really, in burning her business. No financial paper trail showing her buying the means to start the fire. You got a hole of reasonable doubt big enough to drive an 18-wheeler through."

Franklin slammed his fist down on the conference table. "Dang it! I still think she did it. I mean, what was her motive for burning the first building?"

Rob shrugged. "I can't say, sir. The judge hasn't unsealed her records."

Franklin glowered at Chase. "Get on that. Right now. I want those records unsealed by close of business. *Today.* I got people breathing down my neck on this."

"Yes, sir," Chase said meekly. He shot

a sharp eye at Rob, as if to say, "Thanks, buddy."

"And you!" Franklin jabbed a long gnarly index finger at Rob. "You go back to that woman, and you question her about that first fire. Leopards don't change their spots. Whatever her motive was on that, you can bet that's the reason she burned this building down."

# CHAPTER TEN

ROB FOUND HIMSELF at Kari's mom's back door, his hand raised to knock, just as he realized his spirits were lifting at the prospect of seeing Kari.

*Or maybe that's the sugar high you're getting already from the smells wafting through the door, bud*, he warned himself. *Get it together. Franklin may have a point. You don't want it to be Kari.*

But even with such a stern lecture, he couldn't tamp down the way his heart leapt at the sight of her face: flour on her nose, a strand of blond hair strafing her check, her eyes that blue-gray that he found so arresting.

"Oh, it's you—uh, come in—I can't—can you close the door behind you?" Kari sprang back toward the stove, where she knelt down and squinted at a thermometer clipped to the side of the pot. "I miss my digital thermometer. This is my mom's candy thermometer, and it's not as reliable, and certainly not as easy to read."

Rob eased into the kitchen. Cake layers and cupcakes and pastries and bread loaves were everywhere—across the counters and empty burners on the stove, on the table, spread out on a couple of TV trays, jammed onto a shelf that had been emptied of a small radio now on the floor. What counters weren't filled with delicious-smelling baked goods were crammed with kitchen gadgets. The sink was full to bursting with pots and bowls, and the open dishwasher looked crammed full, as well.

"Wow. I like what you've done with the place," he teased her.

She darted a smile in his direction before fixing her attention back on the thermometer. "I'm trying like mad to get some orders done before five o'clock, so you'll have to forgive me if I don't pay strict attention to you. It seems to keep the peace around here better if I can have the kitchen cleaned up before Mom walks through the door."

"Got to be tough."

"I have to admit, it makes me feel all of eleven again. I miss being master of my own place." She straightened up in a hurry.

"Okay! Cream!" She snatched up a measuring cup and started pouring cream into the pot, then stirring like mad. The contents of the pot bubbled up to the edges, threatening to spill over, but just in the nick of time, the boiling mass receded.

Rob meandered over and peered in. "What's that?"

"A ganache for a cake—it's to fill it."

"Huh? You mean, hollow it out and pour it in?"

Kari chuckled. "You don't know much about baking, do you? Good thing you've got your chicken and egg business to fall back on."

"No, my expertise pretty much ends with eating the baking."

Kari kept stirring but grinned.

"I do make a mean brownie from one of those box mixes. Hey, don't make that face. It does the job. We can't all be five-star cooks. And what else are you supposed to do at midnight when you want a snack?"

"Well…" Whatever she was beating had thickened into something that smelled divine and crawled out of the pot into a bowl with the slowness of perfectly cooked grits. "I'd bet you'd be surprised how easy it is to cook brownies from scratch."

"You'll have to teach me sometime. And I'll teach you all about chickens. Oh, and growing beans and tomatoes, and Ma could show you a thing or two about preserves. Hey, you mind if I lick the pot?"

Her slim shoulders, bare except for the thin spaghetti straps of her shirt, shook with laughter. "Go ahead, but watch it. It's still pretty hot. That's molten sugar in there. I swear, I'm going to have to stop letting you come around. You can't possibly have any time to do all your investigating and help out at what sounds like a full-time farm."

Rob got a spoon from the drawer—realizing with a start that he'd hung around Kari so much that he actually knew where to look—and dug into what was left of the ganache.

"Oh, man. Ohhh, this is good. I'm glad Daniel can't see me eat this. He's on this push for all of us firefighters to stay fit. And the reason I can eat all this good stuff you have tempting me is that I do my fair share on the farm." Rob let the spoon clatter against the side of the pot. "So how is it that you manage to keep so slim?"

"Because," Kari replied primly. "Unlike

some people I might name, I *don't* eat everything that I cook. I just test it."

"Who? Me? I'm just testing it." He dug the spoon through a stream of ganache and popped it in his mouth. "And it needs…"

"What?" Kari was at instant alert, her frame at attention, focused on what he was about to say. "More vanilla? More salt? Wait, cinnamon, maybe it needs a touch of cinnamon?"

"Relax. It's great. You're…" He cut himself off before he could finish the sentence with "great." Because this was rapidly falling into that easy, breezy conversation they always seemed to end up in…and that was not why he was here.

No. If he really thought Kari was innocent, he would do her no favors by soft-pedaling this. He needed to clear her. He needed to convince Franklin that Kari had no hand in this.

"You're just trying to talk your way into more dessert," she said, waggling a finger at him. "I've got your number, sir. I know what a guy is really after."

"Yeah? So what's my punishment?"

"Those dishes." Kari gestured toward the sink as she reached for a spoon. "I need some help, and I'm not too proud to swap pot-licking privileges for scullery-maid services."

"Oh, you are not putting that stuff in a 13-layer cake, are you? Please, please tell me that some of the Monroes ordered that sucker?"

"Dishes!" she snapped saucily. "And, no, I'm afraid not. This goes to a teacher over at the middle school."

"Dashing all my hopes today, aren't you?" He set the now cleaned-out pot beside the sink and turned on the hot water tap. "Well, I'll have you know that Ma trained me early on how to wash dishes. A dishwasher is an honorable profession."

"Darn straight, and if that's how well you scrub, you can lick my pots any old time," Kari told him.

For a while they worked in a companionable silence. But as the minutes stretched on, and the sink emptied out, the weight of what he had to do pressed in on Rob. He hated to break this spell. Why couldn't it be like this? Why couldn't he have wandered into her bakery months before it burned down, met her when nothing was wrong?

Kari must have read his mind. "So…as much as I'd like to believe it, I know you didn't come by here simply to eat my cooking and wash my dishes. Something up with the investigation?"

He noticed how carefully she asked that question, and yet how a tremble in the last few words gave away her nervousness. "I've been trying to track down the source of the tank used to start the fire—"

"Oh, thank you, by the way," she interrupted brightly. "Jakayla told me that you gave her my number. I really appreciate that. It was for three dozen cupcakes, and the teacher was so impressed that she ordered a birthday cake for her son. Oh, and then another teacher that she knew has asked me to cater a reception for the high school Beta Club. So that was three—no, counting this cake, four orders. All because of your goodwill."

Were those tears in her eyes? They were. They gathered along her dark golden lashes like tiny jewels. She turned away, but not before he could see one trace its way down the curve of her cheek. His hand itched to stop that tear in its tracks. He remembered how soft her cheek had felt when he'd done that very thing at the farmers market.

"You're welcome," he husked. "It was my pleasure."

"So? Did you? The tank, I mean? Did you find it? That could lead you to who started the fire, right?" Kari's circling back to his earlier topic nearly threw him.

"No. I'm afraid not."

Was that relief that caused her frame to sag? Or disappointment? He couldn't see her expression now, as she was bent over the cake, spreading out the ganache with quick and efficient moves. She was halfway done now, the layers assembling quickly and easily.

"Oh. So…" She didn't finish her sentence.

Rob cleared his throat. "You still haven't come up with anyone who might have a grudge against you?"

Kari shook her head, and flipped another cake layer atop the ganache.

"I don't see why this has to be about me," Kari told him. "Why am I the focus of your investigation?"

Then she blushed—a beautiful shell pink that sprang from her cheeks and suffused her face to the baby-fine curls wisping from her headband. "Oh. Right. My record."

Here it was, the perfect juncture to ask

about that fire. He couldn't square the woman standing before him with someone who could burn down a building, willfully destroy something, ignoring the possibility that people could be hurt or killed.

"Er, actually, no," Rob heard himself saying. He kicked himself for his cowardliness.

"Really?" She paused, spatula in midair, her eyes wide with surprise as she looked over at him.

He rinsed out the last bowl and stacked it on the drainer. "Really," he said. "It's where the fire started that makes me think it was about you. Someone wanted to make a point, you know? They had, what, six other doors they could have leaned their weapon against. So why you? Don't tell me that you haven't wondered the same thing."

Kari sighed and flipped the last layer on. "I have. And honestly, I can't answer that. Maybe there were security cameras at other businesses? Mine was in the middle of the block, so maybe they felt more secure? I really have no clue, Rob. I've stared at the ceiling many a night asking myself that same question. Why? Why me? Why now? What did I ever do to deserve—"

She bit off her last words. The answer to

that question was patently obvious. Karma could be vastly unkind.

"Oh, shoot. I didn't make enough." She raked at the last scrapings of the ganache bowl and tossed the spatula into it in a fit of frustration. "I knew it didn't look as though it would stretch, but I thought, maybe... Now I'll have to make another batch."

"Is it that hard?" he asked, feeling guilty for the healthy amount of ganache he had scraped out of the pot.

"Just tedious. I have to carmelize the sugar. It's a caramel cream ganache, and you have to be careful or you're sure to scorch it— oh, well. Nothing for it but to get it done." Kari squared her shoulders and reached for some of the measuring cups and spoons he had just washed.

"Hey, I'm sorry," Rob said. "Maybe if I hadn't—"

"No, no, it wasn't you. I needed at least half again as much to frost the outside of this cake."

"Well, one good thing, I get to see the magic in the making. Do I get to lick the pot again?"

"Only if you'll agree to wash the dishes I'll dirty. I had to let my part-time helper go because…well… Charlie's still making me pay rent, believe it or not."

"Huh? Is that even legal?"

"He said that if I wanted that space, I needed to keep up with the terms of my lease. And…I want that space. It was perfect. Exactly the right size. And it was mine, Rob. Just like I liked it. Just like I needed it." Her words broke with emotion.

"You'll get it again. Or something better." His attempts to jolly her into a more cheerful mood seemed wholly inadequate.

She dug into a cupboard, sorting through a few small saucepans until she came up with one that satisfied her. Setting it on a unit, she switched on the electric coil, then reached for a canister of sugar. Rob watched with interest as she sprinkled a thin layer of sugar onto the bottom of the pan.

The sugar melted as she peered into the pot, then began stirring the small amount.

"That's enough?" Rob asked. "That doesn't look anything like enough to finish frosting the cake."

"No, no. You have to add the sugar a layer at a time—about an eighth of an inch," she explained. Now Kari reached again for the sugar, dashing another dusting of granulated sugar into the pot. "That caramelizes the sugar, and that's the base of the frosting."

"So how much sugar do you have to cook this way?"

"Only two cups. That should be plenty."

"Two cups! At this rate, you'll be here all day."

Kari glanced at the kitchen clock. "Not all day—but I might be pushing it to get this cake finished by five o'clock like I'd originally hoped to." She sighed and swiped at her forehead with the crook of her arm. "I knew I should have made more. Oh, well. But you were telling me about the investigation—no, I was whining—oh, what *were* we talking about?" Her eyes crinkled at the corners and she lifted a brow. "I have no conversation skills when I cook. You'll have to forgive me."

"That's okay. We were talking about the investigation. And…well, I have to ask you a few things."

She scraped at the pot with her spatula. "I don't know what else I can tell you. I know I keep saying that—"

"Actually, about this, you can. I need to know about the first fire."

Kari had reached for more sugar and was in the process of sprinkling it into the pot when he asked. The question made her jerk, causing a small shower of sugar to settle on the stove. The smell of carbonized sugar filled the air. "The first fire?" she repeated.

"Yes. The one you confessed to."

Kari had recovered, though, smoothly pouring the sugar into the pot in an even layer. "It's all in the records. I thought by now you would have made it required bedtime reading."

"The records are sealed. I admit, I've asked a judge to release them, but…it would save me time if you would tell me about it."

Now why did he feel so awkward about asking her this? This was his job. More than that, if Kari were innocent, he was the one person in an official capacity who was actually motivated to look beyond the easy answer.

Kari's jaw tensed—she was actually clenching her teeth. "I thought you said my record didn't matter." She shook more sugar into the pan with less control than she had before.

"Look, I'm trying to clear you," he shot back. "If I can show my boss that the two fires were totally different, maybe—"

She jutted out her chin, her elbow jerking

stiffly as she whipped the spatula through the sugar. Some of the mixture dribbled down the side of the pan in a thick, taupe-colored rivulet. "Maybe what?" Kari demanded. "Maybe he'll quit trying to pin it on me? Because that's it, isn't it? You're not looking for the real culprit. You're looking at me."

"That's not fair, Kari. I'm trying, and you're not helping—"

She whirled around to face him, the spatula trailing a thin stream of molten sugar. "No, the way you want me to help is to point the finger at somebody—anybody—and heaven help them if they're actually innocent—"

"What if they're not? What if they intentionally burned your shop? What if you telling me how—*why*—you burned that other building can free me up to really help you—"

"I don't want to talk about it, okay?" Anger pulled Kari's skin taut and compressed her lips. "I did it. I confessed. I went to jail. I was a stupid fourteen-year-old, and I did a stupid, stupid thing that ruined my life and I'll never get it back—never—"

Suddenly out of the corner of his eye, Rob spotted a curl of smoke winding its way lazily toward the vent fan. "Hey—Kari—is that—"

But before he could utter the word *fire*, a bright orange flame sprang up, licking at the trail of sugar that had spilled from Kari's spatula down the outside of the pot. He'd seen plenty of fire in his time, but the quickness of this fire still startled him. It was like an animal unleashed, jumping from unit to pot to sugar.

"Fire!" Kari screamed. Her face went white as she saw what Rob did, the flames leaping toward the vent fan in an oxygen-hungry quest for fuel.

A smoke detector somewhere deeper in the house blared out, joined by another one, this one screeching, "Fire, fire, fire, please evacuate now, fire, fire, fire—"

Rob reached for a pot lid to smother the flames, but before he could, he heard the unmistakable sound of a fire extinguisher being cocked. He turned to see Kari wielding the extinguisher, laying down enough foam on the stovetop to blanket the burning pot—and all of her baked goods cooling on it. He just managed to snatch the 13-layer cake out of the way before she aimed the extinguisher at it, as well.

He set the cake down in a perch of relative safety, turned back and grabbed Kari, putting a hand on the extinguisher. "Whoa! Kari! The fire's out! See? Enough. It's out, so you can stop."

He tightened his grip and locked eyes with her. "It's over. It's done. You put it out."

She looked wildly from first him to the ruined stove and then back at him. A pulse thrummed in the hollow of her throat, and she was shaking—hard shivers as though they were standing on a windswept glacier. "Are—are you sure?" Kari quavered.

Rob gently pulled the fire extinguisher from her clenched fingers. "Based on my professional firefighter's opinion, I have to say, yeah, I'm pretty darn sure. But I'll check if it will make you feel better."

"Please?" she whispered.

He made a show of moving the pot around on the stove, checking the chemical-covered baked goods, inspecting the underside of the vent fan. "Yep. That fire is a dead soldier."

Kari closed her eyes and wobbled backward to the table. She sagged against it. Then, just when Rob thought for certain she was going to faint on him, her eyes flew open and her face turned a curious shade of green.

She bolted for the back door. He followed

her, but she waved him off as she knelt down on the porch steps. "No—please, I just need—air—"

He reached for her. She turned away and began to retch, tears streaming down her face. Still she waved him away.

Pride. Instantly he understood why she'd motioned for him to leave her alone. It was Kari's pride. She wanted to hold onto her last shred of dignity by not having him witness this.

Rob went back in, switched off the smoke alarms and stepped to the kitchen sink to dampen a paper towel. By the time he'd retraced his steps to the back stoop, Kari had gotten hold of herself. She leaned against the house, pushing away the wisps of hair that clung to her damp forehead.

"I hate fire," she muttered. "Oh, how I detest fire."

# CHAPTER ELEVEN

KARI GULPED AT the clean, fresh air scented by her mom's backyard roses. Out here, the sky was blue, the grass was green, and there was not a hint of smoke or fire or ashes. She took the dampened paper towel from Rob and swiped at her face.

"Try putting it on the back of your neck and your head between your knees," Rob suggested. He was down on his own knees beside her, a concerned expression etched into his features. "You've had a shock."

"I had a complete loss of good reason, that's what I've had," she retorted. She let her face drop into her hands. "I know how flammable sugar can be, and I let myself get distracted—oh, how could I have nearly burned my mother's kitchen down?"

"Hey, you handled it. No lasting damage," he assured her. "Maybe you should train to be a firefighter. I've never seen someone with such quick responses."

His joke couldn't budge the sick queasiness that kept rippling through her. All she could think about was what it would be like to be a firefighter—actually walking into a burning building, surrounded by hungry flames...

Kari still had nightmares about fire even now as an adult. As a kid, first locked up in juvie, she'd been plagued with horrific dreams of fire surrounding her, burning her alive. She recalled waking up in her cot, screaming, soaked in sweat, sure she'd been left to burn to death.

She shuddered. No, thank you. No firefighter's job for her.

"Better?" Rob asked.

He tipped her chin up so she had to meet his eyes. He was the last person she wanted scrutinizing her. Would he guess, what with the way she freaked out about a little kitchen blaze, how crazy scared she was of a fire? Would he figure out that it hadn't been her who'd set that first fire?

It hadn't been Jake who'd burned the downtown. She'd asked her brother about that propane tank, and he'd told her he'd gotten it to grill steaks for a buddy's birthday ages ago.

But if Rob had found out about that tank, and he knew about Jake's involvement in that fire so long ago, he'd put two and two together and get five.

What else would an arson investigator think? Of course he'd believe Jake had something to do with this one. Wasn't that why Rob had focused on her so much? Why he kept coming around? Because he really believed, despite what he kept assuring her, that she had started the downtown fire?

Kari groaned, disgusted with herself over how much that hurt. She had to admit that it would be nice if Rob Monroe were just a normal guy who dropped in for normal guy reasons…to steal her baked goods. To talk with her. To flirt with her. So that the two of them could let time take its course and turn them into a normal, everyday couple.

But as she felt the pressure of his fingers under her chin, she had to be honest with herself. She and Rob were never going to be a normal, everyday couple. Not ever.

She was a convicted arsonist.

And Rob?

He was an arson investigator.

An arson investigator who had lost his own father in an arson.

Kari pushed herself up off the rough pebbly surface of the steps and wobbled into the kitchen. She nearly ran out again. It was a disaster zone—half her morning's work lay under the fire extinguisher's foam.

But at least Rob had saved the caramel cake that had been the cause of the whole mess.

No, that wasn't true. *She'd* been the one to start the mess. She'd been the one careless with the caramelized sugar.

Just like that, and she could have destroyed her mother's house. As it was, she'd burned up her precious profits by wasting all the raw materials and labor that had gone into the now-trashed baked items.

"I can call over to the fire station and see if we can borrow one of the ventilation fans," Rob offered.

"Thanks, but I can't bear the thought of anybody knowing I've nearly burned down a second kitchen in as many months—" Kari held up her hand. "That was not a confession, by the way. I meant—"

"I know what you meant, Kari. Why are you convinced I believe the worst of you?" Resignation ate into Rob's words.

He didn't belabor the point, though. Instead, he began opening the windows and parting the curtains. He reached over and flicked on the vent fan over the stove. Then, without a word, he grabbed a trashcan and began sliding the ruined baked goods and foam into it.

Something about the quiet way he went about helping her made her heart ache all the more. If he'd yelled at her or accused her of carelessness, she could have benefitted from the numbing anesthetic of anger. His kind forbearance had the opposite effect. She wanted to melt into a puddle of tears and confess everything.

*I'm not an arsonist*, she wanted to tell him. *I didn't set any fire. I hate fire. It terrifies me.*

If she told him that, though, she'd be putting Jake squarely in the center of the investigation. Suspicion would fall on him, fairly or unfairly. That boss Rob had mentioned a few minutes earlier would take one look at Jake's past criminal mistakes—nothing big except the fire, but a lot of dumb, idiotic arrests—and he wouldn't rest until he'd slammed the prison gates behind Jake.

And if she did that, what were those four years in torment for? What good had that sacrifice meant? It would have all been in vain. Her mother would have to live through another of her children behind bars—the shame of it, the agony of the forced separation, the worry that something might happen to that child, something she would be powerless to fix.

No, better for Kari to keep her mouth shut and let Rob prove her innocent. She hadn't done this. There was absolutely nothing that could tie her to that fire. Rob Monroe could look as deeply as he wanted, and he'd never find evidence that she started the downtown fire.

But Jake? The worry that he could be mixed up in all of this nagged at her. She prayed that when all was said and done, Jake could just as easily bear Rob Monroe's scrutiny.

ROB SURVEYED KARI'S mom's house as he switched on the ignition of his truck. He couldn't figure out what to make of Kari's reaction to the fire. He'd seen fear before, but never pure blithering panic like she'd shown in there.

A glance at his watch told him it was five minutes to five. Too late to head back to the office—and his head was crammed full of the case anyway.

But his apartment in town held little appeal for him. He didn't want to be alone with his thoughts, either.

No, what he needed was some manual labor to burn off the mental fatigue and confusion his brain was bogged down by.

He pointed the truck to the farm. He'd use the last few hours before dusk to cross off some chores for Ma.

Ma waved from the back porch as she snapped what looked to be green beans.

"Well, I'm glad to see you," she greeted him. "It was a mite lonesome out here. Maeghan's off for training, and Andrew's on duty—and of course, Daniel seems to always be working these days. And the grandbabies are all back in school. Sometimes I worry about the way I talk to myself."

"As long as you're not answering back, I guess you're okay," Rob told her. He pulled up a chair and started by sheer habit helping her snap beans.

"You come by to get those eggs for that Hendrix girl?" Ma asked.

"Er—no, why would you think that?"

"Because I see you've got a spot of what

looks like caramel cream frosting on the corner of your mouth, and I seem to recall she makes a mighty fine caramel cream cake." Ma's brow arched in question. "Did she decide she had to have organic eggs after all? Ours wouldn't do?"

Rob wiped at the telltale spot. Sure enough, his finger came away with some of the ganache. It occurred to him that he'd never told his mom about his decision on supplying eggs to Kari. "No, she's all for it. But you know…ethics and all. I need to wait until the case is closed before I start swapping money and eggs with…"

What was Kari? A victim? A witness? A suspect? He didn't believe that, didn't want to believe that. But even with her honesty and her warm and open heart, Kari Hendrix was hiding something.

Ma gave him a shrewd look. "This case is a hard one, huh?"

"It's panning out to be that way. I've just got to keep thinking of angles of attack, that's all."

"Well, while you're doing all that cogitating, you mind pitching in? Daniel's sure to be in late, and I know he'd appreciate someone to help with the chores. Besides…the hens always perk up with their egg production when you come around." She winked at him and laid a gentle hand on his arm.

IT WAS MIDNIGHT before Kari got her orders done and the kitchen cleaned up. Her mom had sprung for pizza and had washed dish after dish for her, all of which made Kari feel all the worse.

Maybe she should just give this dream up and find a job and try to pay her mom's retirement money back. With the edge of a fingernail, Kari flicked open the lid of the pasteboard box holding the caramel cake. The golden frosting glistened underneath the kitchen's fluorescent lights, perfection for any sweet tooth.

Was it really worth it? All the work? All the sacrifice? All the stress? Maybe an office job or a retail position would be easier.

But then, who would hire an ex-con? So many times, the moment she had to confess that she was a convicted felon—regardless of how long ago it had been—the job offer evaporated. And even more often she didn't even get as far as the interview if the application had the question, "Have you ever been arrested for and/or convicted of a felony?"

"It's okay, honey," her mom told her now. "We're okay."

Kari looked up to see her mother standing in the door to the kitchen. Without her makeup, wearing her glasses and a scruffy bathrobe, her mom looked inexplicably younger than she did all dolled up—younger, but still more tired.

Kari closed the lid on the box. "It nearly wasn't. I can't believe it—how quick that fire spread."

"You must have been terrified. Oh, I wish I had been here—I know how you are about fire." Now her mom bit her lip.

Kari hadn't always been phobic about fire. But after her mom convinced her to confess, something about all she went through had made her terrified of anything that burned. They didn't talk about it.

They never talked about that other fire. Talked around it, sure, but never about it.

And that suited Kari just fine, thank you. She didn't want to think about it—or where it had sent her. Those four years she'd spent locked up were better off forgotten.

But what if Rob—or Rob's boss—decided she was good for the downtown fire? What if she wound up behind bars again? She'd seen enough of that sort of thing when she was in juvie, girls who were in the wrong place at the wrong time, and had their whole lives upended because of it.

Hadn't she been just such a girl?

"Mom—I'm really afraid," she confessed quietly.

Her mom closed the gap between them, the shuffle of her bedroom shoes the only sound. She wrapped her arms around Kari and pulled her close. "I won't let them take you away again, Kari. Not even if I have to confess myself. That's what I should have done the last time—if it hadn't been for me and my bright ideas, you wouldn't even be a suspect in this fire."

Kari pushed her mom away. "No! No more false confessions! That's not the answer, Mom, and you know it. You couldn't have known what the judge would do."

"Yes, but, Kari… I should never have put you in that position to begin with. I'm your mother. I should have seen the danger for what it was."

"If we want to place blame, Mom, let's place it where it belongs. Jake. Jake should have never started that fire."

"He was a kid! A kid, Kari! In with the

wrong crowd. A prank gone bad. You really think Jakey wanted to cause that much—"

Exhaustion rolled over Kari. She didn't want to refight this battle. There was no coming between a mother and her child. She listened to her mom until her mother ran out of steam. No point in arguing. No point in trying to change what couldn't be changed.

"Like you said, Mom. We're okay. It will all be okay."

"I think so," her mom told her in a brighter, more cheerful voice. "That young investigator certainly seems nice enough—he's always dropping in." She'd injected a teasing note into her words.

Ah, but Kari knew things about cops and how they operated that her mom couldn't know—she'd heard too many tales from her fellow inmates about how cops would cozy up to you just to get you to trust them.

Maybe Rob wasn't like that. He did seem nice. More than nice. He did like her cooking. She was certain of that. And if they weren't each who they were…

She saw that her mom was waiting expectantly for her to respond. "He *is* nice. But don't get your hopes up, Mom. He's just doing his job, okay? Nothing more to it than that."

Her mom gave her a pat on the shoulder. "I can hope. Not just that he likes you well enough to give you the benefit of the doubt… but that you'll meet the right man. If it's not Rob Monroe, then somewhere out there, there's someone for my girl. Someone who will cherish her dreams."

Kari tried to joke. "He'd better like to wash dishes, then, because to me, nothing says 'I love you' more than an empty kitchen sink."

With an ache, she pictured Rob Monroe standing at the sink, happily scrubbing pots and pans. She couldn't be doing this. She couldn't be wasting her time and her heart falling for a guy who was just doing his job.

## CHAPTER TWELVE

A RAP ON ROB'S apartment door pulled him away from the file in front of him. He knew that knock—the classic shave-and-a-haircut twice was Daniel's signal from the time they were kids.

Sure enough, when he swung open the door, there was his brother, standing patiently on the porch of his duplex.

"Hey. Something up?" he asked Daniel.

"I was about to ask you the same thing. I thought you were going to eat with us tonight. But I see you've already made it to dessert."

Rob looked from Daniel to the crispy rolled confection he'd carried with him when he answered the door. It reminded him that he had indeed swung by Kari's again, which made two days in a row, this time with the dozen eggs Ma had insisted he take Kari as a sample.

"Oh—I was planning on eating with you and Ma—what time is it?"

"Just about half past eight. Don't tell me that's your supper."

"Half past eight? That late? I got that case file from Chase right before I left for the day, and I thought I'd take a gander at it. I guess the time just slipped by me."

Daniel cocked his head sideways and raised an eyebrow. "Not like you to miss the dinner bell's ring, Rob."

Rob instantly understood what Daniel meant. It rankled him that his brother, too, was convinced that he was too close to the case to be objective.

"Nothing about this makes sense, Daniel. Come on in and take a look at the file for yourself."

"Only if you've got any more of those— whatever that thing is you're munching on. It looks good. Let me guess—Kari?"

Rob shut the door and followed his brother into the small living-dining room of the duplex. "Yeah. She said they weren't pretty enough for the customer who ordered them and that she'd made some new ones—you oughta try 'em. They've got this chocolate hazelnut filling that's mind-blowingly awesome, and the cookie—really crisp, but really buttery."

Daniel settled into a dining table chair, pulled the file over with one hand and reached for a cookie with the other. "Hmm. They are good. If she's as good at setting fires as she is cooking, we'll never catch her."

"Daniel!" Rob protested. "You're as bad as Franklin."

Daniel swallowed the mouthful of cookie and pointed to Rob's empty milk glass. "Got any milk left to go with this? Or did you drink it all and are all out as usual?"

"I have milk. I go shopping. Sometimes. I am a grown-up." Rob got two glasses out of the cupboard and poured the milk.

"Cookies for supper. Could have fooled me," Daniel ribbed. "So this is it? The whole file? It's…kind of thin."

Rob set Daniel's glass of milk on the table. "I thought the same thing. Of course, she pleaded guilty from the start, so there wasn't much in the way of investigational notes or trial transcripts. These courtroom confessions usually are pretty scripted. But the confession in court was word for word the same as her statement. The convenience store owner accused her of shoplifting, so she got mad and went back and burned the building down. It was more than a little short on detail."

"It doesn't say how she got the tank. And…" Daniel flipped back through the file to her arrest paperwork. "She was all of eighty pounds when she was arrested. A skinny kid. How'd she tote a full propane tank all the way to that convenience store in the middle of the night? She wasn't driving yet—at least, she didn't have a license and she didn't cop to stealing her mom's car."

"I know. I saw that, too. And Daniel— something more. Something even weirder. Kari is flat-out phobic of fire. I mean, cold sweats, throwing up, complete freak-out."

Daniel glanced up from the file. "Yeah? How do you know that?"

Rob told him of the afternoon kitchen blaze the day before, how she'd blanketed the stove with foam. "It was fast and aggressive, but small enough to be contained. All it would have taken to put it out was a lid over the pot. But before I could get to it, she'd gone all Rambo with the fire extinguisher. Plus, I had a look at the house when I went to switch the smoke detectors off. That house? It has five smoke detectors—one in the hall off the kitchen, one in each bedroom, and one in the living room. The kitchen? Not one, but two fire extinguishers. And the bedroom that Kari is in? Her own personal baby fire extinguisher was propped up by the dresser."

"That's a lot of smoke detectors and fire extinguishers. I wish we could convince everybody how important that is."

"Yeah, and ordinarily, I wouldn't think anything of it. Maybe it's part of an alarm package. Maybe a previous homeowner put them in. But…"

"Something else?"

"Yeah. When Chelle got in, she wasn't mad with Kari. You'd think that if someone burned down a building and then later on started a fire in her mom's kitchen…"

"That Mom would be ticked, at least, or alarmed," Daniel finished. He tapped a finger on the laminate surface of Rob's table.

"Not in the slightest. It was over-the-top, but not anger. It was…guilt. You know how when Taylor was little, she was petrified of thunderstorms?"

"And DeeDee would just make it worse by going on and on about it if she'd left Taylor with Ma?" Daniel nodded, picking up the shared memory of how their sister had reinforced their niece's fear of bad weather.

"Right. Exactly. It was like that." The two of them sat, silently munching on the gourmet cookies as they both considered what this might mean.

"Not what you usually see," Daniel conceded.

"No. I haven't met a teenage firebug who ever outgrew his fascination for fire—that's how it gets started. They like to watch it. Like to play with it, even as little kids. And they get turned on by its destructive power."

"But not Kari?" Daniel settled back into his chair and rubbed his chin. His eyes had a faraway look.

"No. Even after an hour or more had passed, she was still a bundle of nerves. Hypervigilant. Kept checking the stove, must have wiped down the top and the drip pan three separate times."

Daniel shook his head. "That's not a firebug's habit. A firebug is confident around fire, sure he can control it. He wants to see fire."

Rob nodded. "It doesn't add up."

"This confession…" Daniel leaned forward and tapped the spread out contents of the file. "It doesn't add up, either. But I tell you what it does remind me of—"

"Dad's fire." Rob beat his brother to the punch. "I thought the same thing. Two big arsons that summer, both of them started with propane tanks."

"Did she do both?"

"No. She was already in juvie when Dad's fire started."

"But she knows. She's got to know who started that other fire, Rob. She knows who killed Dad."

Rob didn't want to think about that—it had already occurred to him, and he didn't want to believe it. He covered his mouth with his hand and shook his head. "No. I could believe she toted that propane tank a half mile in the dead of night as a skinny fourteen-year-old before I could ever think she would stand by and let a killer go free."

"So why else confess to a crime you didn't commit? Because that's what you're thinking she did, right? That she's not good for either fire?" Daniel pressed. "What's her payoff?"

Rob shrugged. "I haven't the foggiest. But this file isn't anywhere close to having the answers I need, and she won't talk about it."

Daniel flipped back through the thin collection of notes and transcripts and forms. "Who investigated this? Rocky?"

"Yeah. Rocky did. I've already called him."

Rocky Gambrell had Rob's job before he'd retired and started doing freelance work for insurance companies. He was, in Rob's opinion, a fine investigator, one who didn't jump to conclusions.

Daniel pursed his lips and drew his brows together. He drummed his fingers on the table. "Well, if it was Rocky, something besides a fourteen-year-old's confession had to tip the balance. Maybe he can fill in the blanks, Rob. Because we both saw how agitated Franklin was yesterday, and I hear he's just as wound up today. He's catching some heat from somebody, and we know what that can lead to."

Rob sighed. He picked up another delicate cookie and snapped it in two. "Yeah. Any conviction, just as long as it *is* a conviction."

THE NEXT MORNING, Rob parked his truck in the driveway of a home a couple of towns over. The arts-and-crafts bungalow bore the scars of a recent fire—soot and smoke damage covered the front and side eaves, and a blue tarp covered what had to be a sizable hole in the roof. Windows on the side of the house were broken, as was the glass inset in the home's front door.

He slid out from behind the wheel of the truck, Kari's file in his hand, and slammed the door, looking around for Rocky. The investigator's truck was there, parked beside Rob's. But there was no sign of life coming from the house.

"Hey, Rocky!" Rob called out a greeting.

From the back yard, Rocky's reply came. "Back here! Come on around."

Rob followed the sound and a privacy fence bordering the property line. He soon found Rocky poking through debris around the back stoop. The older man, still as long and lean and sinewy as he had been when Rob had first met him years before, straightened up and offered a hand.

"Hey, buddy," Rocky greeted him. "Ready for a job with good benefits for a change? I can hook you up. Not a bad gig. Mostly home every night, no 3:00 a.m. callouts."

Rob grimaced. "You know me. I don't do corporate very well. But it looks like it suits you to a tee. What have you got here?" He gestured at the house and debris.

"What I think and what I can prove, two

different things. The lady of the house said she thinks the fire started when she left a flatiron on in that back bedroom. Mind taking a look with me? Just doing a walk-through? You were always good at this stuff, spotting the inconsistencies."

"Sure." Together they tramped through the kitchen door and into the hall that opened onto the back bedroom. "So, wait, this is where she said the fire started?" Rob gazed around the smallish room, heavily damaged with smoke, but still structurally intact. He spotted a dressing table with a mirror and chair by a window on the farthest wall—again, with heavy smoke damage, but no direct scorch or burn damage.

Rocky nodded. "Yep. I'll keep my trap shut and not let anything I think mess up your conclusions."

"Just with this quick look, I don't think the flatiron is the cause of the fire. I mean, see?" Rob pointed to the door behind him. "The fire damage to this room is mostly on the hall side, like maybe it came from the room next to it. But, hey," Rob crossed over to the dressing table for a closer inspection, "fire has been known to do crazy things."

"Yup." Rocky hung back in the doorway. "That it does."

Rob knelt down and studied the dressing table at eye level. There was definitely heat damage to the varnished finish...and, yeah, he'd been called out to any number of fires started by a forgotten curling iron or flat-iron, but...

"Wait, Rocky, you see this?" He beckoned for the investigator to join him. "This thing here—you can just make out the words *auto shutoff* on the side. Even if she had left it on, it would have switched off."

Rocky came to stand beside him, sticking his hands in the pockets of the cotton twill pants he wore. "Yup. Saw that myself."

Rob straightened. He did a slow 360, taking in what he could tell about the bedroom in its post-fire state. There were no photos on display, no change or pocket litter on the dresser or the nightstands, no jewelry or makeup scattered. It was as bare of personal touches as a hotel room.

"The family come through and try to salvage anything?" he asked Rocky.

"Nope. This is just like we found it."

"And the fire happened...when?"

"Middle of the day. Well, not quite the

middle of the day. Lady of the house left about eleven o'clock, off to run some errands, she said."

"Hmm." Rob crossed back into the hall, following the trail of fire damage as it grew worse and more obvious. He poked his head into the room next to the bedroom.

It had been a bathroom—a tub with plastic shower doors, toilet and sink jammed into the space. The plastic shower doors were melted and in shards. The suspended ceiling, which had been added sometime in the 1970s from its appearance, had its asbestos tiles moved over to reveal gaping holes, where firefighters had obviously shoved them aside to gain access to the space above. Scorch marks shot up from the burned and blistered plastic tub surround that had been added to the original cast iron tub.

"Whoa. This is where the fire started. Hey—you can still see something in the tub. Clothes?" Some scraps of cloth—from the looks of it, men's pants. A sleeve of a leather jacket had escaped the worst of the flames.

"She says she was soaking them. To get stains out."

Rob narrowed his eyes and studied Rocky

to see if he were pulling his leg. "A leather jacket? Are you serious?"

"Yup."

Rob bent over the heap and sniffed. The faintest whiff of kerosene wafted up. "You take samples?"

"You know I did. And sketches and photographs. This is just what's left. Nope, I did it just like I taught you, Rob, in the scientifically approved manner." Now Rocky couldn't quite hide the grin that threatened his poker face. "Take a look through the rest of the house, tell me what you see."

Rob did as Rocky suggested, noting suspicious voids where pictures, books and other items should have been. True, the television and the electronics were all there, reduced to pretty much junk between the fire and the water, but there were telltale signs that things important to the family were gone.

Rocky followed him out onto the bungalow's front porch. "So?"

"Based on what your samples tell you, someone used kerosene to soak clothes in the tub and start a fire. Now I *guess* they could have been using kerosene to do some DIY dry cleaning, but it would have sure messed up that leather jacket." Rob grinned at Rocky. "The fire ignited the bathroom walls and the wooden framing and spread into that atrocious suspended ceiling...where it moved up into the attic," Rob added.

"And you came to that conclusion how? Don't give me bunk about V patterns on the walls or pour patterns on the floor. We know that fire leaves strange marks on a floor. I taught you better than that, Rob."

Rob grinned. "You did. I know better than to treat a fire scene like a fortune-teller would tea leaves. No, the main damage was to the bathroom, not to the bedroom. It had to be a fairly hot fire to melt that plastic tub surround and to leave scorch marks on that asbestos tile. And I know you'll tell me it's not actual physical evidence, but...where are the pictures? The photo albums? The jewelry? And I noticed that there were empty hangers in the closet, at least in the section that contained lady's clothing. And shoes... what lady has only four pair of shoes in her closet?"

Rocky beamed, pride evident. He clapped Rob on the shoulder. "You were my best student. Always could see in a three-minute walk-through what other guys never could see in a half hour or more. Would you be surprised if I told you that this was the husband's house before they got married? And that the neighbors told me they'd heard loud fighting over the previous few days? Something about a woman?"

Rob rolled his eyes. "Sheesh. He can't keep his pants zipped up, so she throws all his clothes in the tub, soaks 'em in kerosene and tosses in a match."

"That's what it's looking like. Plus, the neighbor across the street said that the lady came back not once but twice before she left for good. And it was only after she left the last time that the neighbor happened to see smoke coming out of an attic vent."

Rob shook his head. "People always underestimate the effort it takes to light kerosene or gasoline. They think it's like they see in the movies, all they've got to do is pour it out and toss a match in. What they don't know is it's the vapor that's flammable. It's a pure wonder the woman didn't blow herself up, coming back in to relight the clothes. So...what are you going to do?"

"I'll file a report to my bosses. And send a copy of it to the authorities here. Too bad you're not the arson investigator in this county. I could save myself some time and trouble," Rocky said. "But enough about this case. What's on your mind? What was so all-fired-up important that you drove two towns over?"

Rob extended Kari's file toward Rocky. "I needed to pick your brains about this one."

Rocky flipped open the manila folder and swore. He patted his front pocket and pulled out a pair of reading glasses. "Hate getting old. But at least this time I didn't lose my specs. Can't tell you the number of times the things have fallen out at a scene." Glasses perched on his nose, he peered at the open file. "Yeah. I remember this. Weird case. Didn't make a dab of sense at the time."

Rob's heart did a double beat. He tamped down hope with a ruthlessness he hadn't had to use on himself since he was a teenager. "It didn't?"

Rocky read through the file, flipping through the pages with nods and monosyllabic grunts. He said nothing until he came to the last page and then closed the file and folded his arms across his chest. Even then, he regarded Rob with a fixed, unrelenting stare.

"What's this about, Rob?" he asked. "You're not thinking this is related to your dad's fire, are you?"

# CHAPTER THIRTEEN

"WELL, YEAH, SORT OF." Rocky's leap ahead took Rob by surprise. "I mean, both were started with a propane tank. Both in the same summer. But that's not what got my interest started."

"Yeah?" Rocky ran the ball of his thumb along the edge of the file folder. "So what's your interest, then?"

"I'm going to do the same as you did a few minutes ago—not let my thinking cloud yours. What do you remember about this case?"

Rocky closed his eyes and drew in a breath. When he opened them, he stared past Rob, his eyes fixed on a point far in the distance. "It was a kid—I remember she was a shrimpy little thing, all hair and skin and bones, and I didn't think she'd have the strength to drag a filled propane tank five feet, much less a half mile. But...she confessed. The owner told me he'd had words with her the day before, so I naturally went looking for her. Her mom at first swore there was no way her kid could have done it, that she was asleep in bed at the time, and that the mom had even looked in on her."

"And then?"

"Well, a couple of days later, I'm not getting anywhere, and the DA is all over me because he and the store owner are golfing buddies, see? So I go back to the one lead I had—the girl. A long shot, right? I'm thinking maybe it was her brother, because he'd had some scrapes with the law. But no. The girl answers the door, her mama standing right behind her. I don't even get to ask where I might be able to find the brother before this little sprig of a girl takes this deep breath and blurts out that she's the one who started the fire."

"And you believed her?"

Rocky shrugged his shoulders. "At that point? Why not? She told me exactly where the propane tank had been set up, exactly how she'd started the fire. She even told me how she got into the convenience store—she'd seen the guy leave a key on the back window ledge to let himself in. The DA was happy and the owner could collect his insurance, so it was case closed."

"It was her first offense. How did she wind up in juvie? She'd never been in trouble before."

"I recommended that she get probation and some counseling—she really did seem very remorseful." Now Rocky's lips thinned and he shook his head in regret. "But it didn't happen like that."

"Why not?"

"Judge wanted to come across tough, set an example. The papers couldn't put the girl's name in the paper, but they could write the case's disposition. So he spouted off some drivel about her being unredeemable since she'd resorted to such violence and destruction at a young age and told her he wished he could try her as an adult. And then he gave her the longest sentence he could. You would have thought…that girl and her mama…man, they couldn't have been more crushed if a dump truck of bricks had fallen on them."

A wave of nausea pulsed through Rob. He could imagine the scene—a girl confessing, thinking she was going to get off lightly in return for her cooperation, then being dragged off, away from everything she'd ever known.

"Yeah," Rocky told him. "I felt just like you look. I apologized to the mom—she couldn't even get a word out, she was so speechless. But what could I do? Exactly zip, that's what. The funny thing is…if the girl had said nothing, if she'd kept her mouth shut, I didn't have one single concrete piece of physical evidence to tie her to that fire."

"Maybe the evidence burned up?"

"Nope. The smoke detectors were hard-wired into the alarm system, so an engine got paged out PDQ. The back room was pretty well toast, but beyond that, the building was in fairly good shape. And the door she'd gained entry from? It was still intact."

Rob felt that prickle of awareness course through him, the one that always told him where to look for clues and evidence that others might have overlooked.

"You dusted it for prints?" he asked Rocky.

"No fingerprints of hers. Not even a partial of hers—and it hadn't been wiped down. There were plenty of prints on the jamb, on the door, on the doorknob. Not hers, though."

"What about the key?"

Rocky dipped his head and gave him a

mock salute. "Thought of that myself, and the ledge where the key had been hidden. No dice. Not one of her prints on it. Not so much as a partial match."

"You're kidding."

"It gets stranger. We tested the clothes she said she wore to start the fire. No residue on any of her clothes, no sign of rust or dust—and she pulled them out of the dirty clothes hamper, plus the store owner and the video footage positively ID'd the clothes as the ones she'd worn into the store the day before the fire. The *only* thing we had was that the mom said the propane tank was hers from a backyard grill. But we didn't even find prints on what was left of the tank. I mean it. We had zip."

"That doesn't seem possible," Rob murmured.

"I know, right? How could a kid—one who had never done a crime before, so she didn't even know what *not* to do, if you catch my drift—get into that building and not leave a scrap? Not a fiber, a fingerprint, even a hair—it was as though she could teleport herself." Rocky handed the file back to Rob. "Either that…or…"

"She didn't do it in the first place," Rob said flatly.

THE CAKE WAS a gooey mess. Never mind that it had been baking for an hour. Never mind that Kari had used that same recipe a hundred times before at least.

She poked the toothpick in it one last time, in the vain hope that this time, the cake batter would magically have cooked and wouldn't stick like glue to the toothpick.

No luck.

"Oh, Kari…" her mom moaned. "What now? Oh, wait! You can run it over to Sarah's—use her oven—"

"No, Mom. It doesn't work like that. I have a cottage industry permit—I have to actually *live* where I cook, remember? I can't run around borrowing people's ovens."

"Surely they'd understand if your oven is broken—"

"Right now? Mom, I've got Rob Monroe breathing down my neck about both fires. I can't take the chance that—"

"What do you mean, both fires?" Her mom's voice wavered into a high register of alarm. "What fire, Kari?"

"Oh—" Kari kicked herself. She'd purposefully been keeping Rob's latest round of questions to herself. She didn't want her mom worried about Jake.

"Tell me, Kari. You have to tell me," her mom insisted.

"They're looking for similarities between…well, the old fire and the downtown fire. You had to know they would—"

"Your record's sealed, though. They can't use that against you now. Not after all these years." Her mom claimed a chair at the kitchen table and wrung her hands, the crimson tips of her nails flashing in scarlet streaks.

Kari scoffed at her mom's continued naïveté. "Yeah, sure. It's sealed, all right. Only it keeps coming up in every job interview I have, any criminal background check. And you can bet your bottom dollar that they'll figure out a way to use it at the trial."

"But, honey, you're innocent. There's not going to be a trial. You didn't do this."

"I didn't do the other fire, either, Mom."

Her mother's face crumpled. "I know. I know exactly what you sacrificed. I tell Jake all the time how grateful he should be, how much you gave up so that he could go free. I tell him how much he owes you—that he should at least finish his degree and get a good job—"

"Mom." Kari held up a hand. She couldn't

bear to hear a rehash of how Jake had blown the scholarship he'd had and dropped out of college not even a year into her sentence, when that was his big reason for wanting to avoid prosecution. "I know. It's okay. But I have to think about the oven, now, all right? I have to work this out."

"I'm sorry…hey, wait—Janine George has a little countertop convection oven—let me drive over and see if we can borrow it." With a jingle of her keys, her mom was out the door before Kari could point out that a countertop oven was nowhere near big enough to hold the bottom tier of the supersized wedding cake Mattie Gottman had ordered.

That was Mom, always rushing to fix things, and nine times out of ten making things worse than they had been to begin with—but who could be angry with someone like her?

Kari had removed the oven door and had her head all the way up inside the cavity when she heard the back door scrape open.

"Whoa! Hey, things aren't that bad, are they?"

Instantly she felt hands on her as Rob Monroe dragged her bodily out of the oven.

"What?" She blinked at him. "I don't—"

"You—you weren't…uh, well, you had your head in an oven."

Kari burst out laughing. "It's an *electric* oven, Rob. Unless I'm trying to electrocute myself, I don't see it as a viable way to commit suicide. And no, by the way, I'm not trying to end it all."

Rob sat back on his heels. "I—sheesh. I feel stupid."

Kari sagged back against the cabinet doors. "Don't. I appreciate the concern. I'm sure I looked like a complete basket case the last time you were here. And I am the idiot who nearly burned down her mother's kitchen."

"So what's the deal with the oven? Are you cleaning it?"

"I wish. It's stopped working. It's baking, but not at the right temperature. I was checking the elements to be sure they were still working, and the convection fan. Know anything about oven repair?"

Rob lifted his shoulders. "Sorry, no. The extent of my knowledge of ovens is how to turn 'em on and how to put out any fires they may start."

"Exactly how does anyone start a fire in an oven?" Kari marveled.

"A million different ways, believe me. There's the sugar boiling over into the bottom. There's the oh-I-didn't-realize-parchment-paper-really-didn't-need-to-be-over-420-degrees fire. One lady turned on the oven without checking it, all the while completely forgetting that she'd done one of those quick clean-ups where you stuff all your dirty dishes into the oven. Let me tell you, plastic cutting boards can stink up a kitchen in an awful hurry."

"I don't feel like such a total doofus, then," Kari told him. "Unless you're completely fabricating this to make me feel better about myself?"

Something about her words cast a shadow over his face. "Well, no…but…I needed to go into more detail about that first fire. I've read the report. I've talked with the original investigator."

Kari fixed her gaze on the floor. "Then you don't really need to talk to me. You have everything you need."

"No, I don't." He reached out and touched her arm. "Kari, it leaves me with a million questions. What gave you the idea to burn the place? How'd you know to start the fire that way? How'd you get the gas tank unhooked from the grill and down to that convenience store?"

A chill ran through her. She couldn't answer any of these questions because they weren't part of what Jake had told her—not anything she'd rehearsed or memorized.

For lack of anything better to say, Kari shot back, "That's one subject that is absolutely closed for further discussion. I've done my time. I've told the authorities all I need to. I don't want to talk about it, Rob. And what's more, I don't *have* to talk about it."

"Kari...I want to help you out. I'm on your side, believe me—"

"The last time I believed that an investigator was on my side, I wound up doing four years with hardened criminals. Do you know what juvie is like, Rob? It's not boarding school. There were some seriously violent girls I was locked up with. And I'd never done anything—"

She bit down hard before she could spill out the rest of it. Why was it so important that Rob Monroe think well of her? Why did she want him to know she was not an arsonist?

It couldn't help her now. She'd been convicted and sentenced, and the blot was on her record forevermore. If she could tell him everything that had happened, and if that could simply shift the suspicion off her, that might be one thing.

But all her story would do, even if Rob believed her, would be to pin suspicion on Jake.

She couldn't do that to Jake. Or to her mother—especially her mother.

Kari rubbed her eyes. "I don't have time for this. This cake is for the mayor's daughter, and I have to get it done."

"I thought she wasn't getting married until…when is it? I got an invitation."

"Oooh, touch you. I just get to deliver the cake and set it up—if, that is, I can get this stupid old oven to work." She rammed the appliance in question with the toe of her sneaker. "I don't know what's wrong with it. And as for when the wedding is—this weekend. I need to bake the layers ahead and freeze them—it makes them easier to decorate. Plus, this is one mama-jama of a cake. It will take me a while to decorate it."

"I'd guess Mattie Gottman's cake would be a doozie."

"Four tiers. With alternating layers decorated in Cornelli lace and Swiss dots. And a cascade of tons of roses, orchids and a beaucoup of other flowers. Plus I have the groom's cake to do. So I really, really need this blasted oven to work." She gave the oven another not-so-gentle kick with her toe.

"Feel better kicking a defenseless appliance?" Rob teased.

"Well, my toe hurts now, so it's a great distraction." Kari drew in a deep breath, concentrating on how good the kitchen smelled: vanilla and sugar and butter and chocolate and cinnamon mingled together to make her favorite perfume in the entire world. "And now I need to get back to my surgery." She wriggled her head into the oven, peering at the various mechanisms.

"So you've repaired ovens before?" Rob asked her. Kari realized with a prickle of sensation that he was beside her, trying to peer into the oven with her. He splayed a hand out on the bottom rim of the oven for support, and Kari found herself fixated on it. The hand was huge, the kind that could make a basketball disappear into its grip, with strong lean fingers and neatly trimmed fingernails. She fought the urge to slide her own hand over his, to measure the vast difference in size, to feel the way bone and sinew and muscle combined to make a human hand look like the work of a sculptor.

"I said, have you worked on—" he repeated.

Embarrassed at the way her thoughts had run away with her, she cleared her throat and hurried to answer. "Minor repairs, sure. I can replace an element. My old boss could pretty well take an oven apart—and that was a gas oven. I'm—I don't take chances like that. Gas scares me. Electric, though, as long as it's unplugged..." She reached up, tested the connection that the element made with its socket.

"Why does gas scare you?"

Something about the way he said it, a studied casualness that seemed a little too casual, put her on alert. How could she tell when he was just making conversation rather than interrogating her?

*Easy. Remember: anything you say can and will be used against you.*

She pulled back. Space—she needed space away from him to think, to figure out the right answer to his question. Kari studied his profile, with its strongly chiseled features, the stubble across his jaw, the deep cleft in his chin. What was he really asking? "Well, it can blow up. And catch fire. I should know that, right?"

Now Rob pivoted in his half crouch to face her. If looking at his profile had unnerved her, staring into his inky blue eyes was even more disconcerting. It was an unflinching gaze, one that peered into her very soul, weighing her, sifting her parts to see what was wheat and what was chaff.

"Sure. You *should* know gas can blow up and catch fire. What are you not telling me, Kari? I thought all firebugs loved to talk about their work."

He was definitely in cop mode now.

She crossed her arms, tried to swallow and found her mouth parched. And still she couldn't pull her gaze away from his.

"If you're here to cheer me on, you're welcome to stay," Kari managed finally. "But if you're here to interrogate me..."

"Yeah?"

She tore herself away from his eyes and pinned them on her mom's engineered hardwood floor. Impractical for a working kitchen—you needed something you could clean more easily and that wouldn't scratch. But that was her mom, all fluff and appearance and making everything look right.

With a sinking heart, Kari realized that no matter how she tried to better herself, she would always be a convicted arsonist. The honey-blond finish on the floor was like her—if you scratched it the least little bit, the real core would be laid ugly and bare.

And she couldn't stand for Rob to know that about her.

This relationship—if it even was a relationship and not some elaborate con to get her to trust him and confess all—was going nowhere.

Kari felt herself physically wince from the pain of that realization. How vulnerable and stupid must she be to fall for the guy who wanted to put her behind bars?

*Finish this*, she commanded herself sternly.

And so she did. In a tone she wished was a little less bleak, she still managed to get out, "If you're here to interrogate me, I guess I'll have to invoke my right to remain silent."

## CHAPTER FOURTEEN

"YOU'RE GOING TO wear a hole in that wood if you keep pressure washing one spot, Rob."

Ma's gentle reminder yanked him back from his wandering thoughts. "Sorry. I was just—had my mind—" He began directing the spray of water across a wider swath of the front porch's ceiling, keeping it in motion.

"A million miles away." She smiled and settled back into her task of scraping paint along the top of the porch rails.

He hadn't minded coming out and helping Ma with the porch. Daniel and Andrew had already done their share. Daniel had painted the rest of the exterior of the house, while Andrew had stripped and refinished the back deck and pool fence. The porch project seemed like a piece of cake compared to the other jobs.

Besides, it would give him something else to think about besides Kari.

Only, of course, it hadn't. Here he was, still tangled up in the case.

In Kari.

After today's set-to with her, he didn't know what to think. He wanted to believe she was as innocent as pure driven snow. Still, who but a guilty person invoked her Fifth Amendment rights?

"So what's got you so busy that you miss supper?" Ma asked. "You still working on the downtown fire?"

"Yes, ma'am."

"Did you ever get Kari those eggs? Do you know if she liked them?"

"I didn't think to ask her when I saw her today."

"Hmm. Daniel tells me you've been seeing a lot of Kari. So why all that hem-hawing about waiting to supply her eggs until the case is over?"

Ma never slowed the rhythm of her scrape-scrape-scrape, but Rob could tell she was waiting with more than idle curiosity for his reply.

"Not seeing her, exactly," he corrected. "She's part of the investigation, so I am talk-ing to her a good bit. But I really meant it when I said I didn't want my actions to be questioned. I want people to know I wasn't biased. And Kari could be... She..." What could Rob say? Her juvenile record was sealed, so he really couldn't talk about that with his mom any more than he could go into details about the current investigation.

"I know about her confession all those years ago, Rob. How she said she burned that convenience store."

Rob let his finger slide from the pressure washer trigger and turned to his mom. "How? I mean—how do you know?"

"Your dad. It was not long before he died, you know? That fire?" Ma swiped her forehead. "Gracious, it's hot! I think everybody will have to be satisfied with sandwiches for supper."

"Dad told you about it?"

She smiled at him, warmly. "Yeah. Does that surprise you? Your dad needed someone to talk to, a sounding board, I guess you could say. And it bothered him, that case. He didn't think she'd done it. Plus, you guys were about her age—a little older, but it's just so easy to feel a parent's pain. I didn't know Chelle Hendrix except to recognize her when I saw her on the street, but I could tell she was going through a lot. You want your kids to be okay, to do well, to avoid trouble. You want to be able to rescue them and save them from themselves."

"Why—" Rob hated the way hope sprang up at the mention of how his dad hadn't believed in Kari's guilt. She'd confessed, after all. She'd stood in court and told a judge she'd burned that building down. "Why did Dad doubt her confession?"

Ma shrugged her shoulders. "I can't remember all his reasoning now…maybe he never went into detail about it. I just know he thought there was more to it. And your dad was very rarely wrong about things like that. He was like you, Rob. He could always figure out who was lying and who wasn't. A human lie detector, people called him."

Rob shook his head and went back to pressure washing the clapboard siding. "I'm not like him. I can't tell up from down anymore, Ma. I'm so confused about this case—" He clamped down on his words before he could say too much.

"Well, I'd give Kari Hendrix the benefit of the doubt, if it were me," she said. "Even if she did set fire to that store all those years ago—"

"She said she did, Ma. She still says she did," Rob interrupted.

"People *say* they do a lot of things," Ma reminded him. "And for a variety of reasons."

"But that's still lying. That's still not being truthful. Plus, it's allowing the real criminal to go free."

"If she did lie about it, or if she did set that fire, it doesn't matter now, Rob. It was years ago, and she more than paid society's price for it."

"You sound as though you like her— I didn't even know you knew her."

"Only by reputation. DeeDee got to know her right after Kari first opened the shop. She was really impressed with Kari's willingness to make things corn-free for Taylor— you know how hard it is to find bakers who are willing to go to the trouble of cooking for a kid with a food allergy."

That squared with what Rob knew about Kari. She took care of the people around her, took care of her customers as though they were family.

His mom continued. "And Kari has baked cupcakes and other things for Taylor's cheer squad. It sure does make it easier on me. Baking is hard work, especially to decorate it all fancy like the girls want it to be."

"But, Ma, an ugly cake is the best tasting cake, you know that."

"Spoken like a true Monroe—you've got your dad's sweet tooth, that's for sure. You aren't picky." Ma knelt down and started working on the bottom runner of the porch rail. "Even so, Kari has a real talent for decorating. Her goodies looked as beautiful as they tasted. I hate to see anyone's dream destroyed, especially since Kari was putting a lot of effort into it. It's too bad about her shop. I thought she'd make a go of it."

"She's still baking—just at her mom's. She *is* good at it. No offense to your cooking, but Ma, some of the stuff she's made…" Rob whistled in admiration. "I've probably gained ten pounds just nibbling on her samples. But I won't be getting any more of those for a while—her mom's oven is broken."

"Good gracious. That girl has the worst luck."

"Yeah, and right in the middle of trying to get Mattie Gottman's wedding cake done. Kari says she has to get it baked ahead because it's going to take some time to decorate."

Ma laid down the scraper and stood up. "That wedding is this Saturday. And

Mattie Gottman won't be shy in airing her complaints if that cake doesn't get done to her exacting satisfaction. You have a number I can reach her with, Rob?"

"Mattie's?"

"No, Kari's."

Rob pulled out his phone. "Uh, yeah—but why—"

Ma took the phone from him and swiped through his contacts. "Ah, there it is."

A moment later, a bemused Rob looked on as his mom was in full conversation with Kari. There was a lot of talk about layers and buttercream versus whipped versus fondant and tier supports and oven temperatures and sizes.

"Are you sure, Kari? I have a perfectly good oven..." His mom sighed. "That is a problem. So you think it's the thermostat? I'll bet Rob would be glad to help you with that."

Rob was gobsmacked. He was the least mechanical of all the Monroe boys. Chemistry, he got. Fire, he got. Nuts and bolts? That would be Daniel and Andrew's department.

"Well, now, if you see a way around it, you just call me. My oven's not new, but it would do in a pinch, and this sounds like a pinch to me." Ma rang off with a cheerful goodbye and handed the phone back to Rob. "No good. State regulations and such. If she uses an outside kitchen, it has to meet commercial regulations."

"Ma—I wish you'd asked me before you did that. It could get—awkward, you offering your house to a suspect in one of my cases."

"A suspect?" She arched one brow. "Now, Rob. You know you don't think she's really the one who set the downtown fire. You're good at your job, I know that—you're as good at investigating as Kari is at baking. It's what you were put on this earth to do. If in all this time you hadn't been able to find any evidence tying Kari to that fire, it doesn't exist."

"I haven't been able to convince Franklin of that," he muttered, frowning at the memory of the DA.

Ma rolled her eyes. "Sam Franklin, bless his heart, was an idiot even when we were in grammar school together. You find the real culprit, and he'll be happy enough. He just wants somebody to convict, Rob. And I'm fairly certain—no, I'd stake my best cast iron frying pan on it—Kari Hendrix did not set that fire."

"Maybe not the downtown fire, but Ma, she's still a self-confessed arsonist."

Ma compressed her lips and went back to her scraping. For a moment, all Rob could hear was the blade rasping loudly against the wood. When she did speak, it was in her firm, no-nonsense tone that told him for Ma, the debate was over. "I know people. If there's one thing I know, it's people. And that girl? She hasn't burned anything—at least not intentionally."

A COUPLE OF days later, as Rob was finishing up a mandatory training exercise at the station, his phone went off.

"And we have a contributor to our cell phone jar fund!" Daniel announced to the crew. "Rob, you keep leaving that phone on while we're training, and we'll have that new television paid for with your money alone."

Rob dug in one pocket for his phone and the other for the five bucks' penalty. "It's not fair, folks. I have to keep my phone on—people call me back about investigations."

His brother Andrew clapped him on the shoulder. "That's why we insist on having you train with our crew—you're always good for an Abe Lincoln at least."

But Rob didn't take the bait. He'd spied the number on the screen: Kari's.

She'd hung up before he could answer it, so he hit the call-back button and walked out past the engines into the station's driveway. The phone rang once, twice, three times before she picked up.

"Kari? You needed to talk to me?" he asked.

"I'm sorry—I dialed you by accident," she told him. She sounded flustered. He could hear her huffing and puffing, as well as the sound of something metallic screeching in protest. "I...was..."

A loud clatter on the other end of the line made him yank the phone from his ear. He replaced it. "Kari? What's going on?"

"Oops—dropped the phone—I'm...try-ing...to...move...this...blasted...stove."

"By yourself?"

Now she had obviously paused in her efforts, though she was still breathing heavily. "Yeah. Jake was supposed to come help me, and that was who I was trying to call. But as usual he's nowhere to be found."

"Give me five minutes. I'll be right there." He hung up and raised his hand to get Daniel's attention. "Hey, Daniel, we're done, right?"

"Yeah, sure." Daniel waved him on. "You gotta go, go."

Guilt surged through him as he realized Daniel thought his sudden departure had to do with the investigation. He hadn't clarified exactly why he was leaving. Daniel would rag him to no end if he found out that Rob was dashing off to move a kitchen appliance for Kari.

*Hey, Ma told her that I'd help her.* But he knew that wasn't the reason he was dropping everything to move heavy appliances.

Kari was waiting for him at her mother's back door. "I am sure you have better things to do than come shove my stove over," she said apologetically.

He fell back on his earlier justification. "Well, Ma did offer my help."

"Oh, yeah. I remember that now."

Did Kari's face fall as she said that? He couldn't tell for sure if it actually did or whether it was more of his infernal hopefulness.

The moment passed before he could sort it out, and she graced him with one of her sunny smiles. "Thanks! I hate being so scrawny. I've tried everything, and I can't get the stupid stove to budge."

He followed her into the kitchen. "So… why do you have to move it? Why not wait for the repair guy?"

She laughed. It was a musical laugh, one that started out low and twinkled its way up a musical scale. "Because, speaking of waiting, the repair guy won't wait for his money, and besides, I think I can do this and save myself a bundle. Well—" Kari paused and glanced at him over her shoulder, that dimple in her cheek showing itself to full advantage. "I guess it would be more accurate to say 'we,' since I failed to get this thing out from the wall on my own, huh?"

"Wait…you're really working on this range by yourself? Because I have to tell you—" Rob threw up both hands. "I'm no Mr. Fix-It. In high school shop, I barely squeaked by with a passing grade. Heck, I even take my car to someone else to get the oil changed. Daniel and Andrew, now, they're the ones good with mechanical stuff."

Kari lightly punched him in the shoulder. "Ah-ha! I've found your kryptonite. Relax. A strong back is all that I require, that and maybe someone to cheer me on."

"If you're sure…"

"I'm sure. Besides, what's the worst I can do? The stove can't get any broker, can it?"

Rob pursed his lips. "Uh, you could get electrocuted? Last I heard, 240 volts is more than a tickle."

Again her laugh danced up that musical scale. "Trust me, I'm just looking. I've watched a few videos online, and it seems pretty simple, but if I get into it and things don't look like the video, I'll stop. I know my limits. First, let's get this bad boy pulled out." Kari patted the stove's top. "I've put some old carpet scraps down to protect Mom's floor, so I guess we just have to drag it out."

"No hand truck?" he asked. "No dolly?"

"Uh…that would be a no."

"Okay…let's see if I can wriggle it out."

Together they struggled with the ungainly appliance—to Rob's surprise, it wasn't as heavy as he'd thought it would be, but it still wasn't a piece of cake. Two mashed fingers and three scraped knuckles later, though, he had it slid out into the center of the kitchen floor.

"So what exactly are you trying to fix?" he asked.

"The temperature sensor. I checked the

continuity on the element, and it's fine. I think…" Now Kari's face became rosy pink. "I screwed something up with the electronics when I sprayed it all down with the fire extinguisher. I had foam dripping down into the oven cavity, believe it or not."

"Uh—you sure we don't need to call a professional in for this?" Rob asked.

"We don't need no stinkin' professional." Kari wiggled her slim body through the tight opening formed by the back of the stove and the kitchen cabinet. With a flourish, she wrestled the heavy plug out of the outlet. "There. We can't get electrocuted now. Hand me that screwdriver—yeah, that one."

"Just how many stoves have you worked on?"

"Hmmm…" She bent over the galvanized metal cover on the back of the stove and started backing out the sheet metal screws. "I have to confess, this will be my inaugural thermostat sensor repair, but you've gotta start somewhere, right? Whoa! This is slipping on me—can you reach over—"

Before he knew it, Rob had wedged himself in beside Kari in the tiny space between the wall and the stove. Together they worked to unfasten the back cover. He lifted it up, careful to avoid grazing Kari with its sharp edges.

"Oh, man…that's a lot of wires. How will we know what we've got to replace?" he asked.

"You really are phobic when it comes to repairs, aren't you?" Kari shot back. "The video made it look pretty simple. All we have to do is take this mounting bracket off…" She crouched down again, nibbling on her bottom lip as she concentrated on getting rid of still more screws. "And we take out the old sensor." She slid a long metal probe out of the back of the oven. "Voila!"

"So now you just stick the new one in?"

Kari twisted around, first one way and then the other, squinting her eyes. "Uh… yeah…if I could remember where I left it. Boy, some expert I look like, huh?"

Rob thought she looked adorable, especially with the smear of grime on her nose and a dust bunny in her hair. He reached down to pluck the dust bunny from its nesting spot, but found his fingers sliding over her cheek.

Kari's mouth parted. She tilted her head back, and Rob thought maybe she was going to say, "Stop," or "Kiss me," or something in between those two.

She didn't, though. She just swallowed hard, her eyes losing their merry light. "Rob…"

He couldn't seem to stop the ball of his thumb from tracing that path along her cheek. Her skin was soft and warm and silky smooth, her eyes wide, her soft pink lips infinitely kissable. He could definitely kiss her.

But then all the reasons he shouldn't came flooding back to Rob. Slowly he dropped his hand. "You…uh…had some dust on your cheek," he fibbed. To add a little authenticity to his prevarication, he plucked the dust bunny from her hair. "And your hair."

"Oh." Kari ducked her head. Was she disappointed? Or grateful that he'd not tried to kiss her?

Just like before, when he'd tried to gauge her reaction, she didn't give him the chance. Kari lifted her chin, her smile a tad impersonal and maybe a watt or two too bright. "There it is—over there on the table. I'll just slip out and get it."

He felt her absence as much as if it had been a lost coat on a cold winter's day—not just the space between them, but her sudden aloofness. Gone in an instant was the joking tomfoolery, the banter between them.

All because he'd not been able to keep his hands to himself.

Or maybe because he *had* been able to.

Kari returned with a padded shipping envelope. She pulled out a bright and shiny new sensor and began feeding it through the hole. With quick and efficient movements, she fastened the mounting bracket back on and snapped the wires together by way of the plastic clip. "There. All done. Now we just put the cover back on, plug it back in and check the calibration."

"Don't you think we need to leave the cover off until you know it works?" he suggested.

"Oh, yeah, that's a good idea. I'm getting ahead of myself, huh?"

Rob watched her as she went through the motions of preheating the oven and tinkering with the calibration. "I had no idea you could adjust an oven temp like this. I'll have to check Ma's. She's always complaining that her oven is too hot."

"See? You are a Mr. Fix-It after all." Kari touched him on the arm, then jerked back. He noticed how her bottom lip quivered the tiniest bit. "But you'd better check for her specific model—each brand has a slightly different technique, I think, based on what I saw online."

"I will. You've inspired me. I have to admit, I thought it was beyond my pay grade," he confessed as he tightened the last of the screws on the back cover.

"Apology accepted. Desperation will make you do crazy things, I guess." Kari's hand flew to her mouth. "Oh, no. That's not the kind of thing you say to an arson investigator."

He reached over, pulled her hand from her face and squeezed it. "Kari...maybe I'm wrong. Maybe you're playing me in some elaborate con...but...look at you. You're smart. Handy with a wrench and a screwdriver. You figure out how things work. If you'd wanted to burn that building down, I have no doubt you could have worked out a better, much more clever way than a propane tank and a road flare. So...maybe I should be on the job, but right now, could you think of me as...well...a friend? Because that's why I came. That's why I'm here. To help you. I just want to help you."

Misery seemed to ooze from her. Her face

crumpled, despite her efforts to recover her poise. "I—you have no idea how much I wish I could believe that, Rob." She swallowed, lifted that chin again in the way she did when she was trying to compose herself. "I wish I could. But thank you anyway."

# CHAPTER FIFTEEN

At least the oven was working again, and it hadn't cost her a fortune to get it back in operation.

Kari yawned, glanced at the wall clock and piped out another rose. Only three hundred more of the suckers to go, or at least it felt like it was another three hundred. Plus she still had all the baby calla lilies and the orchids and the hydrangeas to make. She'd never get them all done.

It was almost midnight. She'd baked the bottom two tiers of Mattie Gottman's cake, but she had to finish the rest or the leavening in the batter wouldn't do its job. Maybe it hadn't been the wisest course of action to start baking the cake right after Rob had left.

But then again, her brain had been complete mush by the time he'd walked out the kitchen door.

She'd stood there like a complete idiot, willing him to kiss her. What sort of a cow-eyes face had she made at him, and all he was doing was brushing dust off her face?

It hadn't felt like that. It had felt...

Warmth sped through her, and her heart beat faster at the memory of his touch. Gentle. Patient. As if he'd been waiting for her to give him permission...

That was important to her, that permission. For four years, her body had literally not been her own. Guards had told her when to shower, when to eat, when to sleep, when to work, when she could even have a bathroom break. They'd yanked her into line, yanked her out of line, did routine searches of her and her paltry few belongings...and that didn't count the invasions of privacy she'd suffered at the hands of her fellow inmates.

Too many times when Kari had dated before, guys would get pushy and impatient and try to rush things. All it did was turn Kari off.

To try to explain that meant trying to explain her record...which wasn't something she felt comfortable trotting out by even the second or third date.

But Rob knew. He knew, and he still wanted to touch her that way.

The timer beeped. She sighed, glanced at the clock to see it was ten minutes after midnight, and laid the pastry bag on the table. Time to check on the cake.

The door behind her rattled as Kari peered in the oven window. Jumping at the sudden sound in the otherwise silent kitchen, she felt her heart settle when she realized it was Jake at the door.

She swung it open. "Hey. Pretty late for you to come wandering by for a visit."

He pushed by her, a waft of beer and something that didn't smell altogether legal in his wake. "Yeah, well, me and the guys, we were at this club, got a little wasted, y'know? And so I didn't think it would be a real good idea for me to drive."

"That was…smart, at least the not driving part. But you know if Mom sees you like this, she's going to worry—"

"Oh, shut up, Saint Karina," he snapped, invoking his childhood nickname for her. "Not everybody can be so freaking awesome like you all the time. Give me a break. I can't stand my job—stupid boss thinks he's smarter than me, and it's all because he's got some piece of paper from a two-bit community college. I just want to, you know, blow off some steam."

He slumped into the kitchen chair and popped one of Kari's piped roses into his mouth. He spat it out in his hand. "God, that's too sweet! I thought it would be good like your usual stuff."

"Well, no, not those. The buttercream recipe that I use for flowers is pretty sweet. But I'm glad you didn't like it—each one of those takes a good two minutes to make, and I've got a lot more to do," she said. Just to be on the safe side, she moved the flexible cutting board of piped roses to the counter, away from Jake and his appetite. "I got the oven working, by the way."

He slapped his palm to his forehead. "I was supposed to help you! Crap. No wonder you're miffed, huh?"

"I'm not miffed, Jake." She used oven mitts to pull the cake layers out of the oven and move them to the stovetop. She slid the next two pans in and shut the door. "But I have to admit, it would have been nice for you to have—for once, anyway—actually shown up when you said you would."

"I'm here now?" he hazarded. "No, wait, I came too late. Okay, so what can I do to get out of Saint Karina's doghouse?"

"Not wake Mom up, for one thing. I didn't tell her."

"Tell her what?" He was instantly alert, the spaced out expression evaporating and wariness taking its place.

"That you didn't show up. I didn't want to worry her."

"That's like telling the Statue of Liberty to put her arm down," Jake joked. "Mom always worries."

"I guess we've given her good reason to. Don't you think?"

"I require hazardous duty pay for thinking at this time of night, the way I feel. I'm gonna crash in my room—you know if the bed's made up?"

Kari bent back over the roses, feeling her hand ache as she squeezed out another petal. "You know it is. I wish you wouldn't mooch off Mom so—half the time she pays your rent, and you wind up staying here anyway—"

"Me? Hey, I'm not the one who borrowed thousands of Mom's retirement money and then, after it all went up in smoke, moved back here rent-free, all the while raking in big bucks for all this frou-frou cake stuff." Jake sneered as he pointed a finger at things around the kitchen. "Yeah, we all have got to be sooo nice to Saint Karina, you know? Because she went to jail for you, Jakey! She took the rap for you, Jakey! I can't tell you how many times she's shoved that down my throat. I am so sick of it."

"Yeah, well, I was pretty sick of actually doing the time for you," Kari shot back.

Her anger surprised her. For so long, she'd literally been afraid of what she might do or say to him if she had laid eyes on him. Kari's reaction now must have surprised Jake, too, for the sneer melted. He had the grace to give her a sheepish grin. "You're a good egg, Kar. I know how much I owe you. I do. It's just—well, nobody wants it shoved down their throat. All. The. Freakin'. Time."

"I know. And I tell Mom that. It's not like I *intended* to go to jail for four years for you. Honestly, if I'd known that going in..." Kari trailed off.

"Yeah, well, who could blame you, right? Besides, it was Mom's not-so-brainy idea, not mine."

"And she feels horrible about it. That's why—" Kari shrugged. Her mom's guilt explained a lot of her motivation. "Please don't worry her anymore. She just wants both of us to be…"

"Tax-paying productive citizens," Jake finished with his mom's usual line. "Though why anybody who makes as little as I do has to pay taxes…" he groused.

"Speaking of work, you must be off tomorrow—since you stayed out so late," she said.

"Nah, I gotta drag my butt in. We've got inventory. Man, I hate that. So boring. Count this container of widgets. Now count that bin of whatchamacallits. Why? You need me to do something? I can blow work."

"You can*not* 'blow work,' as you so elegantly put it." She paused in midpiping to gape at him. "Besides, it was nothing really."

"No, what is it? If it's any better than counting washers and bolts, I'm in," Jake told her. He stretched out his long legs and planted his flip-flopped feet on the opposite chair. He yawned, not bothering to cover his mouth.

"Really, it's nothing. I just thought you might go downtown with me and help some of the merchants. A few of them have got their insurance checks, but you know how it is—they're trying to do a lot of the demolition work themselves to save some money. I thought we could help."

"Help? Dang, Kari, I thought it would be something fun, you know, like ride down to Savannah and pick up something from that cooking supply store." He wiggled his toes in his flipflops and yawned again, running his hand through hair that Kari itched to take a pair of scissors to.

"They're like me, Jake. They're all having to pay rent to keep their space. Charlie's threatening to yank our leases if we don't."

"That old jerk. Hates spending his money so much. Shoot, the night that block went up in flames, I'm surprised he coughed up the gas to come back early from his vacay—I hope he couldn't get his money refunded for his hotel room." Jake threw his head back and dissolved into gales of laughter.

A cold tingle drifted down Kari's spine. "What do you mean, Charlie came back early, Jake?"

"Yeah, you know. He told us, right? That he was going to be gone."

She laid the pastry bag down. "No. He didn't tell me that."

Jake became as still as she was. "Sure, he did. The day before the fire. He came in, and you started nagging him about the repairs, and then y'all screamed at each other..." A flicker of awareness crossed Jake's face. "Maybe that was after."

"You talked with him after that, Jake?" Kari's mouth went dry. She clutched the edge of the countertop.

"Maybe. Or maybe it was some other time," Jake said vaguely. "I get mixed up when I'm this wasted."

"I went in the back..." She didn't say, *to wash the tears off my face.* "I heard the bell on the front door, and I thought he went out. And when I came back, you were gone, too."

"Maybe that's when he told me he was going to be on Jekyll Island." Contempt flooded Jake's face. "He acted like it was Hilton Head or the Cloisters on Sea Island, the way he talked so big about going 'down to Jekyll.' Bet he stayed at a roach motel with sand in the sheets, as cheap as he is."

"But you told...you told me that you told Rob you didn't know that Charlie was going to be out of town."

Jake stood up, stretched so long and leisurely that Kari could hear his shoulder joints pop. "Yeah, so. No biggie. What? You think I torched the place? Like I keep telling you and Mom—it gets old, this business of you two thinking I'm responsible for every fire that gets started around here."

Then he wandered off, but not before he reached around Kari and helped himself to another of her painstakingly piped roses. "Night, sis. Don't stay up too late, huh. You need your beauty sleep."

But sleep was the furthest thing from Kari's mind. She was awake—achingly awake, with every nerve ending screaming. Jake had bought a propane tank. And he knew when Charlie was going to be out of town.

Had he impulsively decided to wreak revenge on her behalf?

EVEN AN EXTRA-LONG hot shower did not make up for having just three hours of sleep. Kari stumbled into the kitchen the next morning to see her mom pouring coffee in a mug.

Mom took one look at her and handed over the cup. "Here. You look like you sorely need this. I'll get me another."

Kari slurped the heavenly brew down. "Thank you. I'm so tired I need toothpicks to keep my eyelids open."

"What time did you finally go to bed?" Her mom began pulling out eggs and milk.

Kari groaned. "About three. I got the layers baked and in the freezer, and all the roses done. Now I just have to make the rest of the flowers. Hey, I made egg cups and blueberry muffins for our breakfast. I wasn't sure I would be up to cooking this morning, and I figured if our breakfast was ready, it would help."

"Great. We'll just have those, then. So where'd you put the other roses?"

Kari took another welcome sip of her coffee. "What do you mean, the other roses? They're all laid out to dry on the cutting board over there. All one hundred of them. Mattie wanted a waterfall of flowers cascading down the side of the tiers, and I needed to get a head start on the roses."

"Oh, honey…" Her mother wheeled around, her eyes wide, her mouth open. "There's not nearly a hundred here."

Kari lurched to the counter and peered down at the cutting board. Sure enough, just as her mom had said, only about half of the roses were still there. Telltale crumbs of buttercream icing littered the flexible cutting board where the other roses had been.

"Jake," she snarled. "Jake ate my roses. And he didn't even like the way they tasted."

It all flooded back to her, the alarm she'd felt the night before when he'd revealed he had known Charlie Kirkman was going to be out of town, now mingled with fury that he'd sabotaged her hours of hard work.

"Jake? Kari, Jake wasn't even here—" her mom protested.

"He was. He came stumbling in the door last night at midnight, half-wasted."

"Oh, I didn't hear him—has he left already?"

Kari flicked the buttercream icing crumbs. "If he hasn't, he'd better start running for the door," she said grimly. "I told him these roses were for a cake—"

She marched to his bedroom, or what had been his bedroom when he'd lived here. At least her mom had not left it in its teenage glory of martial arts posters and video consoles and piles of dirty clothes—now it had been turned into a gender-neutral spare bedroom.

No sign of Jake, save the rumpled bedclothes, remained. She felt her mom brush up against her as she peered into the bedroom.

"He's gone? He could have at least waited and had breakfast with us."

"He had breakfast—my roses. I hope they

give him a mouthful of cavities," Kari muttered.

Her mother's hands fluttered and her bracelets clattered against each other as she put her fingers to her temples. Kari shook her head. "Don't even think about trying to defend him."

Back in the kitchen, Kari grabbed the plastic bin of muffins—obviously Jake hadn't dug around enough in the kitchen to find them—and got the egg cups out of the freezer. She nuked the egg cups in the microwave, trying to get a grip on her temper.

The microwave beeped. She pulled out the steaming mini-omelets, not even cheered by the scent of eggs, onions, bacon and oozing cheese. "Mom…has Jake said anything to you about where he was the night of the fire?"

"You mean, the downtown fire? Why, he told us. Remember? He said he crashed on somebody's couch. You can't think he did that. There's a big difference between your brother thoughtlessly helping himself to your roses and burning down your bakery." Her mom reached for a muffin and an egg cup. "These are really good."

"Thanks," Kari said absently. She crumbled the muffin in her hand for a moment before popping a bite into her mouth. "It's just something he said last night…he lied to Rob, Mom. Did you know that? He told him that he didn't know Charlie was going to be out of town, and last night he let slip that he did know."

Her mom frowned, clearly wanting to drop the unpleasant topic. "I wish we weren't so ready to blame Jake. He tells me all the time how I jump to conclusions because of that first fire."

"Well, your past *does* define you. It sure defines me. One choice. It's funny how you can trace your life back to one solitary decision."

"I was the one who—"

But Kari ignored her mom's protest. "I'm not talking about the confession, Mom. Neither of us could have known that the judge would throw the book at me. No, if I just hadn't asked Jake to take us by that dumb store that day."

Her mom stared out the window at the bright morning sunlight filtering through her kitchen curtains. Kari followed her gaze and spied a mockingbird dive-bombing a gathering of sparrows. "You never talk about it," her mom said.

"You never wanted to," Kari replied.

"All Jake said was the guy was mean to you."

"He was. It was…awful, Mom. About the worst humiliation I'd experienced ever—well, at least until I went to juvie." Kari pushed aside her own egg, and rose to drop her plate into the dishwasher. "Funny thing was, Jake didn't want to stop at the convenience store. But it was me and Chelsea Boynton and Kai Williford, and we all begged him to. You'd asked him to pick us up from cheer practice, you remember?"

Suddenly an awful pang of regret flooded through Kari—she was fourteen again, pumped up and excited that she had made the cheer squad and that her freshman year was going to be full of adventure. There'd been weeks of hard work and practice— she'd been a flyer, or she would have been.

"And the owner accused you of shoplifting," her mom tagged on. "That's what Jake said. The guy practically strip-searched you there in the store."

"I swear, Mom, I hadn't so much as thought about shoplifting. I don't know what he saw. Maybe it was because we were a group of young girls and he'd seen things go missing—that's a common age for shoplifting, and the girls I knew in juvie talked a lot about how they stole in packs." Kari glanced down at the half-filled cutting board of roses and sighed. No help for it. She had to mix up more icing and start re-making those roses.

She began beating the pasteurized egg whites, the mixer thrumming along at low speed as she sifted her pricey organic powdered sugar. It lumped like nobody's business, and she dared not push the big rocklike clumps through the sieve—she'd learned the hard way that one little sugar crystal could stop up a piping tip.

Over the sound of the sifter and the mixer, she heard the glug of her mom's second cup of coffee. Her mom came to stand beside her.

"Careful of your jacket, Mom—this powdered sugar is going everywhere, and it will get all over that black blazer," Kari warned.

"Jake said that man was a pervert—that he seemed to genuinely like patting you down."

Kari shuddered at the memory. "Compared to other searches I went through after that…no. But it was still mortifying. I wanted to melt into the floor—there I was in front of my friends, and that guy going ballistic over a dollar candy bar that I had not even taken to begin with." It had been the first time that anyone but a family member or a medical professional had touched her in such an invasive way. "Jake snatched me out of there and told him to keep his hands to himself. He even threw a dollar down on the floor, said if the man was so greedy for a dollar, there it was."

"He was just trying to look out for you, Kari. He said the guy deserved what was coming to him."

Kari shook her head. "Nobody deserves his business burned down, Mom. If I didn't know that then, well, I know it now. But… I believe Jake when he said he got carried away with his buddies, defending my honor. I wish he hadn't."

"He…he cares, honey. He doesn't always show it the right way, but he cares. And— and if he did start the downtown fire—I'm not saying he did, mind you, but *if*—well, he was probably just getting back at Charlie. It was the same thing, right? He saw two men putting their greediness ahead of his little sister's best interests?"

Leave it to her mother to try to put the best spin possible on criminal activity. Kari stopped the mixer to check the progress of the batch. The icing was whipping up into a fluffy off-white froth that would have to beat slowly for another ten minutes to become the pure white she needed it to be. She ran a finger through a fluffy peak and tested it: sweet, but not quite light enough yet. Kari slid the switch back on. She met her mother's gaze.

"Mom…he can't keep doing this. He's within spitting distance of thirty. He needs help—professional help."

Her mother recoiled in horror. "Kari! You know—you of all people know what happens when you confess to a crime. The authorities aren't in the business of getting people help—not to say Jake needs that kind of help. He only needs to, you know, grow into his own, settle a little. If you go to Rob Monroe and tell him—" She put her hand to her mouth and set the coffee mug down with a thud. "The stories you've told me about being…in that place. And that wasn't even a real prison, not where they'd send Jake if they convicted him of the downtown fire—oh, honey, please, please don't do this! Not to me, not to Jake."

Lack of sleep and her mom's desperation fed the beginnings of a serious tension headache behind Kari's eyes. The whine of the mixer wasn't helping matters. Her mom was right about one thing, though. "Okay. You win. You're right…they'd slap him behind bars quick as lightning. And I wouldn't wish prison on my worst enemy."

Instantly her mom relaxed. She reached over and gave Kari a peck on the cheek. "Thank you, darling. I knew you of all people would understand. He just needs time, you know? He just needs to find…well, what *you've* found, with your baking. Something that he's good at and enjoys, something that fulfills him."

With a fluff of her hair and a smoothing of her jacket, her mom was out the door, leaving Kari to ponder her mother's words.

Sure, Kari had her baking. She stared down at the fluffy peaks and valleys of the buttercream. On one level, tackling a project as ambitious as Mattie Gottman's wedding cake *did* fulfill her, and she honestly hoped that Jake could find something like that.

But…

Inexplicably a sense of loneliness inundated Kari. Here she was, alone in her mother's kitchen, talking to mixing bowls and spatulas instead of real people. Even in her old shop, she could go for hours without talking to anybody.

*Not always. Rob Monroe stops by a lot these days.*

The thought made her even lonelier. She hated the way she'd come to look forward to his calls and texts and even more to his visits and the time they spent together. She'd come to relish the prospect of seeing his goofy grin, how he seemed to know to give her space and wait for her to come to him.

Once this case was over—even in the best-case scenario—he wouldn't be coming around anymore. She couldn't fool herself into thinking otherwise.

And worst case? He was just stringing her along, giving her enough rope to hang herself.

Or Jake.

She shivered.

She couldn't let that happen.

# CHAPTER SIXTEEN

ROB LINGERED OVER the boxed brownie mixes in the grocery store, turning first one and then another over in his hands.

The brownies-in-the-box, he had to admit, were a stopgap measure for dealing with Kari withdrawal pains. Rob figured if he could treat himself to something sweet and chocolaty and fresh from the oven, maybe he wouldn't be so tempted to drop by Kari's mom's.

The aisle was thick with shoppers stopping by after work. Unlike him, they seemed to know exactly what they wanted. He started to ask one lady which brownie mix was the best, but she hurried off with what she needed before he could stop her.

Just as he was about to give up and pick a box at random, a flurry of activity out of the corner of his eye attracted his attention.

He turned and blinked in surprise. Was he missing Kari so much that he was seeing her wherever he turned? Kind of like a man dying of thirst in a desert stumbling toward a mirage of an oasis?

But no. That blond curly ponytail *did* belong to Kari—she was feverishly scooping up every plastic bag of organic powdered sugar off the shelf.

"Whoa. That's a lot of sugar," he commented. "Your dentist know about this?"

Kari whirled around. He was gratified by the big smile that spread across her face and lit her eyes. "Hey, you," she said. "What are you doing here?"

Then her gaze fell on the box in his hand.

"No, no, no," she said firmly. She plucked the offending carton from his fingers and pushed it back on the shelf. "Honestly, it's just butter, sugar, eggs, flour, cocoa and vanilla. You don't even need a mixer. Pinky promise."

"But I've tried it," he admitted. "I went home and went online and looked up a recipe, and it was awful."

Her blue gray eyes shone with compassion. "You tried to bake? From scratch?"

"Proud of me?"

"I am. But I'm sorry it didn't go so well for you. I—" She looked down at the powdered sugar in her cart. "If I wasn't neck deep in trying to rescue myself from Mattie Gottman's wedding cake, I'd show you myself. Everybody needs to know how to cook brownies."

"How's it coming? If you're here and not in the kitchen, it must not be going well."

Kari put a palm to her forehead. "I realized that I'd miscalculated on how much icing I would need—plus Jake ate up half of the roses I'd made ahead of time, and I still have orchids and hydrangeas and calla lilies to make."

Something about her panicked desperation pulled at him. He found himself saying, "I don't know much about decorating cakes, but Daniel says I'm a good gopher."

"Gopher?" Kari wrinkled her brow in puzzlement.

"Yeah—I go for that, and I go for this."

She laughed. "At my house, we call that guy Stepin Fetchit."

Rob half expected her to say thanks, but no thanks—while the other half of him was wondering what had possessed him to volunteer to help. He couldn't seem to resist, though. The truth was he missed her.

"I'll be your Mr. Fetchit," he offered again.

She seemed torn. He saw her buy time by

grabbing yet another bag of sugar off the shelf, hold onto it longer than she needed to when she put it in the cart.

"Okay," Kari said finally. "My mom is having to work late to get through an audit at the medical office she works at, so I could really use a spare set of hands. But...can we not talk about the case? No questions about the fire? Either fire? And in exchange, once I get done with the cake, I'll show you how to make my not-so-secret brownie recipe."

"You won't have to kill me after you show me, will you?" Rob fell into step beside her as she headed for the checkout.

"Nope. I'm not telling you *all* my secrets," Kari joked. She must have realized what she'd said, because she bit her lip and looked away.

Rob let it slide. He began tossing the packets of powdered sugar on the conveyor belt. "This all you need? Nothing else?"

"Oh, two more experienced cake decorators to help me dig my way out of this hole would be nice."

"I think they're on aisle four if you'd like me to go check." He gave her a wink. "Then again, maybe I'm—"

Just then, he looked past her. There, staring hard at the two of them, was Sam Franklin.

The district attorney was standing just behind Kari, a loaf of bread and a jug of milk in his hands.

"Mr. Franklin." Rob stuck out a hand in greeting.

Franklin gave him a sour smile. "Kind of got my hands full, Rob. I see you're hard at work solving the downtown arson case."

Kari's face turned as green as it had the day she'd caught her mother's kitchen on fire. She pushed past Rob and snatched one of the bags of powdered sugar out of his hand. "Thank you for your help, Mr. Monroe," she snapped. "I'll take it from here."

Franklin smirked. "Looks like it's my lucky day. Lane four just opened up with no waiting."

Kari didn't watch him go, just ducked her head and shoved her credit card through the scanner. Rob found himself in a fast trot to keep up with her as she took off for her minivan.

"Kari! Wait!"

She spun around. "No, you wait. I thought you were genuinely offering to help, not spy on me."

"I wasn't spying on you—"

"Yeah? Tailing me to the baking aisle of the grocery store?"

"I was here before you, thank you very much," he pointed out. "Remember?"

For a moment, she was completely flustered. She fumbled for the keys to her van, dropped them, and knelt down to scrabble for them on the pavement. Rob bent down beside her. His hands slid over the wayward keys, which he handed to her. "Here," he said. "And I really was offering to help. Ma says you'll never hear the end of it if you screw up Mattie Gottman's cake. And believe me, I'm in a position to know. I dated her for all of thirty seconds about three years ago. My name's still mud in the Gottman circle of associates. I can't imagine why I rated an invite to the big day."

Kari unlocked the door and pulled it open. The ancient hinge squeaked in protest, and Rob could see that the worn fabric on the door's liner had given way. Specks of orange-colored foam spilled out of the tattered upholstery.

"I don't know..." she said.

"Do you or do you not need that help you were talking about?" he pressed.

"Why do I think I'm going to regret this?"

"Because I'm the world's worst at frosting any sort of cake known to man."

Kari chuckled. "You think I'd let you anywhere near Mattie's cake?"

"There are dishes to be washed, right? And things to be handed? And I can hold a cup of water with a straw—you can prevent dehydrating that way."

"You are a goofball, aren't you?" Now the hesitation and worry had evaporated from her eyes.

"Hardly words to motivate me to help you— first, you call me a spy, and then a goofball."

"Maybe I should just quit while I'm ahead and call you a godsend." She tossed the bags into the passenger seat. "Okay, you want it, you've got it. I hereby deputize you as my assistant cake decorator. Get ready for the crazies."

*IF DANIEL AND ANDREW could see me now.*

Rob was most certainly glad they couldn't, not as he tried for the fourth time to imitate Kari's deft moves with a stick and a pastry bag.

"I give up," he groaned. "My rose looks like a lump of modeling clay left in the dryer, and yours—well—yours—"

Hers had taken all of sixty seconds to whip into shape. He couldn't even follow her moves when she'd slowed it down.

"No, no, don't give up...you can do this, you're getting the hang of it." Kari closed her eyes and drew in a deep breath. He could tell her tension was mounting, and that she was in an even deeper panic than she had been earlier at the grocery store.

Otherwise, she'd never have taken the time to try to teach him how to create a rose out of the best frosting he'd ever tasted.

They'd been at this for two hours. He admired her persistence, not to mention her patience with him as she taught him what to do.

"How did you ever learn this?" he grumbled. "How were you ever brave enough to tackle the main event of somebody's big day?"

Kari stopped mid swirl of what she called the crumb coat. "I guess it was just being naive and maybe even a bit foolish? Maybe I just didn't think through all the things that could possibly go wrong? At least, not until I stared down three large unfrosted layers and that doesn't even touch the first time I delivered the cake to the site."

"But you'd been trained how to do it, right?" Rob prompted. "You worked at a bakery?"

Suddenly she dissolved into giggles. "Yeah, but I was in my second week at the bakery when I did that first wedding cake. It was…oh, a nightmare. A disaster. I'd offered a—well, a friend that I would bake her wedding cake for her wedding present. She'd seen me do really simple birthday cakes, and she was always blown away by my designs."

"I'm thinking it was a little more involved."

Kari swiped at her eyes with her forearm, tears of mirth threatening to spill over onto her cheeks. "AJ would have been fine with just this really simple cake, right? But, no, I had to go all fancy on her, and I promised waaaay more than I could deliver. I had no idea how long any of it would take, no idea how much icing to make. I must have made three different batches of icing. I stayed up all night to bake that thing, and then I fell asleep in the wedding."

"You fell asleep?" Rob could imagine the scene. "Tell me you weren't the maid of honor."

"Nope. You know, I've never been a maid of honor, or a bridesmaid for that matter.

Girls come into my shop all the time fussing about what a bother it is, but I think it could be kind of fun."

Rob gave her a dubious look. "From the experience my sisters have had, I'd count yourself lucky. They must have been in a gajillion weddings by now."

Kari dragged her spatula through the cloud of white frosting and sighed wistfully. "I don't know. It must be nice to have someone want you to be a part of your big day. How about you? Have you ever been a groomsman?"

"Yep. I've been roped into wearing the old penguin suit more than once. I guess the guys have it easier than the girls."

"And…you said you'd never been married."

This, Rob noted with a prickle of awareness, was delivered with a studied casualness while Kari made a big deal of focusing on the icing. "I came close. Once. She was my high school sweetheart. We'd dated all through our junior and senior years, and everybody always assumed we'd get married eventually. I guess it finally hit her that I was really going to be a firefighter after she went off to college and I stayed behind to sign up for the academy. I think she was convinced Ma would talk me out of it."

"What's so bad about being married to a firefighter? Didn't she want her own personal hero? I mean, you came in handy the other day when I nearly burned the kitchen down." She winked as she slathered on still more frosting.

Rob paused. "Sheesh. People will die of a diabetic coma after one slice," he observed. "That's a lot of sugar."

"I know." Kari grinned like a kid with her hand in the cookie jar. "But what's a cake good for but gobs and gobs of frosting?"

Rob chuckled. He admired how she'd managed to keep a positive attitude and her sense of humor through everything that had happened lately.

Their laughter faded. "She really didn't marry you just because you wanted to be a firefighter?" Kari asked.

"Really. I can't blame her. It's a lot of stress, and for guys who aren't used to it, it's not much of a family life. You're on a twenty-four-hour shift, then off for forty-eight. And that's not counting the potential for…well, the worst that could happen."

"You're thinking about your dad, I guess."

"Yeah. Well, no. I'm thinking about Ma. Dad was prepared. He knew the stakes going in. And Ma…she was the epitome of what it took to be a firefighter's wife—cool and calm and unflappable. She just always concentrated on the positive and tried to remember that Dad was trained to do what he did. She wasn't a drama queen about it. It was hard at the time, but I realized it was a good thing that Charlotte took a hard look at us and decided to pull the plug when she did. She said she couldn't do it, couldn't face it, which was fair enough. I respected her honesty."

"Still, like you said, it must have been hard."

"It stung at the time, but when I look back on it, I think I knew the way the wind was blowing long before we broke up."

"How was your mom? You know, when… the fire happened?" A shiver visibly ran through Kari's slim shoulders.

"While he was in the hospital, she was great. Pillar of strength. Never showed him how scared she was. But she'd come home to, you know, check on us, get fresh clothes, and I'd hear her crying her eyes out. And after Dad was killed, she was a wreck for a real long time."

"Fire ruins everything," Kari muttered.

Rob nodded. "Yes. You're right about that."

AN HOUR LATER, Kari was anything but quiet. She was freaking out over not having enough roses for the cascade. It seemed there was only so much frosting two people could do with a looming deadline.

"There's nobody else you can call? No 911 alert to fellow bakers? What about that friend of yours, Alice?" he asked, staring at the stick in his hand with its less-than-optimum rose. "I just don't want to let you down, okay? I'm trying, but I don't want to mess up this cake."

"You won't. You won't. You're doing great. Besides, let's face it, I can't afford to lose you now. And Alice, she'd be glad to help out, but she lives two hours away. So it looks like it's just you and me." Kari laid her tools aside and put her hands over his. Her fingers were so incredibly tiny compared to his. She smiled up at him. "Let's try it this way. Maybe I can show you another way to do it."

Together, they worked through the making of a buttercream rose. At first, all Rob could think about was how good her fingers felt on his, how close she was to him. He wanted to kiss the worry that was etched into her face, tell her it was all going to be okay—but it wouldn't. Not unless some fairy godmother with a magic wand that spat out buttercream roses came and bopped him over the head.

And then suddenly he got it. Rob beamed at her.

"Look at you. And you said you weren't a Mr. Fix-It. You're very good with your hands," she said primly.

What he wanted to do with his hands was sweep her up and kiss her senseless—but first he had to help her make about a jillion roses.

They worked until his hands screamed in agony. "Okay, I think that's enough roses for now…" she said. "I've got to get started decorating the cake proper. She wants Swiss dots and scrolled Cornelli icing on alternating layers—I can teach you that pretty quick—don't worry, it doesn't have to be perfect."

At 9:00 p.m., when Chelle Hendrix came in with bags of fast food, Rob could have hugged the woman. How he could be starving in the middle of all this frosting and cake, he couldn't figure out.

They pushed aside the plethora of tools on one corner of the kitchen table and fell on the burgers with the enthusiasm of the famished. Chelle stared at first them and then the cake, which stood at attention on the other end of the table.

"I thought you would have it nearly finished by now," she told Kari. "You've only got the bottom two tiers done, and you haven't even started on the cascade."

"I know, Mom, but it is a big cake. And I ran out of powdered sugar, plus I had to start back over on my roses, and those calla lilies didn't transfer like I hoped they would."

"It's looking good, though," Chelle said. Rob chuckled at the brave face she was putting on. "What you've got done, that is. Rob, I'm so glad you were able to help her."

"I think I'm more in her way than anything," he replied.

Kari closed her hand over his. "No, no, you're a natural. I couldn't have gotten this far without you."

Chelle shuddered. "Not me. I have a complete phobia about decorating cakes. Remember that time I tried to learn?"

Kari's shoulders shook as she bit into her burger. She put her hand to her mouth and swallowed, got choked and had to have Rob pound her on her back. "Mom, that was awful—I hate to say it, but I wouldn't let you lay a pinky finger on Mattie Gottman's cake."

"I wouldn't dream of trying. I just—oh, give me numbers. I can definitely do numbers, but anything with a pastry bag?" Chelle scoffed and then asked, "Is there anything else I can do?"

He and Kari soon started back on the intricate scrollwork and the infernal Swiss dots that made Rob's hands cramp and his shoulders ache. He hoped Mattie Gottman was planning on having lots of champagne with her wedding—otherwise she might look a wee bit too close and see that the scrollwork wasn't completely up to Kari's usual exacting standards.

As the clock hit 11:00 p.m. and they were only starting the fourth tier, Chelle yawned. "I'm leaving it with y'all. Kari, I've cleaned out the fridge like you asked—took the shelves out, too, so it ought to be tall enough for the cake to slide in. But I've got to go to bed."

By midnight, they were beginning on the cascade. Rob was so bleary-eyed he was seeing double. "Have to admit my hands haven't hurt this badly since my first days training with a fire hose—or maybe even when I was little and had to shell bucket after bucket of butter beans for Ma."

Kari looked up from transferring all his less-than-perfect roses to the side of the cake. She'd pluck them up with a pair of scissors, glue them on with a walloping amount of buttercream, and adjust them to her liking. "Somebody told me that all the Monroe boys were firefighters—that it was a family tradition. Did you actually want to be a firefighter? Or was it something that your family expected?"

The question took him aback. "Well, yeah, of course I wanted to be a firefighter. Ma's got pictures of me when I was little, parading around in a firefighter hat and a toy fire truck."

Suddenly the white monolith of a cake was starting to look like…well, a wedding cake.

Even his ugly roses didn't look so bad interspersed with her much prettier orchids and hydrangeas and lilies.

"Yeah? It must be comforting to have known what you've always wanted to do with your life."

He rubbed at his mouth, considering. "It wasn't comforting to Ma, not after our dad died. She's proud of us, don't get me wrong. But I could have clobbered Daniel when he gave up his shot at the majors to join the department."

"Why was that?" She glanced over at him. "Man, you've got more frosting on you than the cake does!"

It was true. He found himself inspecting his knuckles and licking the sweet sticky stuff off them. "Just taste-testing, that's all. Don't worry, I'll wash up before I come near your cake."

Kari shook a finger at him, but she sported a smile. "You'd better. You were telling me about Daniel. What did it matter that he became a firefighter, too?"

"We'd just lost Dad, see? And Daniel had never wanted to be a firefighter—it was all baseball, all the time. But then

Dad was killed, and Daniel seemed to believe he needed to take up Dad's place. And all I could think was that Ma, as nervous and anxious as she was over Daniel's move, would never stand for me becoming a firefighter, too."

"But that didn't happen? Hand me that spatula over there, please."

He obeyed. "No. I underestimated the stuff Ma's made of. She may not like it, but she's never going to stand in the way of what any of her kids want to be."

"I like her. She's called me several times, you know, to cheer me on. It's really helped me to have folks like Ma and Alice in my corner."

"And me, of course," Rob said grandly, tapping his chest. "You like having me in your corner."

Kari stared at him, unspoken words clearly on her lips. She averted her gaze. "Yeah. Yeah, you most of all. I just hope you'll stay there," she murmured cryptically.

By 1:00 a.m., he was uncapping the last of the pearlescent spray—who knew you could spray paint a cake?—and watching her as she turned the long four-tier cascade of closely bunched flowers into something that looked straight out of Hollywood.

"I'd kill for my paint gun right now," she said as she shook the aerosol can and finished up the last section. "It's so much easier to control than these spray cans. But until I can afford to replace it, I've got to make do."

"Paint gun?" he asked. "Like you'd paint, what, cars with?"

"Yeah. Great for airbrushing cakes. So much better. You hook it up to a compressed air tank and spray away."

"Whodathunkit," Rob muttered. He filed it away, along with all the other unguarded moments she'd moaned over not having exactly the right tool for the job. No, unlike that lady two towns over who'd most likely torched her own house, she hadn't emptied out her shop of her most cherished possessions.

But he had to admire her tenacity—despite not having the right tools, despite how it made the job ten times harder, Kari had stuck with it, made it work with what she had.

She frowned, now, took a paintbrush with a teeny-tiny tip and began tinkering with spots that didn't meet her satisfaction.

Rob endured it for another half hour. But when Kari's fiddling and twiddling seemed never ending, he gently pulled her back against him.

"Relax. It's done. You did it. And it looks… even if I do say so myself, that cake looks fabulous."

She craned her head up to stare at him. "Will it do? You know Mattie…will she like it?"

"She'd be crazy not to. This town has never seen a cake that glamorous. The thing could be on TV, the way it looks."

"Oh, good." Kari turned in his grasp until she was fully facing him. "Now I can start on the groom's cake."

Rob's jaw dropped. "Are you kidding me? We've got another cake to do?"

Kari reached up and tapped an index finger against his nose. "Gotcha! Oh, if I could have taken a picture of that face of yours. It was priceless. No, the groom's cake is done—he's a huge Georgia Bulldogs fan, so all I had to do was decorate a chocolate cake with the Georgia emblem. Easy-peasy."

Rob sagged against her with relief. "That's cruel and unusual punishment, ma'am. Geneva conventions have distinct prohibitions about teasing poor exhausted assistants in the wee hours of the morning."

"What about poor exhausted cake decorators?" She giggled. "I'm so tired I don't dare let go of you because I might fall. You're the only thing still keeping me upright."

"What are you talking about? *You're* the only thing keeping me upright." Kari roared with laughter as Rob swung her wide, lifting her off the floor and twirling her. "No, wait, maybe that's my second wind kicking in. Got another cake that needs decorating?"

"That's the sugar high talking—I think you may have licked one too many bowls of buttercream," Kari said. But her eyes were sparkling, and Rob knew it wasn't the buttercream that made his heart do a triple beat.

"There's sugar, and then...well, there's sugar," he whispered. He bent down to kiss her and was gratified to realize she was on tiptoe, stretching up to her full height to meet his lips.

She tasted of sugar—vanilla buttercream, to be exact. She smelled of the stuff, which suited him just fine, because for that moment all he wanted to do was drink in the scent of her, the taste and the feel of her. If he'd had to decorate a thousand more cakes, give him a kiss like this, and he was game.

Because it was plain and simple. He was addicted to the sugar high that was Kari Hendrix.

# *CHAPTER SEVENTEEN*

KARI HAD LOST her fool mind.

Or maybe she was the one who'd been hopped up on buttercream frosting.

Why else was she kissing an arson investigator whose job it was to put her away?

And why couldn't she seem to stop kissing him now that she'd started?

For one thing, he was really, really good at this kissing business…much better than he'd been at making roses.

For another thing, she felt…safe.

Her heart, her lying, lying heart, promised with every thrum against her ribs that she could trust Rob Monroe not to hurt her.

And maybe he wouldn't mean to. But in the end…

In the end, he'd remember who she was, who she'd said she was, anyway, in a court of law, in front of a judge.

An arsonist.

Regretfully she let logic and reason and

bitter experience kick back in. She pulled away from him, but couldn't quite bring herself to let her hands slide from his strong, finely sculpted forearms.

"Wow… I don't quite—I guess I let the sugar get to me, too," she whispered.

Rob seemed unsure of what to say. Was he regretting kissing her? Was he thinking of all the reasons he shouldn't have?

The image of Sam Franklin and his smarmy expression earlier that evening in the checkout line came crashing back in on her. Of course Rob didn't need to be kissing her, any more than she needed to be kissing him.

Unless… Was all of this some elaborate trick? Some game?

She dismissed it as paranoid. No investigator would go to that much trouble to win her trust.

Again, it was like their brains were working in tandem.

"Kari, I know we said we wouldn't talk about the fire."

She yanked away as if he had become as hot as an overheated oven. "Yes, we did."

"The cake's done, so I feel like I've held up my end of the bargain. I've been thinking—

I've had a lot of time to think tonight. Watching you while you worked. If you didn't set that fire—okay, okay, you *didn't* set that fire." He held up his hands to ward off the protest bubbling up to her lips. "Logic dictates that *somebody* did, and that *somebody* knew you. Knew your past. Knew that you would be an easy suspect. They even knew to use a propane tank. How?"

Her mind instantly went back to Jake. But Jake couldn't have meant for her to take the blame for this. If he'd done this—and that was still a big *if*, even for her—he'd done it to seek vengeance. He hadn't wanted to get her into hot water.

"I don't know." She slid to the floor of the kitchen, against the cabinets. "I keep telling you, I don't know. Maybe it's just coincidence."

He knelt down beside her, close, too close to ignore how his proximity always made her feel. "No. You're involved in two fires that had a propane tank? That's not a coincidence. People don't use propane tanks. Amateurs pour gas or kerosene or lighter fluid and light it—or try to, anyway. A pro will wrap cotton gauze around a cigarette and leave it near something flammable—in between couch cushions, in a drawer full of clothes. But a propane tank? That scares the amateur, and it's too obvious for the pro. So why did *you* use a propane tank?"

She'd been right. Even after that kiss, he was still thinking of her as an arsonist. No matter what, this would always be there, hanging between them. And she couldn't tell him and put Jake in harm's way.

Maybe she didn't owe her brother anything...but she could at least spare her mom pain.

"I can't tell you," Kari got out. She twisted away from him and put her face in her hands. It was the honest truth—she couldn't tell him why Jake had used that propane tank. Just as she hadn't been able to answer the question when the other investigator had asked her all those years ago. "It was there, okay. It was...*there*. Please. I was fourteen, Rob. Fourteen and foolish and I didn't think things through. If I had, you can believe I would have never..." She couldn't bear to say she was an arsonist, not again. Not when, if only in her heart, she could still think of herself as innocent. "And I learned my lesson, okay? Do you know how hard it was for me? How much I paid? Those four years weren't merely any four years. They were my high school years, Rob. While my friends were all thinking about learning how to drive and passing Spanish and hoping someone would ask them to the prom, I was just hoping to survive, to get the time over and done with, so that I could move on."

She hadn't told anybody this, not Alice, not even her mom. Alice would have told her not to feel sorry for herself—good advice—and her mom would have felt guilty.

Now that Kari had begun to pour out her bottled-up feelings to Rob, she couldn't seem to stop. "But it's never been over—do you know how it is to apply for job after job and no one will hire you? Before I got hired at the bakery, I had nothing. At least in juvie, I had a roof over my head. There were times when I missed that place, and in a weird sort of way, it made sense, Rob—how screwed up is that?"

Rob's features softened. His voice was almost a whisper when he spoke. "You were only a kid, Kari. I look at Taylor and I think about how you were practically the same age as her when you got sent away and I say to myself, 'How could any girl survive and come out as whole as Kari has?' But as much as I respect that, as much as I want to leave you to your privacy, this case dictates that I can't. So tell me how someone else would know to use that method. Maybe you told some of the girls you were with?"

She shook her head. "No, I made it a point not to talk about why I was there. I just kept hoping that I could lock it all away, forget it, never think about it again. And I'm still hoping that. Please, Rob. Don't make me relive the worst mistake I ever made. None of the girls at juvie could possibly know about that fire."

"Well, somebody thinks it's your signature. Or maybe…maybe just maybe they got the idea from you. Later that summer somebody used a propane tank to start another fire. A bigger one."

Her heart rat-a-tatted in her chest. "Not the one that…that killed your dad?" she whispered. "Are you sure? A propane tank?"

"Yeah. They didn't use a roadside flare—in fact, I've taken a closer look at that case. I've resubmitted some of the evidence for more testing, and I'm waiting on the results to come in. But whoever set that fire definitely used a tank—a tank almost exactly like the other two. And that stretches credulity, Kari. Propane tanks? In three major arsons in the same town?" Rob scoffed. "I don't believe in coincidence. Someone got an idea from that first fire. From *your* fire. The one you said you started."

She couldn't process what he was saying. Had that second fire been another one of Jake's? Had, after all her sacrifice, he repeated his crime?

Or was Rob right, and it was a copycat?

That didn't make it any less horrific. If that was the case, Jake's original crime had, directly or indirectly, still led to Rob's father's death.

She managed to drag her focus back to what he was saying, even if she couldn't meet his eyes.

"Kari, It's too pat, this last fire. Too in your face. Too personal, somehow. This is revenge. Somewhere, somehow, you've ticked somebody off, and they're out for revenge. They're using your past against you, and they know too many details for it to be a coincidence."

She shook her head, not bothering to lift it. The only people who knew even part of the details of the case were Jake and the buddies he'd hung out with back then…and her mom.

And the buddies were long gone. Some had actually wound up in the system, others had straightened up and finished the business of growing up—at least according to her mom.

So the only one who could possibly know about that old crime—every last detail, anyway—was Jake. And Jake, flaky as he could be, didn't want to hurt her like this. It was just as her mom had said. He'd wanted to help her. That's why he'd done it.

"I can't believe that," Kari insisted. "I can't. You're just being paranoid."

"You'd better hope I am. Because…think of it like this, Kari." Rob took her chin in his fingers, gently drawing her face to meet his. They were as close they had been earlier when he'd kissed her, but now a different intensity fired Rob's dark blue eyes. "How many times have you worked just this late at your shop? Completely by yourself? With, let me guess, the front door locked with the key?"

"A lot. When I needed to, whenever I had a big order. You see how long it takes. You work until you get it finished, no matter how late that is."

Rob's mouth twisted bleakly. He sat back on his heels, and she was left bereft without his touch. "Somebody could have just as easily blocked that back door with that tank, stuck that flare in it and left you to die. If we'd found you—what with your past—we would have figured you set the fire and it got out of control before you could make it out the front door. And, Kari, if I don't catch them? Well…" His voice was almost tender. He stood up, towering over her. "Next time, they might succeed."

IF ROB COULD find his phone, he'd throw it out the window.

With eyes that felt welded shut, he fumbled for the insistent buzzing of the cheerful xylophone ringtone.

"'Lo?" he mumbled into it.

"Rob? That you?"

Daniel.

"Who else would it be, bro? And why are you calling in the middle of the night?"

"Middle of the night? Bud, it's ten in the morning."

"What? No way." Rob forced his eyes

open—just a sliver. Sure enough, bright sunshine flooded through the apartment windows. He rocked forward on an elbow and peered at the bedside clock. The numbers didn't lie: 10:05. No, 10:06.

He collapsed back against his pillow with a groan. "Oh, man, I am too old for this."

"Too old for what? And what were you doing that meant you haven't even rolled over until the middle of the morning?"

"Wait, I wasn't supposed to pull a shift at the station, was I?"

"Nope," Daniel answered.

"Something for Ma?" Rob asked, racking his brain.

"Not that, either. I figured something was up when you didn't show up for supper again last night. Ma's kind of worried about you. She has this idea that you're turning into either a skeleton from not eating or a blimp from eating too many of Kari's desserts."

Rob swiped his hand over his eyes, trying in vain to rub what felt like a gravel truck's worth of sand out of them. That was two family suppers he'd blown off for Kari.

*And* he'd kissed her.

Blast.

He didn't need to be thinking about that,

or his way-too-perceptive big brother would have guessed that Rob was in over his head.

"So? What's up?" Daniel pressed.

"Uh…it wasn't with the case. Not, er, exactly," Rob evaded his question.

"But…it *was* Kari."

"Yeah, she needed help. With Mattie Gottman's cake."

Daniel snorted. "Like you know how to decorate a wedding cake."

"I'll have you know I made at least half the roses that went on that thing," Rob shot back hotly, and then realized his mistake.

"Wait, *you* decorated a cake?" Daniel asked. Rob could hear interest humming loudly from every syllable. "You mean those little flowers and stuff?"

"Uh, yeah. And Cornelli lace and Swiss dots."

"What the heck is that?"

"The Cornelli lace is this scrollwork you do with royal icing—kind of like a lace doily on buttercream, or some people use fondant, but Mattie insisted on—"

"Whoa, bro. I didn't understand half of what you just said, but I'm thinking it means you got a crash course in cake decorating courtesy of Kari." There was a beat of silence before Daniel tagged on, "Which, on the whole of it, is pretty cool because maybe you can save us some bucks when it comes time for me and Kim to have a cake. You know, when we get married. But…hey, it's *Kari*. You know. *Your suspect*?"

"Tell me something I don't know," Rob said. "What the heck has gotten into me? I keep telling myself I can't keep doing this, and yet, I keep finding reasons to spend time with her."

"You ought to have her investigated thoroughly by now at least," Daniel ribbed.

Rob flashed back to the sweet feel of Kari's embrace, the way she'd stretched up on tiptoe.

Oh, yeah. He'd thoroughly investigated Kari Hendrix, all right.

"Right. I get your point," Rob conceded. He rolled over and reached for a pair of blue jeans from his dresser drawer—a benefit to having a cramped apartment bedroom. "So were you just checking to see if I was alive and kicking, or is there something you need help with?"

"I could always use help around the farm, you know that. There's okra that needs cutting and a few last green beans to be picked, and Ma says it's time to plant turnip greens and kale, though for the life of me, it can't be that late in the year and still be this hot—"

"Whoa, wait—Mattie Gottman's getting married today!" It hit him with a thud.

"Yeah. You can't be regretting that you let that particular barracuda get away—and please don't try to save that fool she's marrying from himself. The mayor likes him, and whatever makes the mayor happy makes me happy. He signed off on a full-percent increase over last year's budget."

"No, no, bless him and may they be happy forever or for at least thirty minutes, but that's not my interest in Mattie's wedding. The cake, Daniel, the *cake*. It's got to be delivered. I'll bet Kari needs help with it. It's pretty big, nearly two feet tall when it's on the stand."

There was a long pause on Daniel's end that Rob didn't notice at first because he was throwing on clothes and raking a comb through his hair. He took one look at himself in the mirror, and decided that the reflection belonged to a sleep-deprived zombie.

"Uh, Rob…did she ask for your help?"

Rob gave up on trying to tame the cowlicks out of his hair and yanked on a ball cap from his closet. "What do you mean? You say it like I don't have a stake in this here cake—didn't you hear me? I made at least half of those roses, and they were irritating little suckers."

"And this has nothing whatsoever to do with you wanting to ride to the rescue of a damsel in distress?"

Now it was Rob's time to guffaw. "Buddy, that's the pot calling the kettle black, since I seem to dimly recall a sibling of mine pulling himself in pieces trying to rescue, hmm, who was it? Could it possibly be my future sister-in-law Kimberly? Nah, because that would make my brother—"

Daniel said something rude and reminiscent of the kid he'd been as a ten-year-old. Then in his more usual grown-up voice, he said, "Hey, no problem. It seems like I can't save you from yourself. Go check on your roses and frosting."

"Icing. It's icing. Frosting is what—"

But Daniel was hanging up—laughing and hanging up. Rob threw the phone down, yanked off his cap. A minute later he was sticking his head under the shower, gasping at the cold water because he'd been in too much of a hurry to wait for the water to heat up.

Five minutes more he was out the door, dialing Kari's number as he slid behind the wheel of his truck.

KARI, TO HIS DISAPPOINTMENT, seemed to have the business of delivering the cake completely under control.

"I'd ordered this box—it's great. Keeps things from sliding around if I have to hit the brakes," she said. "It was designed by an engineer for his wife, and I had a couple that got burned up in the fire. I knew I'd need replacements for them for this wedding, so I ordered new ones. They came in yesterday, thank goodness."

Indeed, the cakes were all boxed up in their plastic incubators, looking more like a museum display than parts of a wedding cake. Rob couldn't quite hide his wince as Kari shoved the long metal probe through the center of the wedding cake. And he gasped as she tilted the box.

"See? As long as you've got everything secured with the proper framework—"

"Don't do that!" Rob put a hand on the cake box. "It could fall apart."

Kari's dimple deepened. "Hmm, you're just a wee bit proud of this cake."

"I am. Also, my hand is still cramping from all those infernal dots and details."

She raised one brow. "Did you maybe want to see what the cake looks like all set up?"

Rob's insides went to jelly when her eyes twinkled like that—it was as if she had his number, but she was too kind to call him on it.

"Uh, yeah," he said. "I guess I did."

"What if I let you, with your big strong firefighter's biceps, take the wedding cake box to the van for me? Feel brave enough for that?" She gave a final check on the box's various clamps. "And I'll get my delivery kit put together."

"Your what?"

"My delivery kit. Used to—before the fire—I had a separate bag of tools I used for wedding cake deliveries. Any cake setup, really. You want to be ready for the worst."

Rob gripped the corner of the box more tightly. "We are going to remember just how hard those roses were to make, and we are not going to mess up this cake. We are going to drive exactly ten miles an hour and avoid all potholes. I don't care how safe that thing is supposed to make carrying cakes."

"But…" Kari's lips came together in an adorable little pout that made him want to kiss her again.

*The cake, man. You're just here for the cake.*

"But what?" he asked.

"But what if we're going so slow that someone rear-ends us?" There it was again, that same flirtatious teasing that had bubbled up the night before—and that had tempted him into kissing her.

"Is this any way to treat a guy who learned how to make roses just for you?"

Her laugh was infectious. "Come on, let's get this cake delivered. I remember how nervous I was about the first cake I had to deliver—not the one I made for my friend, but the very first delivery, a three-tier wedding cake. I actually told my boss, no way, no how, I won't ever do that again. I guess I'm not much of a risk taker."

Kari's comment fell between them like a piece of hot lead, neither anxious to touch it. It just pointed out one more aspect of her character that didn't jibe with her earlier crime.

*She could have learned her lesson too well.*

The devil on his other shoulder whispered in his ear, *Even if she didn't do that fire, she's still lying. What's she got to hide? Why can't she trust you?*

Rob tried to ignore the awkwardness that had sprung up between them. Instead he put his hands on the plastic box.

"And you're sure this contraption will keep the cake in one piece?"

"I've used one just like it for all my cake deliveries—never had a catastrophe yet. It works, as advertised."

He sucked in a deep breath. "Okay. Here goes nothing." With that, he hefted the box up off the table, amazed at how much all that cake weighed. Shoot, half of it had to be pure sugar, as much icing as had gone on it.

He didn't really breathe again until he'd set the box down in the back of her van, centered on the white tarp and the piece of slip-stop padded cabinet liner she'd put down.

"See?" Kari told him as she slid the smaller box containing the groom's cake in beside it and then dropped a large bag down from her shoulder onto the tarp. "No problem."

"That thing's got to weigh close to fifty pounds. Just how would you have manhandled that cake to the van?" he pointed out. "Or into the hall?"

She blushed. "Okay, so I was hoping you'd call. Because I couldn't count on Jake showing up. I used to have a wheeled baking cart that I used…only…"

"The fire," he said grimly.

He'd heard those two words the night before until he was sick of them. "The fire" had taken this tool. "The fire" had destroyed that piece of equipment. "The fire" had burned this ingredient.

He knew the power of fire to destroy. It had, after all, taken his dad.

And Rob had, in his work as a firefighter, seen the shock and desolation of families when they'd lost everything.

But he hadn't seen them in the aftermath, in the weeks following such a calamity, when they'd had time to need or want the things they'd lost.

Man, he hated fire. He really, really hated fire.

"It's okay, Rob." Kari put a hand to his arm. Her touch brought him back to the present. He looked down at her. "I'm okay. Even if I never get a penny of that insurance money, as long as…" She swallowed. "I can rebuild things, okay? I may have to make do. I may have to beg and borrow and rely on other people to help me. But…I can do this. I *will* do this. And you helped me—you have no idea how your help last night…"

Her eyes were shiny, but this time she didn't cry. She lifted her chin in that defiant way of hers and didn't say another word. Instead, she waved him back and slammed the door. "Let's go deliver Mattie Gottman's dream cake, shall we?"

AFTER ALL THAT, setting up the cake was pretty anticlimactic. They hefted it up the back steps into the church's fellowship hall, past all the teal ribbons on the banisters and doors that proclaimed a wedding would soon be taking place. Then they slid it onto the serving table, and Rob could actually breathe again.

Even so, Kari fussed with it, turning it this way and that until it met her satisfaction. She took out her little bag of tricks and began doctoring all the imperfections that she saw—Rob couldn't see any. Out came the last can of the pearl spray and the little pointy brush and even Kari's pastry bag, which she used to pipe on some last-minute roses and leaves.

The door to the fellowship hall swung wide and Rob heard the swish of fabric. There came Mattie, in full wedding attire, marching out to inspect the cake.

She put her hands on her hips and bent down to stare at their creation. Rob felt a strange sense of defensiveness—on both Kari's and the cake's behalf—at such a hard scrutiny.

"I was afraid it was going to be too dinky," Mattie said, not bothering to greet them. "You said eighteen inches, and I just could *not* sleep last night because I was afraid it was going to be this itty-bitty cake."

"That's eighteen inches of cake," Kari told her. "The flowers and the stand—not to mention your topper—make it taller. Do you like it?"

"No," Mattie said emphatically.

Rob's heart fell, and he fought the urge to snatch the cake off the table and take it to some other bride who would appreciate all the hard work that went into it.

"You don't?" Kari asked, her face white. "What's wrong?"

Mattie turned, grinning. "I love it! It's perfect! It's even better than I thought it would be!"

Rob's knees went as weak as they had when he'd succumbed to the urge to kiss Kari.

"Oh, great, then! Now, your photographer will get me a photo, right?"

Mattie nodded. "For that discount? Sure! I'm so happy—I know I was a witch when it came to planning, but I wanted it to be perfect."

Kari took Mattie's hands in hers. "It's your day. Of course you want it perfect. Now go. Spend some time with those bridesmaids and your mom. I've got this."

As Mattie departed in a swish of satin and lace, Rob bent down and whispered, "Do you ever get the urge to kill your customers?"

Kari's lips didn't falter in their wide curve. "Only on days that end in *y*," she said archly.

She fussed with the groom's cake only a little less than she had the actual wedding cake. By the time she'd satisfied herself with the setup and delivery and had stowed her gear into the van, strains of the prelude were wafting out of the church doors.

"Come on," she said, grabbing Rob's hand. "Let's go spy on the wedding. I know the perfect spot where we can watch without being seen."

But he didn't watch Mattie Gottman tie the knot. He had no interest in how she did her unity candle or the vows she exchanged with the poor sap who was marrying her or the long flowing white dress she wore that had so much lace, it bore a striking resemblance to one of Ma's tablecloths.

He only had eyes for the girl beside him—the one peeking out behind the alcove wall, in her dark chef's pants and her white chef's jacket and her hair yanked back in a slick bun. Her eyes were bright and shiny as she watched the ceremony unfold. She was enchanted with the wedding.

And he was enchanted with her.

Monday and all of its challenges would roll around soon enough. He'd be back at the investigation, trying for any lead.

But when he went back to it, he'd go back with one sure instinct. Ma was right.

Kari Hendrix, the girl who loved beginnings and was so optimistic about finding her way out of the ashes, had not burned anything. Not the downtown. Not that convenience store all those years ago.

And he knew what that meant.

Kari was covering up for the person who had really set those fires—and maybe, just maybe, that person had one more fire to his credit.

The fire that had killed Rob's father.

# CHAPTER EIGHTEEN

AFTER THE CHAOS of getting Mattie Gottman's wedding cake done, even a double batch of croissants seemed easy to Kari. She slept until noon on Sunday, her usual custom post-wedding-cake-delivery, and spent the rest of the day in an ebullient fog.

One that, if she had to be honest, featured a lot of stolen thoughts about Rob.

But of course it was the massive relief of having the cake done that had lifted a ten-pound weight from her shoulders. Because nothing had really changed between her and Rob.

He was still an arson investigator.

She was still a convicted arsonist.

And Jake…

Kari had pushed away *that* thought at least a thousand times by Monday morning when she'd tackled the croissant dough she'd mixed up Sunday in the hopes it would occupy her brain and her hands.

By lunch, the croissants were well into the laminating stage. Her shoulders and arms ached from rolling, turning the dough, rolling, turning the dough, rolling.

If Kari had thought the project would engage her wayward thoughts as much as it engaged her biceps and triceps, she had to admit she was wrong. She slid the laminated dough into the fridge for another rest period, and sat down at the table with a sigh.

Okay, so she was a trifle blue. She was coming down from the post-wedding-cake high, that was all. It had nothing at all to do with Rob's radio silence all day Sunday and—she glanced at the clock as her tummy rumbled for lunch—half of Monday.

Maybe that kiss was just what she'd said— the product of exhaustion crossed with one too many turns at a buttercream bowl.

*But he came back. To help. I didn't even have to ask him. He magically appeared... so where is he now?*

Kari didn't want to want Rob this much. She'd learned—the hard way—that the minute you let yourself want something this badly, life had a way of kicking the stuffing out of you. Her bakery was only the latest example of that.

What did she want from Rob, anyway? Someone to talk to? Someone to keep her company? To help her decorate cakes? Eventually she could hire someone part-time again to help out. Unlike Rob, that person wouldn't tempt her to spill all her family secrets. They didn't even have to know about her criminal past.

Kari used a bread knife to cut a couple of pieces of fresh sourdough bread that she'd baked just that morning, slapped some ham and tomato and lettuce between them for lunch. As she bit down into the tangy flavor of the bread, she found herself wishing she could share it with Rob.

At which point she remembered that she really didn't need to be sharing anything with Rob, lest one thing lead to another.

A brisk knock sounded, and for a minute Kari was sure it was Rob. The surge of joy deflated like a punctured soufflé, though, when she realized the knocking was coming from the front door.

Funny how Rob had quickly become back-door company.

She laid aside her sandwich, wiped her hands and went to answer the door.

A man dressed in a short-sleeve dress shirt

and a clip-on tie stood on the front porch, waiting patiently. "Is this—" he glanced down at an aluminum clipboard "—Kari Hendrix's residence?"

She pulled the door close to her body, instinctively narrowing the gap. "Why do you need to know?" Kari asked.

The man peered over half-lenses. "Name's Victor Miller," he replied. He extended a hand that, despite his innocuous appearance, Kari hadn't much desire to accept. "I'm from your insurance company. You filed a claim for fire damage and work interruption?"

"Yes, I did. I'd tried to get in touch with you—"

"I got your messages." He broke in. "All two dozen of them. Pretty anxious to get your check, aren't you?"

Behind him, her mother's car turned into the drive a little too fast and nearly took out the sego palm in its clay pot. Kari managed to reply to Miller's last question with, "I have a business to run, Mr. Miller, of course I'd like my claim settled," as her mom squeezed her car by Miller's four-door sedan.

Miller turned at the sound of the car in the drive. "Who's that?" he asked.

"My mom. I guess she came home for

lunch." Kari tried to cover her surprise—
her mom usually ate a sandwich at her desk.
She couldn't remember a time since she'd
moved back home that her mom had done
this for lunch.

"That would be Chelle Hendrix? Figures.
I just talked to her on the phone. Guess she's
coming home to give you a heads-up." Miller
clasped the aluminum clipboard to his chest.

"Uh, no. I think it's probably just for
lunch. Won't you come in, Mr. Miller? I'm
sure you have some questions you need to
ask." Kari stepped back from the door and
gestured for him to come inside.

He strode across the threshold, stopping
in the entry hall to take in his surroundings.
There was nothing particularly fancy about
the room—a small accent table and settee
her mom had picked up at an estate sale, a
reproduction tall case clock, and a coat tree,
along with some garden prints her mom had
liked. Still, Victor Miller took his time inspecting each item, as if he were assigning
a cash value to every stick of furniture in
the room.

The delay gave her mom time enough to
rush in the kitchen door. "Kari!"

Even to Kari's ears, Mom sounded alarmed.

Again Miller gave sharp-eyed attention to the discomfiture he'd caused.

"I'm in here with Mr. Miller, Mom. There's fresh bread on the table for your sandwich."

"For my—" Mom seemed a bit slow on the uptake when it came to decoding Kari's hint. But a beat later, she trilled back, "Right, yes, lunch. The sourdough?"

Miller had by now decided to follow Kari through the living room into the kitchen, where Mom was hacking away at the bread with a butter knife.

"Here, Mom, let me get that." Kari laid her fingers over her mother's fidgety ones and stilled them. They locked eyes and Kari willed calm into her mother. It would not do for Miller to get the idea they were hiding anything. Maybe he didn't have a clear agenda going on—maybe that was all on Kari. She shouldn't always be so negative.

Her mom took a visible deep breath, and beamed brightly at the dour looking man behind Kari. "So you did find the house, then. My directions are just so hopeless sometimes."

"Yes, ma'am. It would have helped if you'd told me to take a left at the stop sign instead of a right."

"Oh, my, did I do that?" Mom asked with such feigned innocence that Kari was tempted to kick her on the ankle. "I *am* hopeless."

"That's all right, ma'am," Miller told her. "We investigators know how to track down people."

Kari pictured the man fielding a pair of bloodhounds and couldn't suppress a shudder. Quickly she sliced the bread with the proper knife and placed it and the rest of the sandwich fixings on a plate. She forced herself to smile and ask, "Mr. Miller, can I get you something? It's fresh sourdough bread, baked from scratch this morning."

His gaze fixed on the bread, and she could swear she heard his stomach growl. But he shook his head decisively. "I'm sorry. I don't accept any offers of goods or services."

She blinked. "I beg your pardon?"

He inclined his head toward the hump of golden brown artisan bread remaining on the cutting board. "You are a baker, right? And you sell that bread? Well, if I take that bread, it could be you trying to bribe me or otherwise influence my disposition of the case. I make it a practice to never accept any offers of goods or services from claimants."

For a moment, Kari was speechless. "Sir,

if you thought I was trying to bribe you with a sandwich, let me clear up the confusion. I wasn't. I was simply trying to be hospitable."

"She was," Mom rushed to add. "Kari's like that—always trying to feed people. You should try the bread—just pretend I was the one who offered it, why don't you?" She made the whole thing worse by actually winking at the man.

"No, ma'am." His face now took on an impassive poker face except the odd flicker of an anxious smile every once in a while. "I also make it a practice never to accept offers of food or drink in a claimant's house."

"That must get awfully…tiresome," Mom trailed off. At a loss for anything else to do, she took an enthusiastic bite of the sandwich, chewed it and swallowed it. "You don't know what you're missing. My Kari is an excellent baker."

He didn't bother to reply. "If we could get these questions answered," Miller said. It wasn't a question, more of a weary, resigned suggestion, as if this was an intellectual exercise, not the possible key to her future. Was that what it was? Had the people at the insurance company already made up their minds?

"Certainly. How can I be of assistance?" Kari indicated a chair, half-afraid the man would insist on not accepting even that level of hospitality from her.

This must not have been out of bounds, because he perched on the edge of the chair and let his glance slide over the clipboard. He had the twitchy air of a crow on a fence, on the lookout for the next shiny object to snatch between its beak.

When his questions came, they were delivered in his machine gun staccato, straight off the form. He allowed her no latitude in answering them. When she tried to elaborate, he cut her off.

"Yes or no, please, just like a court deposition," Miller told her. "I don't have a lot of room on these forms to put long-winded explanations."

"I'm trying, sir, but you don't understand— I want to answer your questions as accurately as I can."

Miller treated her to another stale expression. "All the explaining in the world isn't really going to make much difference in the end, Ms. Hendrix."

"Sir?" She blinked. Had he just said what

she thought he had? "What do you mean by that?"

"I mean this is a complete and total waste of both of our time, isn't it?" He jammed his ballpoint pen into the pocket protector of his shirt. "Do you honestly think my company is going to approve the payout of a claim on a case that is clearly arson, when you were deep in the hole? And to top it off, you didn't even pay a year's worth of premiums?"

It was as if he'd snatched the breath right out of her. She could do nothing but gasp like a beached fish.

If she couldn't speak, her mother wasn't so similarly stricken. "So I guess no company should expect a favorable resolution of their claim unless they've paid at least a year's premiums and if they were clearly not the victim of arson? What about negligence? Does your company have similar policies regarding accidental fires? Is what you're saying, Mr. Miller, that your company wants to treat a client's money as if it were more of a savings account? You don't collect until you've paid in everything you're claiming as a loss?"

"The timing is an important aspect of any claim investigation," he said primly.

"That's fascinating." Mom inspected her fingernails, perfect little pink ovals that she'd had done earlier in the week. "I'm the comptroller for Levi County Health and Wellness. We have our property insurance through your company, and it's just about up for renewal. I believe our board will be extremely interested to know your company's policy on claims payout. I'm sure they'll want to look into any recommendations I could make about alternate property coverage."

The investigator went a shade pastier than he'd been already, sliding toward a sickly gray-green. He began coughing, clearly alarmed at losing a major client. "Well, now—just hang on a minute—" he sputtered again, still not recovered. "Uh, can I have a glass of water?"

Mom treated the man to an oh-so-innocent bat of her eyelashes. "Oh, my. Certainly. That is, if you aren't afraid that we were trying to, how did you put it? Bribe you or otherwise influence your disposition of the case?"

Kari silenced an inward groan as the man's face went from gray to puce with anger. She rose from her chair and got him a glass of water. He took a swallow of the ice water as if it were laced with battery acid, thumped the tumbler down on the table and stood.

"If I weren't convinced before, I am now. Regardless of your not so subtle threat," he said, directing a sneer at Kari's mom, "you might as well know I'll be filing my recommendation to reject your claim. And I'll be forwarding a record of this to the local authorities. I'm sure they'll find my report—what you'd say? Extremely interesting." He treated them to another contemptuous look before he murmured, "I'll see myself out."

ROB LEANED ON the front counter of the auto parts store and waited for the manager to get through with his current customer. He listened to a complicated litany of carburetor cleaning do's and don'ts the manager was showering on two kids barely old enough to drive. If the car they were working on had a carburetor instead of fuel injection, it was probably a decade older than they were.

Finally the pair shuffled out, bemused expressions on their faces. Rob would have bet anything that they'd be back sooner rather than later with the contraption in a bucket, begging for the guy to help them.

The manager strolled over to greet him.

Now that the man was closer, Rob could read the name Ellis on his name patch. "Help you?" Ellis asked.

Rob flashed his badge, only to have the man hold up both hands. "Hey, we sell only brand-new parts here—none of that chop-shop crap," he protested. "We're legit."

"No, no, I'm not with the police. I work with the fire department," Rob told him. "I'm finishing up my investigation of the downtown fire, and, well, you know how it is. Paperwork." He treated Ellis to his best aw-shucks grin. Over the years, he'd found that it worked out better if people thought he was just going through the motions. They were less likely to warn the target of his investigation.

Ellis relaxed. "Boy, do I know about paperwork. Weren't computers supposed to do away with it? I think it just made it worse. So how can I help? We're not even close to the downtown section."

"I've got to show my boss that I asked some questions about a guy." Rob shrugged, trying to communicate with his body language that this was completely routine. "Bosses, right?"

"Got me a district manager..." Ellis rolled

his eyes. "Thinks I can deliver parts, keep the store ordered and do all that paperwork without any decent help. I'd like to see *him* do it."

"Good help is hard to find these days. Funny, that's why I had to bug you. To ask about some of your help."

"Shucks, you ain't bugging me. Right now it's slow. Only people coming in here are gals picking up oil for their hubbies and kids after school. And you see they ain't exactly banging the front door down. Who you need to ask about?" Now Ellis stood at the counter in an exact mirror image of Rob's posture.

Rob dug a photo out of his pocket and put it in front of Ellis. "Jake Hendrix?"

"Jake? That guy hasn't worked here in… sheesh. Months. And I wouldn't exactly call what he did while he was here 'work,' anyway. Mouthy, you ask me, but then everybody younger than me seems that way. Jake here…" Ellis tapped the photo with a fingernail. "He delivered for me. Said he wanted to do outside sales, but how can you do outside sales if you never get around to making any sales calls?"

"You run a criminal background check on him?" Rob asked.

"Naw, not at first. No reason to. See, he'd checked no on the question that asked if he'd ever been arrested. And he had pretty good references. Plus at the time he had a driver's license. I needed somebody pretty quick, and he looked good for the job—you know, smart, said all the right things, said he really needed the job. I was kinda hoping he'd work out, because, well, he had a wicked sense of humor.

"But..." Ellis flipped his hands palms up. "Then he fails a random pee-in-a-cup test. What can I do? Company policy says I got to let him go. Man, was he ticked about that."

"Yeah? What'd you test him for?"

"Marijuana. Funny thing, after I let him go, my insurance guy called me up and said that Jake's license was suspended. He'd apparently gotten charged with a gas drive-off after he started working here, and boom, they suspended his license. So it was just as well."

Rob wasn't hearing anything new. He'd pulled Jake's criminal check when he'd got in that morning and found it littered with two-bit misdemeanors: drug charges, a public drunkenness or two, several disorderly conducts, plus the gas drive-off Ellis had referred to.

The gas drive-off had actually been Jake's second petty theft—he'd already had one on his record. He'd kept the county busy—and somebody, Chelle, maybe, broke from all the fines and fees he'd been charged.

But he'd always managed to skate on anything more serious. Rob had to hand it to the guy—he might not see his charm, but apparently Jake made a good first impression when he put his mind to it.

At least that's what all his former employers had agreed on. The golden boy would come in, smile his little smile, do his little song and dance, and land himself a job. Pretty soon, though, keeping up with the daily grind of actually showing up to work on time every day apparently grew old.

"So why you looking at Jake? He do something? He start that fire?" Ellis leaned closer. "You can tell me. I won't tell a soul."

Rob seriously doubted that. Ellis struck him as the type that wouldn't wait until the door shut behind Rob to start spreading the news. "Oh, he's just the brother of one of the shop owners. He was hanging around and I had to verify…you know…his employment habits."

"Habits?" Ellis haw-hawed. "He's got a

serious lack of work ethic, that's his employment habits."

"So have you heard where he's working now? Anybody asked you for a reference?"

"Beats me, man. Kind like Jake, they always seem to land on their feet. Now, me? If I got fired? Shoot, I'd be out of a job for months."

Rob was disappointed. That was another constant...nobody seemed to know what Jake was doing to make money. He'd tumbled onto Jake's work trail by checking on a loan application for in-store credit that had shown up on his financials. One employer had been listed, and he'd backtracked over Jake's checkered past.

"Well, thanks. I appreciate your time—"

"Hey, wait a minute. I said *I* didn't know. Maybe Jill in the back knows. Jill! You remember that guy Jake who worked for us?"

A bored-looking woman in the same sort of uniform Ellis wore peered out from around the shelves. "Jake Hendrix?"

"Sure. You know. He failed the drug test, remember?"

"How could I forget? Now I'm stuck doing all the deliveries," she muttered. "What about him?"

"You know where he's working now?"

She furrowed her brow in concentration. "Maybe Jefferson's Parts? Uh-huh. Last I heard, he had a job there, but just part time."

"That's the one on Milton?" Rob asked.

"Yeah, but you need parts, you come here." Ellis pounded the laminate countertop. "Unlike my competition, I get it right the first time, never send you out with something wrong."

Rob thanked him and headed out for the sidewalk. It had been a long, grinding day interviewing all of Jake's past employers. Jake had apparently possessed the staying power of a dandelion, letting life take him wherever it wanted.

The thing was, Rob couldn't even say what he was after with all these questions. So what if Jake had a gajillion crummy little crimes on his record? So what if some people's sneezes lasted longer than some of Jake's jobs? It didn't make him an arsonist.

In the truck, Rob stared down at the inkjet photo of Jake that he'd printed from his mugshot. Even a mugshot photo couldn't make Jake ugly. Rob could definitely see the resemblance between Kari and Jake—

the eyes, maybe, and they both had dimples and golden-blond hair.

Beyond those similarities, though, the two were as opposite as a brother and sister could be.

Jake had a pattern of multiple run-ins with the law, of ticking off law enforcement, of skating on job responsibilities and court dates. And yet he'd never served serious time behind bars.

Kari? She'd put her nose to the grindstone, worked hard and had a steady history of employment. Her record was squeaky clean.

*Well, except for felony arson.*

Rob resisted the urge to ball up the photo of Jake's smirking face. Maybe he simply didn't like the guy, and that's why he was trying to pin not just one arson but two on Kari's brother.

Dislike could cloud your judgment, though. It could make you jam puzzle pieces together in ways that they were never intended to fit.

Rob had to face it. He'd spent all day chasing down info on Jake, and all he'd come up with was a picture of a completely irresponsible guy who ought to have grown up and got his life together. As much as he despised the guy for that, it didn't necessarily follow that Jake was guilty.

*You want it to be Jake simply because you don't want it to be Kari.*

*And maybe it is him*, a part of Rob shot back.

His cell phone went off, interrupting his internal debate. A sucker punch of dread hit him when he recognized the number.

Sam Franklin.

## CHAPTER NINETEEN

KARI SAT ON the rough wooden step as the light from the afternoon sun took on a golden hue. A woman farther down the block grappled with three Shelties bent on tangling up their leashes and barking at every squirrel they saw. Across the street a brother and sister still in grade school played tag on a pincushion front lawn.

Something about seeing the girl and boy playing together reminded her of her and Jake at that age. Before Jake was too cool to pal around with his kid sister. Before Dad had decided being a dad tied him down too much. Before the fire.

Way before the fire.

*This is silly. You have no idea when Rob's coming in. Maybe he's not. Maybe he's on a date.*

The idea of Rob Monroe on a date, teasing some other woman besides Kari, cut her to the quick. She pushed aside the wave of jealousy by peeking into the paper grocery sack sitting beside her.

Butter, sugar, flour, cocoa and eggs. She couldn't wait on Rob for much longer, else the butter would melt and the eggs would spoil.

It had been an impulsive move on her part—completely unlike her. But after Victor Miller had left earlier that day, and she still hadn't heard a peep from Rob, Kari had been driving herself crazy wondering if Miller *had* talked to Rob.

Ergo the thinly veiled brownie gambit.

*I did tell him I'd show him how to make brownies.*

So now she sat in the hot afternoon sun, her free-range eggs threatening to spoil and her butter turning into a drippy mess.

Kari had actually grabbed the bag to leave when she heard gravel crunching in the drive of the duplex. Rob's pickup came to a stop. She clutched the grocery bag to her chest.

He made no move to get out of the truck, just sat there with an agitated expression and his cell phone jammed to his ear. It was rare that she ever saw Rob Monroe with a frown on his face, but this was one of those times.

His mouth was a thin, compressed line,

his brows drawn together. As he listened, his face grew harder, and he slammed a palm down on the steering wheel so hard that she winced for him.

Rob ended the call a moment later and opened the truck door. Kari had half a mind to make her apologies and beat a hasty retreat.

But then he smiled. It was a tired, exhausted smile that only just reached his eyes. He gripped the open door of the truck as though he'd fall over without its support.

"This is a surprise," Rob told her.

"I—uh—I did promise to teach you how to make brownies," Kari said, lifting the bag a fraction of an inch.

"So you did. You're determined to save me from the evils of my own baking, aren't you?"

"Unless…you look tired. I should have called."

"I am tired. But you're a sight for sore eyes. And after the day I've had, I could use a brownie or three. If you don't expect me to be scintillating company, come on in." Rob shut the truck door and led the way up the stairs to the railed porch. As he unlocked his door, he explained, "I was working all day yesterday on some files, so don't mind the mess."

"Really, it's okay if you want a rain check," she rushed to tell him.

Rob stopped, reached out and touched her cheek. He took the bag from her hands. "Don't go. I know there are a thousand reasons why you should, but…please. Don't go. Finding you here, waiting on me, is the nicest thing about the whole bad day."

She watched him for another moment as he headed into his apartment, clearly expecting her to follow him. Then she pushed aside her doubts and joined him in the compact space.

Aside from the small dining table that was thickly covered in files and printouts, the living-dining-kitchen area was spare to the point of Zen-like bareness. A philodendron clung to life in a clay pot on the ledge above the sink, but no canisters of flour or sugar graced the kitchen counters that she could see.

He placed the bag onto the counter by the sink and turned to take the space in, clearly seeing the apartment as he imagined she was. "It's not much, I know, but I'm hardly ever here."

"No, it's nice… I don't know what I was expecting. Big leather couches and posters of muscle cars, maybe."

"Eh?" He lifted a shoulder. "I outgrew those by the time I was old enough to vote. So…how'd you know where I lived?"

Now Kari was mortified. "I called your mom."

"Huh? I should have guessed." Rob shook his head and began emptying out the bag. "Organic wheat, organic sugar. Man, I'll bet this stuff cost a fortune. But hey, I know these eggs—they're the ones Ma sent you."

"I know it sounds like I went all stalker-ish on you," she said, rounding the table to take the eggs. "But your mom had given me her number, you know, when she offered the oven, and she's really nice. And I—well, I wanted to do something nice for you, too. To say thank you."

*And also to see if Victor Miller had turned you against me, but, yes, mostly to say thank-you,* Kari amended silently in her head.

Now Rob held the tin of cocoa powder. He turned it over in his hands at it as though it were some alien artifact he'd never seen be-fore. "I don't know which I like better," he said, "the idea of homemade brownies or the idea that you wanted to make them for me."

"I meant it when I said I'd show you how to make brownies." Kari tapped the cocoa powder, then moved to the sink and washed her hands. Drying them briskly, she asked, "So where's a bowl?"

He pointed to a cabinet door. "Check there. I seem to dimly recall a bowl or two lurking in there."

"Don't you ever cook?" She pulled back the cabinet door to reveal a smallish plastic bowl. "I guess this will do."

"We can go to your mom's and use her kitchen if you like. I probably know it better than my own."

"Don't you know? It's always more fun to play in somebody else's kitchen." Kari set the bowl down and started opening and closing drawers.

"No, and if you're looking for a mixer, you won't find one."

"Don't need one, thank you very much, but I do need—aha! Here you go, one spatula." She extended it to him with a flourish. "I dub thee Sir Chocolot."

Rob swept into a deep bow and accepted

the spatula. "M'lady, I was unaware I was graced with such a utensil."

"An old girlfriend's, perchance?"

"Probably one of my sisters'—they fixed me up when I moved out on my own, not realizing that I knew Ma's cooking was far better than anything I could attempt."

"Well, this is the day that you learn how to make brownies all by yourself. Your first solo baking."

"Wait, I thought you were going to bake them." Rob raised his eyebrows. "If I cook them, they won't be fit to eat, and then what will we have for supper?"

"You need something besides brownies for supper, silly. And I have faith in you. After all, you helped me decorate a wedding cake—not just any wedding cake, but Mattie Gottman's wedding cake. So…what do you maybe have lurking in your fridge?"

He wrinkled his nose. "Help yourself. If you can come up with anything remotely edible…"

Kari peeked into the fridge, as bare as the counters were. "You really don't cook, do you? All you have in here is milk and a block of cheese."

"I have cheese? Wow. The milk's for my

cereal. Breakfast is the most important meal of the day."

"I can make us a cheese omelet."

"Let's wait and eat the brownies first," he told her. "I mean, they have flour and eggs, so can't we think of them as really good muffins?"

She didn't bother to suppress a chuckle. "Oh, all right. We'll get the brownies whipped up, and then we'll make the omelet."

"Don't make me learn two dishes in one night—my poor brain might explode."

"You're a wheedler, aren't you?" Kari asked. "You're going to try to wheedle me into cooking these brownies for you. Well, sir, it won't work. I intend to sit down and supervise." To underscore her point, she skirted the table and sat down on the far side. "So what do you think your first order of business is?"

"Don't I at least get a recipe? The box would have directions."

"It's in the bag. I printed it out for you."

Rob dived back into the bag and surfaced with the slip of paper. "Okaaay. And you really think I can do this?"

"You made roses on a stick. You can do anything, Sir Chocolot."

He busied himself with reading the recipe, something she heartily approved of, but he was too cute to bear watching. Something about a big strapping man wielding a spatula made her heart melt like butter.

So she occupied herself with trying to figure out a way to broach the Victor Miller subject. She had considered and discarded a half dozen segues when something in the paperwork scattered across the table caught her eye.

It was a crime scene report. The foggy edges indicated that the report was a photocopy of a photocopy half-buried in a stack of papers. "...Propane tank was used as an accelerant and improvised explosive device..." she read.

A quick check reassured her that Rob was still engrossed in the recipe. As unobtrusively as possible, she nudged the stack blocking the rest of the report over so she could read what he'd written.

But a few seconds more of reading revealed that it wasn't the downtown fire at all. This was a different fire, one in a warehouse. But the description of it sounded a lot like the downtown fire—and the fire that Jake had set.

A chill coursed through her.

This wasn't any fire. This was—

"The fire that killed my dad."

Kari looked up to see Rob staring at her, the recipe forgotten in his hand.

"I didn't mean to pry—"

"I didn't say you were. I've been comparing those three fires. They're a lot alike, Kari."

"Just because of the propane tank?"

"It's more than that. It's the setup. It's how the arsonist communicated his main message. He wanted to be noticed. He wanted to be front and center."

Kari shivered. "I don't like to think about it."

"Who—"

She held up her hand. "No, Rob. Can't we just bake brownies and pretend all this doesn't exist? Just for tonight?"

Some of the fatigue she'd seen earlier came back to his face. "Sure. But I'm running out of time, Kari. You have to know that. We're both running out of time."

"What do you mean?" Instantly she was at full alert. "Is there something you're not telling me?"

He abandoned the brownies and came

to sit in the chair beside her. "Not to sound more than a little like you have on occasion, but did you just come here to quiz me?" Gentle amusement took the sting out of his question.

"No, of course not—I wanted to see you." Her hands went all fidgety on her.

Now his eyes twinkled with genuine pleasure. "I like the sound of that." He reached for her hands to still them. "But the real question is, why did you feel the need to cook up an excuse to come see me?"

For a moment, she was confused. "But—didn't you want the brownies?"

He leaned over, moved his fingers to her jaw, and she found herself closing her eyes as he lowered his mouth to hers. She let her hands settle on his chest, then move up to his shoulders. One kiss, what could that hurt?

He pulled away. "Kari, I'd have been excited to see you if you'd shown up completely empty-handed, never mind the brownies."

"Yeah?" she breathed.

He kissed her again, the sweetest, most patient kiss, laughing as he sat back. "Okay, maybe, just maybe, you had the right idea with those brownies after all. Otherwise…"

*Otherwise, I'd sit here and let you kiss me*

*for another couple of hours at least,* Kari thought to herself. With hands that trembled far more than she'd like to admit, she pushed herself up from her chair. "Well, then, Sir Chocolot. Let's get those brownies baked."

ROB EYED THE man through the one-way mirror and popped a brownie in his mouth.

The perfect balance of sugar and chocolate brought to mind Kari and last night.

"So how long you plan on letting the poor guy sweat it out?" Lieutenant Tim Clarke asked him. He reached over and helped himself to one of Rob's brownies. "Mmm, these are good. Ma make 'em?"

Rob swallowed the last of the brownie. He thumped himself on the chest. "I did, thank you very much. But I had some help."

On the other side of the glass, the guy was indeed sweating—pale and pasty. He'd pace for a moment or two, then collapse into the chair, then hop back up to resume pacing.

"What's his name again?" Tim scooped up another brownie, hesitated, and then grabbed a third one for good measure. "This has got to do with the downtown fire, right?"

"Sort of. This guy—Ethan Blaire—used to run with Jake Hendrix back in the day.

But unlike most of Jake's crew, he straightened up and flew right."

Tim's mouth curved in appreciation. "I get it. You figure he's got something to lose. I've used that trick myself once or twice."

Rob gave the detective a friendly punch in the shoulder. "Where do you think I stole that move, huh?"

"But what could somebody who doesn't hang with Jake now tell you about the downtown fire?"

"Maybe nothing. But I think Jake did the fire that my dad was in. And I'm betting Ethan probably knows something about that."

*He'd better. Franklin gave me forty-eight hours to show him a viable suspect other than Kari for the downtown fire, and almost twelve hours of that are gone.*

"So...is he done yet?" Tim inclined his head toward Ethan, who had resorted to biting his knuckles.

"Stick a fork in him. You want in on this?"

"Heck, yeah, if you think he's got info on your dad's fire. That's an open homicide."

Once in the interrogation room, the introductions and the Miranda rights taken care of, Rob flipped a plastic chair around and straddled it as if he had all day to chat with the likes of Ethan Blair. "So, Ethan...you know why you're here?"

"Man, I haven't got a clue. I swear. I hadn't done anything—this is the first time I've been in a police station in years." Ethan protested.

"That's right. Last time you were here, you and some buddies were booked on a street-racing charge." Rob tapped the cover of a manila folder he held in his hand. "You were what, twenty?"

"No, man, nineteen. Young and dumb. I got my act together now. But my boss...he's gonna want to know why the cops picked me up."

"So you've got a whole new life, huh? New job? New friends?"

Ethan nodded his head vigorously. "New everything. I had to, or I would have kept getting in trouble. Like my granny always said, birds of a feather flock together."

Tim leaned forward. "And those birds you flocked with...who were they exactly?"

Ethan swallowed. Rob could see the man's Adam's apple bob up and down. "Just pals, man. Guys I hung with back in high school."

"Guys like..." Rob flipped open the folder

as if to study something in it. He snapped it closed. "Jake Hendrix?"

"Maybe, yeah. But I haven't seen Jake in years. We went our separate ways."

"Why was that?"

"I told you, man. I wanted something different. I wanted to stay out of jail." Ethan clenched and unclenched his fingers, his left thumb touching his wedding band as if it were a talisman.

Rob exchanged a meaningful glance with Tim, and Tim did not disappoint. "Yeah? What switched the lightbulb on for you?" the detective asked.

"Huh?" Ethan wrinkled his forehead. He passed a hand through wiry hair that reminded Rob of a piece of steel wool.

Rob leaned forward over the back of the chair he was propped on. "Was there some sort of bust-up between you two? I mean, it was a beautiful friendship, after all."

Fresh beads of sweat popped out across Ethan's face. He swiped at it with the back of his hand. "He got…scary, that's all. Stuff I didn't want to be involved in. Too much for me." Ethan shook his head. "So I said adios and never looked back."

"What sort of scary stuff?" Tim stretched

out his legs and clasped his hands behind his head. "More scary than driving a hundred miles an hour in a fifty-five at three in the morning?"

Ethan blanched. "He got all crazy, you know?"

"No, I don't know," Rob replied. "Crazy how?"

"Ask him, man. You're the cops. I need to get back to work before I don't have a job."

"You help him with any of this crazy, scary stuff?" Rob pressed. "Maybe that's why you wised up? A near miss?"

Again Ethan's Adam's apple bobbed up and down. He ran his tongue over his lips. "Yeah, maybe. Or maybe I was smart enough to know it was gonna be my backside in hot water if I didn't start listening to my granny."

Rob flipped open the folder again, pretended to review its contents. He sighed and shook his head. "Ethan, maybe you've been in hot water all this time and didn't realize it. Maybe Jake pushed you in that hot water, and you just thought you crawled out."

"No, man." Now Ethan was literally yanking at his hair with both hands. "I didn't do squat—nothing, once I heard what he was gonna do—I was outta there. I didn't want any part of that!"

"So you didn't help him, huh?"

"Uh-uh!" The beads of sweat had multiplied on Ethan's forehead. He swiped them away. "No, man, that was all Jake, not me. He was the one who had it in for that guy— just like that guy who dissed his little sister, man. But I ain't started no fires. If Jake torched the downtown, that's all him, bro. It ain't on me."

Rob swallowed the smile threatening to spread across his face. "Now, Ethan, who said anything about a fire?"

Ethan slammed his eyes shut, panted as though he'd just sprinted a sixty-yard dash, and put his face in his hands. He muttered a string of curse words.

"Ethan?" Rob pressed.

Ethan straightened up. "I ain't saying nothing else. I ain't saying another word. Not until I talk to a lawyer."

## CHAPTER TWENTY

ROB GROANED AS Sam Franklin himself swept into the police station, not a hair of his silver pompadour out of place. Chase followed two steps behind him. He'd called Chase to come down here—not Sam.

"Chase says you got a break in the downtown fire." Sam jabbed an index finger toward the closely bent heads of Ethan and his lawyer through the one-way glass of the interrogation room. "That the guy?"

Rob ran a hand through his hair. "Not exactly. I need a search warrant." He glared at Chase. "Which is what I told *you* on the phone."

"So who's this guy?" Franklin asked. "What's he got to do with the case?"

"It's…tangential. Bear with me." Rob took a deep breath and jumped in, knowing Franklin didn't have patience for convoluted stories. "This guy knows something about Jake Hendrix torching a convenience store—the fire Kari confessed to—and the warehouse fire later that summer."

Franklin frowned. "Whoa. Stop right there. Are you telling me that all this guy can do is say *maybe* Jake burned something, what, ten, twelve years ago? You've had all this time, and this is the best you can do?"

"No. You're the one with the timeline—if you'd be a little more patient, I could figure this out. But you've got me in a crunch," Rob snapped.

It was the wrong thing to say to the man. His expression soured even more. "We're on a timeline because people need their money, Rob. And insurance companies won't pay until we tell them who's good for this. Or do I need to send you back to school to learn Arson Investigation 101 again?"

Behind Franklin, Chase was giving Rob a vigorous headshake, a clear plea to pipe down. It took all of Rob's will, but he bit back the retort he wanted to send stinging toward the DA. "Granted. I get that. I understand your position," Rob ground out. "I'm thinking that we can connect Jake to the earlier two fires, and that he's responsible for the one downtown. I managed to check his alibi, and it's got enough holes to make Swiss cheese jealous."

"But this guy here?" Franklin jabbed his thumb in Ethan's direction again. "He can only say that Jake did what exactly?"

"He lawyered up, so I don't know yet what he will say. The attorney's been in there for a while now, but it's a pretty good bet that Ethan can tie Jake to the convenience store fire and the fire later that summer. Both of them were started with a propane tank—"

"Wait. We got a big problem, Rob," Chase interjected. "We've already got a conviction for that convenience store fire—your girl? She confessed. So we can't charge somebody else for the same fire and expect it to stick. There's your reasonable doubt, right there."

Sam Franklin huffed. "That's not the biggest problem, boys. The biggest problem? The reason this is a total waste of my time? Statute of limitations ran out on that fire about, oh, six years ago. Even if somebody saw him personally stick a lighted match to the place, the case is going to get dismissed. You got no leverage. And if that lawyer in there remembers anything from law school, he'll tell him that."

Rob forbore mentioning that he hadn't

called Franklin down to the station in the first place. "You said leverage. I do think this gives it to me. True, we can't try Jake for the convenience store fire, but the warehouse fire, now, that's a different story. I think Ethan here knew about Jake's plans to burn the warehouse—"

Franklin cut him off again. "Let me guess—this Jake's a secret pyromaniac that's responsible for at least half the unsolved arsons in the county," he said in a voice dripping with sarcasm. "You may think that pinning this on Kari Hendrix's brother will do the trick—but it doesn't clear her, Rob. It just makes it easier for me to prove a case against her to the jury. It's *more* likely, not less, that she had something to do with it. How could somebody not know her own brother torched the place? She's at least an accessory after the fact, and probably a coconspirator."

"She didn't do this, sir," Rob insisted. "We've got absolutely no evidence tying her to the downtown fire. No motive. No opportunity. No weapon. And she was in custody when the warehouse fire happened later that summer, so she may not be aware of Jake's involvement. I can't believe she would stand by and knowingly let a killer go free—"

"Boy, I understand you want to find who killed your daddy!" Franklin burst out. "I get that. It's an honor thing. But you got two obsessions that are getting in the way of you solving the one current case I need solved—trying to find somebody to blame for your daddy's death, God rest his soul, and trying to pull your new gal pal outta trouble. Like I told you on the phone, I saw y'all playing house—"

Rob stood toe-to-toe with the arrogant DA, not sure what he'd do next. Chase put a hand on his shoulder and Rob backed away.

For his part, Franklin stepped back, as well. "Boy. I'm warning you. Don't you ever—ever, hear me?—ignore what I say again. I get that this case is a mite tetchy for you, it bringing up all these memories of your daddy. But you got the answers staring you in the face. If you don't do your job—if you don't arrest this pair of firebugs—well, I'll get it done for you, and I'll make sure the county suspends you."

With that, he turned and stalked out of the station.

So much for the power of chocolate. Kari stared down into her bowl full of the rich, dark batter for a German chocolate cake she was mixing and couldn't help but think of Rob.

Not the fire investigator Rob—no, Rob Monroe was more than his job. She liked the way he cared about Ma, the way his affection for his older brother Daniel came across every time he'd recounted a childhood memory. She liked the way he was willing to help her with just about anything.

Yeah, about the only thing troubling her about Rob was that he was an arson investigator.

What had he meant when he said they were running out of time? What did he know that he was keeping from her? Had Victor Miller made good on his threat to turn his report over to the authorities?

*If Rob were going to arrest me, would he have let me stay and bake him brownies?*

As she poured the batter into her prepared pans and slid them into the oven, the silence in the kitchen couldn't drown out her nagging thoughts. She had to stop dwelling on this, Kari told herself.

Not exactly cheered by that, but determined to do something, anything, to get her mind off Rob and the fire, she reached up and switched on the old radio her mom kept in the kitchen. A techno-pop song with an insistent beat filled the air. Instantly Kari felt better.

She started on the decorative chocolate roses for the cake by kneading the decor chocolate she'd prepped the night before, a mix of bittersweet couverture chocolate and golden syrup. Kari had half of the petals formed when the DJ announced the top of the hour news. She pressed her thumb into yet another ball of chocolate, trying to get the form right, only half her attention on the way-too-cheerful newscaster chirping about rising rates for water and sewage.

"And in breaking news, District Attorney Sam Franklin has announced that his office has made a major break in the downtown arson that destroyed five local businesses and resulted in millions of dollars in property damages. Franklin's office named local bakery owner Kari Hendrix and her brother Jacob Hendrix 'persons of interest' in the arson investigation. Hendrix is the owner of a popular downtown bakery damaged in the fire. The District Attorney's office would not say if insurance fraud was a motive in the case, but did say that arrests are imminent. Hendrix could not be reached for comment."

Kari's thumb bore down so hard on the fragile petal that it smashed in two.

*Arrests are imminent.*

In a flash, Kari was back in that nightmare all those years before: the scratchy orange jumpsuit, the bite of the handcuffs on her wrists, the thin mat for her bed, the constant din of noise from miserable inmates being watched by equally miserable guards. She fought to keep herself upright, pressing down hard onto the counter and dragging in deep, ragged breaths.

To think that a few seconds before she'd been wishing she hadn't been alone. How could she have forgotten how claustrophobic being surrounded by people 24/7 had been? No privacy, not even for a second?

She couldn't face it again.

Despair welled up within Kari, that same hopelessness that had first overtaken her when the bailiff had dragged her weeping from the courtroom. How could Rob have not told her? How could he have stood a hair's breadth away from her and let her go on believing that he was on her side? That he believed she was innocent, not just of the downtown fire, but even the fire she'd confessed to?

Bile rose in her throat as she reckoned the depth of his betrayal.

Kari had been wrong, so wrong, about Rob Monroe.

ROB YANKED HARD on the steering wheel of his truck to make the turn into Kari's mom's drive. Slamming it into park, he had the door open and his foot on the ground before he'd even switched off the ignition.

Why hadn't Chase at least given him a heads-up on that confounded press release Franklin had put out? Didn't the district attorney realize that naming someone as a person of interest was tantamount to arresting her? It was a bell that couldn't really be unrung.

He'd made it up the gravel walkway and almost to the back steps when the door flew open. Kari stood there, eyes flashing, hands on her hips.

"You stop right there," she hissed. "Unless you have an arrest warrant, leave. Now."

Rob's heart sank. He'd hoped he could get to Kari before she heard the news from someone else.

"Kari—"

"Don't you 'Kari' me! You—you *slime*.

You let me bake you brownies, and you knew. You…you *kissed* me, and you *knew*."

"No. That's not true." Rob took a step toward her, but she stopped him with the flat of her hand.

"Are you here to arrest me? Do I need to call a lawyer?"

"Of course not! You're innocent—I know you are."

"Right. And innocent people never get convicted, never get sent to prison."

Something about her self-pitying sarcasm needled him. "That was your choice, Kari. You chose to take the fall for your brother."

"It wasn't supposed to be like that—I was supposed to get probation. They would have sent Jake to real prison—tried him as an adult."

"So you admit it. You lied about it. You gave a false confession." Somehow, hearing the truth from Kari didn't hearten him the way he'd thought it would. Maybe she'd had the best of intentions, but it had still thwarted justice.

"What if I did?" she shot back. "Didn't I serve four years for lying? Haven't I been punished enough? I didn't set the downtown fire. And I'm not about to confess to something I didn't do—not ever again."

"You may not have set that fire downtown, but you knew Jake did," Rob told her.

"Oh, no." She clutched the doorjamb, her knuckles turning white from the effort. Her anger dissolved into wide-eyed fear. "No, no, no. You can't pin it on me, so you're pinning it on Jake? What? Any Hendrix will do? So you can get an arrest? That's what all this has been about, all the times you've oh, so, helpfully stopped by. You were stringing me along, trying to get me to incriminate myself or Jake or both of us."

Now she stood up straighter, every inch of her rigid with indignation. "Jake may have some growing up to do—he's immature, sure, and some people would even call him a screwup, and yeah, even a little lazy, but… he wouldn't knowingly hurt anybody, Rob. He's my brother. I ought to know my brother. And if I chose to serve time for him, well, it didn't hurt anybody but me, did it?"

Rob stared at her in total disbelief. "You still don't get it, do you, Kari? There's a reason it's illegal to give false confessions—because it leaves the real guilty party loose in society."

No lightbulb seemed to go off for Kari; she kept drilling him with that same aggrieved expression. He struggled to explain just what her actions had cost him—cost all of the Monroes. "When you gave that false confession, you let your brother go free. Free, so he had the opportunity to set the fire that killed my dad. You took a husband and a father away from his family—forever. And to make matters worse? You seem to think you deserve some sort of medal for being a self-appointed martyr and doing it in the first place."

Rob couldn't bear to look at her another second. He started to speak, couldn't get any more words out, so he turned and headed back down the path toward his truck.

Maybe Franklin was right. Maybe the answers had been staring Rob in the face the whole time and he'd let himself get sucked in by blue-gray eyes and dimples. Maybe Kari Hendrix couldn't ever be the woman he'd hoped her to be.

But one thing was for certain: with or without her help, he intended to put Jake Hendrix away for killing his father.

# CHAPTER TWENTY-ONE

JAKE HAD DISAPPEARED on her again. He didn't
answer her texts. He didn't answer her calls.
He didn't return her increasingly frantic
voice mails.

Oh, the phone rang, all right. If it wasn't
near-hysterical calls every five seconds from
her mom at work, it was a customer. People kept calling to tell her how suddenly
they didn't need those orders they'd been so
desperate for earlier in the week. The customer who'd ordered the German chocolate
cake she'd been working on when the radio
news bulletin had aired wasn't the first. The
woman had rung up and nervously tittered,
"Uh, Kari—uh, hope you haven't started on
that cake yet. Looks like our plans have…
uh, changed."

Kari stared around the kitchen, taking in the hundreds of dollars' worth of
ingredients—not to mention the labor—she
was now stuck with because Rob Monroe

had named her a "person of interest." Fury and betrayal and fear struggled to rise to the top like some inner "king of the mountain" battle. One moment she was weeping, while the next she was slamming doors so hard she endangered their hinges.

And the next? She was frantically dialing Jake's number and pacing around the kitchen.

Kari had just hit redial when she turned to see Jake. She went weak with relief.

"Oh, thank goodness! I've been trying for over two hours to get hold of you," Kari started.

Jake let loose a string of foul invectives. "Why'd you do it, Kari? Why'd you sell me out? Just 'cause you have the hots for that arson cop?"

She dropped the cordless phone on the countertop. "Me? I didn't do anything, Jake."

"You had to have known—didn't your boy toy give you a heads-up? Didn't he tell you he was nosing around in my business? I got two or three calls from buddies of mine—Rob Monroe's been sniffing around, talking to my old bosses and other people. And I just found out that Ethan Blaire, the weasel backstabber, he's been pouring his guts out for two days straight now. I'll show him what it means to cross me just as soon as I get a chance—but for now, Kari, you better tell me just what junk you've been telling that Rob Monroe."

His rage took Kari aback. "I haven't said—" But she remembered her last angry words with Rob, when she'd told him that, yes, she'd taken the fall for Jake on that convenience store fire.

Her guilty expression was all that Jake needed. He sprang toward her, grabbing the neckline of her T-shirt up in a wad. "What'd you tell him?" he gritted out between clenched teeth.

Alarm exploded through her, arcing through her nerve endings. This was a side of Jake she'd never seen before. Sure, his sarcasm could scald, and his thoughtlessness was legendary, but she'd never been afraid of him.

"Jake—" She tried to take a step back, but he'd pinned her between the cabinet and himself.

"Tell me!" he insisted.

"He—he knows about the convenience store fire. And he thinks you had something to do with that warehouse fire that same summer."

Jake shoved her, the counter's edge digging into the small of her back. "Is that all? What'd you tell him to make him think that?"

Kari rubbed the bruising pain flowering on her back. "I didn't tell Rob Monroe anything to make him think that. You're my brother, Jake. I went to jail for you."

"As if I haven't had *that* crammed down my throat ever since," he grumbled. "And how'd he know I torched that stupid warehouse, anyway? Why now? I mean, they leave me alone all these years, and only now are they chasing me down about it?"

Kari's breath caught in her throat. "Jake…"

Jake rolled his eyes. "Oh, don't pretend you and Mom didn't know. Why else would Mom have so many smoke detectors in this place? And a dang fire extinguisher in every room? She honestly thinks I'm itching to burn every building I'm in."

"You didn't." Nausea permeated Kari. "Jake, tell me you didn't burn that warehouse. Tell me you didn't set the downtown fire."

"Why does an old abandoned warehouse matter, anyway? Old coot who owned it wasn't using it—ran us out when we were hanging out there, having parties, not bothering anybody. What was it to him?" Jake's beautifully shaped mouth curled in a contemptuous sneer.

Kari's vision blurred. She'd always heard of people passing out from shock, but it had never happened to her—never before now. She fought against it. "A man died in that fire, Jake—he died, and all he was doing was his job—to put out a fire before it could hurt people." She closed her eyes, hearing Rob's words echo in her head.

*You took a husband and a father away from his family—forever.*

Jake snorted in derision. "He was a firefighter—he knew what he was getting into. If he didn't want to end up like that, he should have had better sense than to run into burning buildings, right? Besides, I'll bet his wife got a pile of money from the county. Bet she was set for life."

Jake's rationalization sickened her. "I went to jail for you—and you swore you'd never set another fire. Do you know what agony I went through? Do you have any clue how bad it was? Did it matter? Did it not mean one iota to you? It must not—not if you could start another fire, what, months? No, weeks, weeks after I went to jail. For you." Tears streamed down her face. "And you killed a man—no, you killed Rob Monroe's *father*."

He advanced on her again, backing her into the corner formed by the kitchen counters. "Yeah, yeah, yeah, St. Karina saved my bacon. I owe you my life. I should make something of myself. I should be just as wonderful as you are. Well, you know what? I never asked you to confess for me. That was all Mom. And if you were stupid enough to do it, well, you deserved everything you got—besides, Mom's been taking care of you—she never would loan *me* money. Oh, no." Jake shook his finger in her face. "It was always 'Jakey, I'm broke,' or 'Jakey, you should have thought about that before I had to bail you out of jail.' But you—you are the golden child. Whatever you want, she gives you. Need ten or twenty grand to start a business? No problem—but she wouldn't loan me five hundred bucks to get out of a hole I was in."

"Oh, no—Jake—you didn't—" Kari swallowed, pushing him back, away from her, needing space to think—or maybe not to think, not if what she feared he'd say came out of his mouth.

He didn't seem to notice her or the patches

of white flour she'd left on his T-shirt where she'd pushed him away from her. Spittle had formed at the corner of his mouth, and his blue eyes were hard and cold. "You didn't deserve that business. I figured if I burned you out, you'd haul off, go somewhere else. We were fine, Kari, fine, until you came back. And then suddenly, Mom was all, 'no money, no how,' and 'Kari says this' and 'Kari says that.' Do you know how sick I got hearing her say that?"

"It's not too late, Jake. You can turn yourself in. I'll tell Rob that you're sick and you need help—not jail. He'll listen to me—I know it."

Jake whirled around. "I'm not going to jail, and I'm not going to be stuck in a psych ward. Not because you couldn't keep your mouth shut. And as for Rob Monroe listening to you? You're a convicted arsonist. I'll tell him it was all you. He can't prove anything about that warehouse fire."

"I'll tell him the truth. I swear."

Jake picked up a heavy marble rolling pin and brandished it at her head. "Just try. Just try. Besides. I'll bet that DA won't be so picky. Way I hear it, he's itching to convict you. He'll listen to me. I'll work out a deal, and it will be my word against yours. Then it will be Mom and me again, and you won't be around to stick your nose in my business. Yeah, that's exactly what I'll do. Just as soon as I have Rob Monroe's attention somewhere else." He slung the rolling pin so hard onto the counter that a tiny piece of marble flew up and struck Kari on the arm.

Her fear didn't seem to touch him in his agitated state. He turned this way and that, and then smiled. "Ha. And here's the way to do that." Jake scooped up a bag of her organic confectioner's sugar and slapped it against the palm of his hand. "Yeah. This oughta do it."

Then he was gone, leaving the door wide open and Kari full of remorse and regret.

Rob watched as Jake Hendrix bailed out of his mother's house in a near run. He had something in his hands—a package? Rob couldn't get a good glimpse before Jake had tossed it in his old beater of a car, slung himself in and peeled out of the drive.

"There he is," Rob told Tim, who sat beside him in the passenger seat of his truck. "One good thing about that press release. It sure has stirred up a hornet's nest," he said grimly. He eased out of his spot by the curb down the street from Kari's mom's house.

Tim sat up. "You said he'd show up here sooner or later. Better not follow too close, or he'll spot you. I knew I should be the one driving."

"Relax. I got this. Just because you're a cop and I'm not doesn't mean I'll completely blow this."

But Jake apparently had his focus ahead, and it hadn't even occurred to him that he might have a tail. He drove aggressively through the residential streets. "I don't think he's checked his rearview once," Rob commented. "I think he's rattled. What about you?"

If Jake *were* this rattled, maybe he'd be desperate enough to do something that would give Rob clear proof that Jake had started the warehouse fire. And at this point? It could be that Sam Franklin was right. Maybe bringing his father's killer to justice was all that mattered to Rob.

Ahead of him, Jake yanked the wheel of the car and turned into a strip mall, an oncoming car laying on the horn in protest. Rob eased by the first drive, then came in the second. As he cruised closer to where

Jake had parked, he saw Kari's brother lope into a hardware store.

"Now what's our boy needing in the DIY department?" Tim scratched his chin and reached down between his knees for the bag of cookies he'd brought along for the stakeout. "He doesn't have the handyman look about him at all."

Rob parked an aisle over, close enough that they could keep tabs on the car and the main entrance of the store. "Got me. I was hoping for something—but I didn't expect this."

Tim offered the bag of cookies, shaking it so that the plastic rattled. "Want one?"

More to shut Tim up than because he was actually hungry, Rob scooped out a couple of the ginger snaps. He bit into one and immediately regretted it. Cookies reminded him of baking and baking reminded him of Kari.

"Here. You can have this one." Rob handed the untouched cookie to Tim. "It's not very good. I've had better."

Tim lifted a brow and munched on the cookie. "Got all snobbish about your baked goods since you've been hanging around that Kari Hendrix."

Rob scoffed. "That was one thing Sam Franklin was right about. She *is* part of this."

"Huh?" Tim washed down the latest cookie with a healthy swallow of a soft drink. "You didn't tell me you found that out. Granted, you hadn't said much at all today since you dragged me out on this stakeout with you, but I'd have figured you would have mentioned a little something like that."

"No—no, I mean—she didn't have anything to do with the actual fires. But she knew, Tim. She knew—and when she confessed to that convenience store fire, Jake was out and loose and set the warehouse fire. We all know what happened there."

"I gotcha." Tim slapped a comforting hand on Rob's shoulder. Rob tried not to notice that it was covered in cookie crumbs. "Listen, buddy. This girl—I can tell, she's something to you. I don't know what, exactly. I'm thinking maybe you don't either, not yet, anyway. But can you really blame a—how old was she? Fourteen? Dang, you got two nieces that age or close to it. Now would you blame Taylor and Marissa if they did something stupid like that? I think what we got here is an unintended consequence."

Rob rubbed a hand over his face. "Maybe

you're right. She couldn't have known then. But…didn't she think it was odd, such a similar fire so close in timing? I mean, Sam's right. How could she have not known it was her brother, especially after the downtown fire?" He drummed his fingers against the steering wheel. Had Jake pulled a fast one and used a back exit to ditch them?

Tim munched noisily on a cookie, his face screwed up in thought. "From what you've told me, she's a born optimist. Shoot, she's been baking up a storm ever since her place burned, right? Kind of girl who'd crawl out with the cockroaches after a nuclear bomb went off, ready to take on the world or at least what's left of it." Tim sunk a hand back into the bag for another cookie. "You oughta give these another go. These aren't half-bad, and I only shelled out a couple of bucks for 'em."

Rob thought back to that last angry exchange. Kari hadn't had the air of 'you've nabbed my brother.' No, she'd been defiant in her defense of Jake. She honestly thought he was innocent, that Rob was simply trying to railroad him. Tim could have it right—she could have convinced herself that her sacrifice had been worth it.

Still…she knew Rob's father had died as a result of that warehouse fire. If she'd had any idea, any suspicion at all that Jake had started it, why hadn't she said something to him the night she'd come over to bake brownies?

"Hey, there's our boy. Stump remover?" Tim pointed across the parking lot. Sure enough, Jake jogged toward his car, a container of stump remover in his hand. "What's a guy who lives in an apartment need with a stump remover? Kari's mom had any trees cut down lately?"

A prickle of awareness crawled over Rob. He pulled out his cell phone and managed to snap one photo of Jake with the container in his hand before his cell phone battery died. "Shoot. Can you take another picture of him? Battery's died and I didn't bring my car charger with me."

"You think we need a shot of this? Okay." Tim lifted his phone and snapped the photo.

Rob waited to switch on the ignition of his truck until Jake's attention would be focused on starting his own car. "Wait—he's not leaving. Where's he going now?"

Tim squinted, shielding his eyes with his hand as he ducked forward to gaze across the parking lot. Jake had dumped his purchase into the car and taken off for the other end of the strip mall.

"Drug store? Yeah, see? He's heading into the entrance to that pharmacy on the end. Kind of odd day to be running errands. Especially the way he left the house a while ago. Man, it was like the hounds of the devil were after him," Tim said.

"I don't think he's running errands. He knows me—he'd recognize me. Can you follow him in there and see what he's buying?"

"Shoot, yeah. My legs need a stretch, anyway." Tim propelled the door open and planted his feet on the asphalt surface. Even this late in the early fall, heat poured in the open door. "What are you afraid he's buying?"

"Petroleum jelly."

"Huh?"

Rob ticked items off his fingers. "Petroleum jelly, stump remover and powdered sugar. You combine those into a ball, and you've got a handy-dandy fire starter. Add matches, and watch it burn."

Tim did a double take. "Listen, don't ever cross over to the dark side. You must know a hundred ways to torch a place."

"It's what I think he used along with the

propane tank to start the warehouse fire. He didn't use a safety flare on that one—but they found traces of all that stuff and bits and pieces of a magnifying glass," Rob told him. "As for the dark side, you'll see my dark side if you let him get away."

"Mite tense, aren't you?"

But the rhetorical question must have been just that, because he didn't wait for an answer. Tim levered himself out of the seat and trotted off to the pharmacy.

It left Rob alone with his thoughts. Tim's words about his nieces kept haunting him. That's how old Kari had been when she'd been locked up—and had stayed locked up for four years. He couldn't imagine Taylor or Marissa surviving that sort of experience with as optimistic an attitude and as generous a spirit as Kari had.

But his dad…his dad would still be with him except for Kari's lie. Taylor and Marissa could have known their grandfather instead of simply hearing stories about him.

An ache filled his heart. If Kari had only shown some remorse, some understanding about what her lie had cost his family, if she'd tried to make things right… He couldn't think about Kari now—maybe not ever.

Jake came out of the pharmacy in a fast walk, his eyes fixed on his car. Rob noted the smirk on Jake's face as he let the bag of whatever he'd purchased dangle from his fingertips.

What was it? He could tell nothing about the shape or size of the contents through the plastic shopping bag.

"Tim, come on. We're gonna lose him," Rob muttered.

But Tim was nowhere in sight. Rob gripped the steering wheel and swore as he saw a plume of oily smoke belch out of the exhaust pipe of Jake's car. For a moment, Jake sat there, the car not going anywhere. A pulsing, relentless beat sounded from Jake's speakers—he must have spent more on the sound system than he had on the entire car, Rob realized.

Jake's car slid out of the parking lot. He wasn't in a hurry now, but almost poky, as though he had all day to do whatever it was that he had planned.

Burn a building. Dollars to donuts, Jake was planning on torching something. He was mad, and when Jake Hendrix got mad, he used fire to get even. But what building? Who did he need to get even with?

Who would be in his way? Who would he blame for his current predicament?

Rob picked up his cell phone to call Tim, and realized the phone was a useless hunk of plastic and glass. He tossed it in the console and swore again. Where was Tim?

Jake's beater merged into traffic, no rush, no hurry, just a smooth right turn that headed back the way he'd come. There were about a dozen different directions he could take in the next five minutes.

As Jake's car disappeared from view, Tim came hustling out of the pharmacy and across the parking lot.

"I was just about to leave you!" Rob snapped. "He's already gone!"

"Well, go!" Tim slid into cab and slammed the door. "We got to get him—you were right. He bought a big old container of petroleum jelly. That boy's planning on a fire somewhere."

Kari. Kari was one of two witnesses who could tell the truth about Jake. And Kari was in the direction Jake had headed.

# CHAPTER TWENTY-TWO

"Mom, Mom... I've got to go, I've got to find Jake!" Kari pulled free from her mother's grasp, intent on getting to her minivan. "I've got to stop him—he's going to kill Rob, I know it."

"No, Kari, wait, don't leave—stay with me—we'll call the police—" Her mother couldn't finish. She sagged against the door, her face red and swollen with crying. Kari hadn't seen her mother in such a state since the night Mom had begged her to take the blame for Jake.

Jake. Who had killed a man.

"Kari, Kari, please..." Mom whimpered. "Wait, just let me think. I've got to fix this, I know I can fix this. If you call the police, they'll arrest Jake—but if you don't—oh, we've got to call them. We've got to tell them to warn Rob."

"I did! I tried. Don't you see? They don't believe me. It's like Jake said—I'm an arsonist. Why should they believe anything I tell them?"

Her mother plucked at Kari. "You are not an arsonist. You did not start that fire. Not *any* fire. I am so sorry—it's all my fault. I was just trying to save my boy…"

She wept still more, but Kari had no time for her tears. Jake was out there, somewhere, and he was planning something awful. She hadn't known about the warehouse fire that killed Rob's dad. She hadn't known Jake was intending to get back at her in some sort of weird twisted sibling rivalry by burning half the downtown. She couldn't have stopped either of those fires.

But she did know he was intent on something terrible now. She could—had to—stop this fire.

Where was Rob? Not at the fire station, not at his office, not answering his cell phone. In desperation, Kari had even picked up the phone and called 911.

But when the 911 operator had asked what her emergency was, and she'd tried to explain, it had made no sense and taken too much time. She'd finally given up and told the operator to forget it. Now her mother was taking up still more precious seconds, seconds she needed to be able to think.

Where would Jake go? What was he planning? What could he do with a bag of sugar?

Sugar that had come from her kitchen.

"Well, you should call Rob, then, he'll believe you."

"I have, Mom, a dozen times. I really did. It just goes to voice mail. He won't answer. He hates me. He blames me…" Kari put her hand to her head. All she could think about was Rob's devastated expression when he'd told her she'd taken his father from him.

*And you did.*

All those papers, all those forms on Rob's table—Rob had been looking for his father's killer ever since it had happened, and it had been Jake, all along.

Wait. The table. Rob's apartment. Did Jake know where Rob lived? How hard could it be to find out? It had taken her one call to get the location, granted from a woman who'd trusted her.

*She won't trust me now. That was before anyone told her that I took her husband from her.*

No. There would be no more deaths. No more fires. Kari would go to Rob's—maybe, even if Jake wasn't there, Rob might be, or someone would. She had to do something.

Because she couldn't stand by and do nothing, not anymore.

KARI STEERED THE car beneath the leafy canopy arching over Rob's street, craning her neck this way and that. People hadn't come in from work yet, and school hadn't let out. It was deserted.

Then, on a side street, she spotted Jake's little two-door sports car. He'd been so proud of it when his mom had given him the key for his seventeenth birthday, but now it bore dings and scrapes and a hasty repair job of a front headlight with a plenteous amount of duct tape.

He'd been after his mom to help him buy a new car, Kari remembered.

*Was that why he torched my bakery? Because I told Mom not to get him the car?*

She parked her own car behind his and got out. Leaning against the window, she peered in. The car was empty of people, but a dumping ground of assorted fast food wrappers, gym shorts, towels, drink bottles, energy drink cans and game discs.

She stood up and touched the palm of her

hand to the hood. The metal was still warm. Jake must have walked to Rob's.

Kari tried dialing Rob's number one last time, but again got his voice mail message: "You've reached Rob Monroe with the Levi County Fire Department. If this is an emergency, please hang up and dial 911. If it can wait a bit, leave a message after the beep."

She disconnected and dialed her mom, who answered in hiccupping sobs. "Please tell me you found him before he's done anything stupid," her mom got out.

"I found his car—it's near Rob's. I'm going to walk down there and try to talk some sense into him—maybe he just went to talk to him." But Kari didn't believe that, not in her heart of hearts. "Maybe he'll listen to you if not me—he's really bitter, Mom, about the loan you gave me."

"Wait—Kari, somebody's at the door—oh! Call me back when you talk to him. I've gotta go."

Kari stared at the phone in disbelief. Once again, her mother was letting her deal with the fallout from Jake all by herself. Still, this time?

*This time, I'm scared. This is not the same Jake I grew up with.*

Rob's truck wasn't in the parking space in front of the duplex when she approached the house. The house appeared empty. At least there was no smoke coming out of it, she told herself.

The door was closed, but it creaked open when she put her hand to the door to knock on it. Her heart sank. Rob had not been one to leave doors unlocked, if his actions the other night had been anything to go by. No, he'd unlocked both the door lock and the separate deadbolt.

"Jake?" Kari called out.

The living room and kitchen area was as spare and neat as she'd seen it the other night—even neater, because now there were no papers scattered across the table.

The difference between Rob and Jake, almost the same age, couldn't have been any more apparent. Jake was still locked into a seventeen-year-old's mentality. Rob valued his space, valued his things.

*I wish he could have valued me. I wish I'd been worth valuing.*

"Jake? Are you here? It's me, Kari," she called.

Still no reply came. She pushed farther into the apartment, past the seating area on the left, opening a closet across from the kitchen to see a broom and some cleaning supplies, but no Jake lurking.

The bathroom door was open—and empty, even behind the shower curtain. It felt strange and wrong to Kari to be seeing Rob's home like this—somehow seeing his brand of shampoo felt like a huge invasion of his privacy. She would hate it if anybody poked through her stuff without her permission.

Had Jake come and gone? Had he changed his mind? Kari ducked into the apartment's one bedroom, with its bed jammed on one side close to a dresser, the closet on the wall opposite the living room. It was neat and undisturbed, the bed even made—surprising for a bachelor.

*But Rob's not like Jake. He understands responsibility. He understands he's accountable to himself.*

How had she missed that about him? No— staring at Rob's well-ordered space, remembering his cheerful willingness to help her with dishes and cakes and deliveries, she realized she *had* known that about him. She'd been drawn to his integrity, to his moral code that showed so plainly in his actions.

Kari had let that moral code down. She had betrayed Rob, not the other way around.

A flash in the dresser mirror caught her eye—just as a hand clamped over her mouth and fingers twined in her hair to yank her head back. She found herself staring into Jake's enraged face.

"Should have known you'd stick your nose into it. Got to rescue everybody, huh, Saint Karina?"

"Jake, please—"

"Jake, please," he mocked her. He twisted her around. "Maybe this is a good thing after all. I'll just leave you here when I torch the place, and they'll think you didn't get out in time. Kill two birds with one stone."

She fumbled for her phone, tried to get it unlocked to dial 911. Jake yanked it from her fingers and slung it against the mirror. The pane of glass shattered. "Oops. Think that gives me seven years' bad luck?" he smirked.

Kari kicked at him in a desperate attempt to get free. She had to get out and find help.

But as she did, he let go of his hold on her, and she went spiraling backward, falling, falling.

She heard a crack as she hit the sharp corner of Rob's dresser and felt a blossom of pain in her head. The last thing Kari saw before blackness was Jake leaning over her, a packet of matches in his hand.

ROB HEARD THE sirens two blocks over. Despite his seatbelt, Tim lurched forward and braced himself against the dash of the truck as Rob screeched to a stop in front of his apartment.

"Hey, buddy—wait for backup—if this guy's gone as five-alarm crazy as his mama says—"

Rob ignored him and almost fell out of the cab. "You are my backup—Kari's in there with that lunatic. He didn't burn her bakery because of insurance. He did it to get back at Kari." He slammed the truck door.

He smelled smoke—the acrid smell of a house on fire. But he saw no telltale puffs. Was it his imagination in overdrive?

Rob pounded up the steps and laid a hand on the door. Cool. He tested the doorknob. It was cool to the touch, too.

He'd paged out the engines and a squad car before they'd left Chelle's—who wasn't making a whole heap of sense, the shape she was in. He had managed to get one coherent thought out of her—that Jake was at his place, and Kari had gone there to stop him from torching it.

Tim was behind him, his gun out. "You need a weapon, Rob, why don't you carry a weapon?"

"Maybe because I'm not really a cop?"

"That's right, you nozzle jockey. Oh, well, the reason they made cops is so that firefighters would have heroes, too." Tim pushed ahead of him, his weapon out in front of him.

"Wait—go around the back, tell me if anything's burning. Or if Jake bailed out a back window."

For once, Tim didn't argue. As he rounded the side of the duplex, he called out, "Wait for the backup—don't be a glory-hound."

The sirens were closer still, a block if he was judging right. But any minute the place could go up in flames—or explode if Jake had cobbled together some other homemade explosive.

And Kari could be in there.

"Hey, we got smoke!" Tim hollered.

It decided matters for Rob.

The crew was coming. They'd have his back. He shoved in the front door with his shoulder and stayed low. Smoke was already pooling in the front room, making visibility hard. He coughed on the pungent taste of it.

"Kari!" he called. "Kari! Are you in here?"

The stove was all right—no burners lit, nothing on fire in the oven. What had Jake used to get the fire started so quickly? Had he had a chance to get a propane tank? Rob stumbled deeper into the apartment.

"Kari!" he screamed.

The smoke was dense and thick, and now there was heat. Rob dropped to his knees and crawled toward the bedroom door. What he'd give for turnout gear.

The bedroom door was hot to touch. Open it? Don't open it? Somewhere outside, over the all-too-familiar sound of crackling flames and arcing electrical currents, came the screech of airbrakes and the rattle of the engines setting up. He heard the volley of calls from one crewmember to another.

"Kari!"

He couldn't leave it to chance—he had to know if she was on the other side of that door. Rob nudged it open.

Fire crawled up the drapes from a mountain of bedclothes aflame in his closet and spilling out into the center of the room. In the eerie yellow light of the flames, he saw Kari's pale crumpled form on the floor.

Rob inched forward, closer, closer, until he could begin to drag her out. Was she dead? He couldn't take the time to see if she was breathing. They had to get out of this place now, before they both succumbed to smoke inhalation.

He had her in the hallway and would have hollered for help from the firemen storming through the front door,

But out of the dim recess of the bathroom a form exploded: Jake. They tussled and fought, hitting, punching. Rob felt his lungs spasm as he choked for breath in the midst of the smoke and dimly wondered where Jake's superhuman stamina was coming from.

Rage. Pure animal rage, from the string of curses Jake was uttering. Now Jake was between him and Kari, and Rob fought back, trying to get past him. He had to get Kari out.

He dug deep for the strength for one last punch, one more uppercut to Jake's glamour-boy jaw. Rob sent him pinwheeling back against the bathroom door, then scrabbled for Kari's limp form.

He had her up in his arms when he heard

a sound that filled him with relief: the thump of boots on the kitchen floor. Rob turned, saw a firefighter in turnout gear and presented Kari to him like a broken ragdoll.

"Get her some help. Now!" Rob shouted over the noise of a fire rapidly becoming out of control.

He turned back for Jake.

But Jake was up again. Kari's brother's face was white and taut as he saw the firefighter secure Kari in his arms and head for the door.

"Give it up, Jake! You got nowhere to go! There's no exit back here!" Rob told him.

Jake twisted with the panic of a cornered animal. "I'm not going to jail!"

Rob lunged for him, but Jake slipped from his grasp.

Instead of the front door, Jake leapt for the burning bedroom.

*No.* Jake Hendrix would not do this to his sister. He'd face up to his crimes, finally. He'd be accountable, if it was the last thing Rob ever made him do.

Rob bolted after him, grabbed him by the thin fabric of his T-shirt and landed a hard hit to Jake's blond head.

The arsonist slumped in Rob's grasp. Only

then did Rob make for safety, dragging Jake Hendrix out with him as he left his apartment burning down behind him.

He'd see his father's killer brought to justice. But had he been too late to save Kari?

# *CHAPTER TWENTY-THREE*

RESTRAINTS.

They had her arms in restraints.

Kari fought, even though she knew it was futile. The guards would write her up, and it might add more time to her sentence.

They were pressing her down, sticking something in her throat—she couldn't scream for help, couldn't get even a syllable out.

"Open your eyes, hon!" one of the guards called. But Kari couldn't bear to. She tried to recoil backward, but couldn't move from the grasp of yet another guard.

"Don't fight, sweetie! Just relax! We've got this breathing tube down your throat. You want it out, right? Open your eyes if you want it out."

Breathing tube? Kari dared to open her eyes the tiniest sliver, sure it was a trick.

But no uniformed guards loomed over her. No inmates held her down.

Instead, a smiling woman in scrubs bent

over her and smoothed a hand over Kari's forehead. "You had us worried there for a bit, yes, you did. You've got a couple of people waiting on us to get this thing out of you, though gracious knows, you're not going to be able to talk for a bit. Okay, you ready to follow my instructions? I'm going to take these restraints off you, but you can't fight me. You listen to me, and we'll have this tube out in a jiffy."

Kari nodded. The woman bent over her again and released first one wrist and then the other. Kari couldn't help it—she held up her hands to see them. Long Velcro strips dangled down from her wrists as she moved her fingers to her face.

"No, no—let me suction you out first. It won't hurt, I promise."

A loud noise came at Kari, and she felt a suction, exactly like at the dentist's office, work around the plastic that was in her mouth, then a far worse pain deep in her chest that made her gag. "Okay, let's get this mess off you—I know this can't feel great. Yep, turn that way so that I can get this unfastened."

Kari turned her head to the side. There

was her mom, wringing her hands, smiling, tears streaking down her face.

And Rob.

She blinked. Rob? Here?

But before she could make sense of it all, the woman had asked her to turn her head back to the other side. More pressure, more fumbling, but she didn't focus on them.

She focused on the fact that Rob was here. And he didn't look angry or disappointed or anything at all like he had the last time they'd spoken.

Where was Jake? Had they found him?

Smoke. Matches. Jake leaning over her.

He had been going to kill her.

Her own brother.

"Okay, you're doing good, so we're going to suction you again—and then I need you to cough, and this time it will be out, okay?"

Kari felt hands grip her head, and realized another person was there, too, holding her. She gagged and coughed and the tube was out and her mouth no longer felt as though it were filled with plastic pipes.

In a flash, an oxygen mask was on her, the cold metal of a stethoscope pressed against her, and the woman in the scrubs was giving her a reassuring pat. "Your throat's going to be sore for a bit, okay? That's normal. Okay, guys, she's all yours, but don't wear her out."

Mom crept up close to the bed and gripped Kari's hands in hers. She was bawling in earnest now. "Oh, Kari, Kari… I'll never forgive myself…"

Kari tried to speak. She could only get a rasp out.

Rob's hand patted her on her other shoulder.

She drank in his face. He was calm and cool. Grinning like a crazy man, but at least he wasn't falling apart like her mom.

"Don't try to talk. We couldn't understand you anyway," Rob told her. He crouched down so that he was at eye level. "I'll bet you've got a lot of questions."

Kari nodded.

"Do you remember the fire?" he asked.

She shrugged. "Not really," she husked.

"Shh," he said. "Save your voice. You'll get it back sooner if you don't talk right now."

"Rob saved you, honey," her mom told her. "You nearly died…" She raised her eyes to meet Rob's over Kari. "I can never, ever thank you enough."

"Wha-what happened? Jake...hurt...you?" Kari managed to croak out to Rob. She reached up and touched a bandage on his forehead, let her fingertips slide to a greenish bruise on his cheek.

"I'm okay...but Jake..."

Another exchange of glances between her mom and Rob.

"Jake is in jail. Where he belongs," her mother told her.

"The...fire?" Kari asked.

"Which fire? The downtown fire?" Rob scratched his head. "I don't know where to start. Jake's been charged with the downtown fire, and with manslaughter...for my dad. And he's got a laundry list of charges in connection with burning my place."

Kari felt a tear slip down her cheek. "Such...a...waste," she whispered.

The tip of Rob's finger caught the tear and wiped it away. "Yeah. He's a smart guy. He could have had so much more. I don't understand why he blew the opportunities your mom and you gave him. But he did, Kari. I'm sorry. I know you love him."

Another tear—this one because the gentleness of Rob's words cut her to the quick.

How could he be so compassionate about the man who had taken his father?

"Oh—I can't—" Her mother sprang up from the chair. "I'll be back!" She ran from the room.

Rob rounded Kari's bed and took the seat her mom had vacated. "Don't be too hard on her," he said. "She really hung tough all this time. You've been on a vent for two days. And—it was her, Kari, who told us where to find you. She told me about Jake. She was terrified for you. It's been hard—but she's been pretty brave about the whole thing. I don't know that I could have chosen between my kids."

For a long moment, he held her hands and didn't speak.

"Could I have some water?" she whispered.

He leapt up, nearly turning the water pitcher and the glass over. "Uh, no water, but how about some ice?" With the same infinite patience that he'd piped on Swiss dots, Rob held a spoonful of ice chips to her lips. Kari sucked them greedily, relishing the cool relief they brought.

"Better?" he asked.

This time when she spoke, her voice was

stronger—still raspy, but more understandable even to her ears. "Am I going back to jail?"

"No!" he said. "You're not under arrest. You're no longer even a person of interest in the investigation. It's over. Like I said, your mom has stepped up to the plate big-time. She's fully cooperated with the DA. She went on record to explain what happened ten years ago. Jake—well, Jake's pretty much been caught red-handed. He's going away for a long time, I'm afraid."

Kari closed her eyes. Four years of pain and deprivation, and it had all been for nothing.

"Not nothing," Rob said. She realized she must have been whispering the words aloud. "Sam Franklin says he'll see what he can do to get your conviction reversed. And the insurance company is satisfied you didn't have any knowledge of the arson…so they're cutting a check."

Kari stared up at him as she tried to take in what he was saying.

"You understand what I've said?" he asked. "You've got this expression on your face like I'm speaking Greek or something."

Kari managed a laugh that ended with a

painful cough that ripped through her. The cough dwindled into a sob she couldn't seem to hold back.

"Shh, shh," he crooned. "It's gonna be okay. It's gonna be all right."

"No. It won't. It can't be all right for you," Kari told him. "You were right. I took away your dad, as surely as if I killed him myself. If I hadn't made that confession—"

"No." His voice was fierce, and he gathered her up in his arms. "That's not on you. Your mom, yeah. But mostly Jake. He was old enough to know the consequences. He was the one who started the first fire…and the second. And all of them. But you were a kid, Kari. You were just a kid."

"I don't deserve your forgiveness—"

"I don't deserve yours. You've been through almighty torment… I have brothers, and I get it. I get why you did what you did. But Kari—" Now it was Rob's eyes that were shiny and bright with emotion. He averted his head. "What I don't know is…can you ever look at me and not see the guy who put your brother behind bars?"

A huge weight lifted off her shoulders, and she felt as light and free as the day she'd walked out of juvie. "Rob… Jake put himself behind bars. Not you. Not me. His choices. His consequences. You believed in me… I think you were the only one who really, really believed in me from the very start."

Kari pressed her cheek to his chest and relished the way she heard the steady, reassuring thump of his heart. It was a good heart, one she could trust with her very life.

"Oh, man… I've been sweating bullets, thinking you'd hate me forever." He held her away from him and beamed at her before he swiped away something that looked suspiciously like a tear. "Got something in my eye," he mumbled.

"Does that mean you'll be hanging around, helping yourself to my baking?" Kari asked.

"As long as you'll let me hang around." Rob engulfed her in another tight embrace. "I nearly lost you. I'm not going anywhere."

"Good," she mumbled against his shirt. "Because I could use a man who knows how to make roses."

Rob lifted her chin and held her face in his hands. "Honey, I'll make you dozens… and all the lace you'll ever need. Just say the word."

She reached up to meet his lips as they slanted toward hers, laughing, crying, not believing how all her bad luck could turn on a dime with the right man. "Rob Monroe, you just consider it said."

* * * * *

# LARGER-PRINT BOOKS!

## GET 2 FREE LARGER-PRINT NOVELS PLUS 2 FREE MYSTERY GIFTS

*Love Inspired*®

### Larger-print novels are now available...

# LARGER-PRINT BOOKS!

## GET 2 FREE LARGER-PRINT NOVELS PLUS 2 FREE MYSTERY GIFTS

*Love Inspired®*

SUSPENSE

RIVETING INSPIRATIONAL ROMANCE

### Larger-print novels are now available...

**YES!** Please send me **The Montana Mavericks Collection** in Larger Print. This collection begins with 3 FREE books and 2 FREE gifts (gifts valued at approx. $20.00 retail) in the first shipment, along with the other first 4 books from the collection! If I do not cancel, I will receive 8 monthly shipments until I have the entire 51-book Montana Mavericks collection. I will receive 2 or 3 FREE books in each shipment and I will pay just $4.99 US/ $5.89 CDN for each of the other four books in each shipment, plus $2.99 for shipping and handling per shipment.*If I decide to keep the entire collection, I'll have paid for only 32 books, because 19 books are FREE! I understand that accepting the 3 free books and gifts places me under no obligation to buy anything. I can always return a shipment and cancel at any time. My free books and gifts are mine to keep no matter what I decide.

263 HCN 2404   463 HCN 2404

| Name | (PLEASE PRINT) | |
|---|---|---|
| Address | | Apt. # |
| City | State/Prov. | Zip/Postal Code |

Signature (if under 18, a parent or guardian must sign)

## Mail to the **Reader Service:**

**IN U.S.A.:** P.O. Box 1867, Buffalo, NY 14240-1867
**IN CANADA:** P.O. Box 609, Fort Erie, Ontario L2A 5X3